Cover design by: GetCovers

Gingerbread GAMBLE

MELODY TYDEN

For every woman who ever felt second-best.

Chapter One

THE HOOK-UP

~**Noelle**~

The thumping bass of the music vibrated through my body as I peered through the crowd at the party, searching for the familiar red hair of my best friend, Eve. Wafts of beer and pizza and a dozen different perfumes and colognes all mingled together in the air as a trickle of sweat dripped down the back of my neck.

My red-and-white sweater dress seemed perfect for a December party when I put it on earlier that night, but the heat pumping out full-blast combined with the press of bodies filling every available inch of space made the small off-campus house feel like a sauna. The hair I'd spent an hour straightening beforehand had kinked into a frizzy mess and my makeup had probably started to run. Heat was not my friend.

"Have you seen Eve?" I asked a group of girls I recognized from one of the classes we had together. They all shook their heads, barely sparing me a glance as I thanked them and moved on in frustration. I'd been looking for fifteen minutes already. Where could she have gone?

When she told me twenty minutes earlier that she needed to use the restroom, I thought she'd be a couple of minutes at most. To pass the time, I made my way to the kitchen to get another drink, and there at the counter, I bumped into Corey Davison.

My mom told me that every girl has one dream guy in college, the unattainable ideal they lust after, and Corey had been mine from day one. We were in the same economics class in our freshman year and I fell hard for him, as did half the other girls in the class. Standing six foot three with dark hair, blue eyes and a jaw you could cut glass with, he could have easily been a model if hockey didn't take up so much of his time. Gorgeous, funny, and smart, he ticked every box I had for my perfect man. Over the years, we moved in a lot of the same circles and my crush only got worse with the passing of time, though I couldn't be sure he even knew my name.

But that night, when he saw me at the kitchen counter by myself, he came over to say hi, proving that he did know I existed after all. "I don't usually see you without Eve at your side," he greeted me with a charming grin that made my knees weak in a way that had nothing to do with the alcohol. "I thought you two might be surgically attached somehow."

That exaggeration had some basis in truth. Eve and I had been born on the same day, to parents who were best friends with each other. We grew up as best friends too, and even now that we were in college, we still spent a lot of time together. I hadn't realized Corey even noticed me enough to make that connection, and it flattered me that he had been paying attention.

"She's just gone to the restroom," I told him honestly, trying to keep my voice from wobbling with nerves. Part of me still couldn't believe he had approached me at all. "She'll be back soon."

"Not too soon, I hope." Still wearing that same grin, he leaned closer to me and for a brief, heart-stopping moment, I thought he might actually kiss me. Could this be the moment I'd been waiting more than three years for? It would be out of the blue, sure, but I wouldn't complain.

Unfortunately, my imagination had gone a step too far. He simply reached around me to grab another beer from the counter, his strong arm brushing against me before, with a wink, he left the room and I exhaled in both pleasure and disappointment.

It might not have been much, but that conversation counted as one of the longest I'd ever had with him one-to-one. I couldn't wait to tell Eve that I'd actually flirted with my dream guy, even if calling it flirting might have been a stretch.

Not that Eve knew the identity of my mystery crush. She knew that I liked *someone*, but I had kept his name a secret even from her, too afraid that somehow word would get back to him and he would find the idea ludicrous. Though Eve naturally had some curiosity about the object of my desires, she respected my privacy enough not to push me on it. We hardly had any secrets from each other, so she understood that if I kept this one, it meant I really didn't want to tell her.

However, after fifteen minutes of searching for my friend, all the excitement of what I wanted to tell her in the first place had faded, replaced with simple worry. Eve never just disappeared without giving me a heads-up. Something felt wrong.

"Hey, Noelle. Have you seen Eve?"

At first, I thought the question was in jest, that someone had heard me asking around for Eve and decided to make fun of me, but when I turned around and saw where the question came from, that thought quickly disappeared. My arch-nemesis, Aaron Speelman, stood behind me, and I would place money on the fact that he had no sense of humour at all.

While 'arch-nemesis' might have sounded a bit dramatic, it fit nonetheless. Aaron and I always seemed to be going head-to-head against each other: for top marks in our classes, on the debate team, and even in the election for student body president, which I had won by the narrowest of margins earlier that fall. When he 'congratulated' me, he made it clear that he thought my victory rested on the fact that Eve had personally campaigned on my behalf with all the sports teams.

I argued back that Corey had campaigned just as hard for him among the sororities, where he naturally had a lot of sway, so Aaron couldn't use that excuse. Aaron and Corey were best friends just as Eve and I were; not only in the sense of being friends, but in the way that Corey and Eve were the extroverted, popular counterparts to Aaron and me. Exactly what Corey liked about Aaron, however, I had yet to figure out.

Unlike his god-like friend, Aaron was closer to my own height, his brown hair messy and his glasses slightly bent, as usual. That evening, he wore a plain button-up shirt that had come untucked from his pants, like he had started to tuck it in but lost interest half-way. Aaron always looked like he had just fallen out of bed, but not in a sexy way. I might not be as naturally beautiful as Eve, or my sister, Olivia, for that matter, but at least I made an effort. Aaron didn't seem to care at all.

"I don't know where Eve is," I answered Aaron's question. "I'm trying to find her myself."

His brow furrowed, making his glasses slide down his nose, and he pushed them back up again. "Where have you looked?"

I told him where I'd checked, which encompassed the entire ground floor and the backyard. Even though the temperature had dipped below freezing, a few people were drinking outside, but Eve hadn't been one of them.

"You haven't looked upstairs?" he asked, and I shook my head.

"It's just bedrooms up there, isn't it?"

He gave me a look that made it clear how foolish he considered that response. "That's exactly why you should be checking there."

He headed for the stairs before I could say anything else, so I hurried after him. "Wait, what are you going to do?"

"Make sure she's not in trouble," he muttered. My eyes were level with his ass as I followed him up the stairs, and I couldn't help noticing it actually filled out his Chinos rather well. I had never looked at it before, for obvious reasons.

Without any hint of embarrassment, Aaron threw open one door after another, surprising couples in various states of undress. As soon as he saw they weren't Eve, he gave a short apology, closed the door, and moved onto the next one.

Soon, only one door remained, and as we moved towards it, it opened on its own from the other side. Eve walked out a second later, stepping almost straight into Aaron who, by that time, stood right in front of her.

"Oh! Hello." She gave him a curious look before spotting me over his shoulder and flashing me an apologetic smile. "Sorry, Noelle, I should have sent you a message. I got distracted."

"Apparently." Although I obviously felt relieved nothing bad had happened, her behaviour surprised me. Hooking up with a random guy at a party wasn't usually Eve's style. Rich, beautiful and confident, she could have any guy she wanted, and she almost always made them work for it. Though she was no virgin, a quickie in someone else's bedroom didn't usually fall within the Eve Stamer playbook.

Before I could figure out what any of that meant, the guy she'd been in the room with appeared in the doorway behind her, and my heart dropped down to my feet.

"Did we keep you waiting?" Corey asked with a laugh, double checking that he'd done his fly up before he put his arm around Eve and walked past Aaron and I down the hall, looking incredibly pleased with himself. "Have fun, kids."

Eve gave me a smile too, letting Corey lead her along. "See you downstairs."

Oh, God, no. Feeling suddenly dizzy, I leaned back against the wall, my head swimming not just from the heat but from the thumping of my heart and the churning of my stomach. Corey and Eve? Out of every guy in the world, why did it have to be him? In a stunned stupor, I watched as Corey's hand moved down Eve's back, palming her ass before they headed down the stairs together.

Even in my disappointment and heartache, I couldn't blame her for a second. She had no idea how I felt since I had never told her, and who wouldn't jump at the chance to be with Corey? I certainly would have.

The situation left me so dumbfounded that it took me a moment to realize what Corey had meant by his comment about keeping us waiting: he thought Aaron and I wanted to use the bedroom ourselves. Self-consciously, I glanced over at Aaron, taking a step further away from him while Aaron scowled at his friend's retreating back.

"Fuck," was all he said before heading into the bedroom and slamming the door behind him, leaving me in the empty hallway while moans and grunts drifted through the other closed doors and the party carried on downstairs.

Though I'd grown used to being the runner-up in so many ways, as I stood there with my back against the wall, my heart breaking inside my too-warm dress and not even my best friend to confide in, I had never felt quite so insignificant.

~**Aaron**~

Standing above my best friend as he slept, his arms thrown wide across the bed and his mouth open as he snored loudly, I couldn't help thinking how easy it would be to cover his stupid, good-looking face with a pillow and put an end to his suffering.

Or maybe just my suffering. To be fair, he seemed perfectly content. He'd probably never suffered a day in his life. The state of his room, filled with dirty laundry and takeout food containers that the maid hadn't cleaned up yet, seemed to support that theory.

With a sigh, I pushed my uncharacteristically dark thoughts out of my head. Killing him would be a step too far. Cutting his dick off would suffice, but I didn't do that either. Giving his shoulder a hard shove, I simply woke him up instead. "Get up, Corey. It's almost nine, we have to get to the airport."

He groaned, rolling over and covering his eyes with his arm. "Fuck off, Aaron."

Not satisfied with that response, I grabbed hold of his covers, pulled them off, and immediately regretted it. "For fuck's sake. You can't sleep with some clothes on?"

"The ladies don't complain," he replied, turning back to me with a grin, not bothered in the least by his exposure. "Neither does your mom."

"So original. You're such a child." I threw the covers back at him. "You've got twenty minutes before we need to leave. I'm going without you if you're not ready."

He ruined my dramatic exit by calling out after me: "No, you're not. You won't leave me behind and you know it."

Just because he was right didn't mean I had to tell him so. We both knew I would have never been invited on this trip if not for my friendship with Corey. The wealthiest, most popular students in our senior year were spending the next ten days together in a massive house in the faux-alpine town of Leavenworth, Washington. Though I didn't qualify as either rich or popular, my status as Corey's best friend got me in by default.

The destination had taken me by surprise when Corey told me where we were going. Wouldn't the Caribbean be a lot more fun, not to mention warmer, I wondered? But when he explained that Eve Stamer chose it because of her love for all things Christmas, that changed things. If Eve liked something, I could learn to like it too.

Besides, Corey said we wouldn't be spending our time going on sleigh rides or baking cookies anyway. Twenty horny college students on a big break together before our final term and graduation would lead to all kinds of adult fun, and he promised me it would be the perfect time to hook up with any of the girls. I only had interest in one of them, though, which I told him shortly before he slept with her himself three days before.

"It just happened," was his only explanation when I confronted him about his hook-up with Eve the following day. "I can't explain it. We've never really been attracted to each other before, but last night, it just clicked."

I had a pretty good idea what made it 'click' for him: the moment when I admitted to him just how much I liked her. Listening to me talk about all of Eve's good qualities, he suddenly paid a lot more attention to her than ever before. Seeing me getting ready to make my move, he swooped in first. He wanted her because I did, and whatever Corey wanted, he got. It never occurred to him that it would be otherwise.

"It's not just a one-night stand," he added, which only made it worse. "I think she might be the real deal."

And now, instead of using this trip to try to make my move with Eve, I would have to sit back and watch the two of them together instead. Given the situation, I had considered not going at all, but the devil on my shoulder pointed out that Corey might easily do something to screw it up, especially with a lot of alcohol involved and other pretty women around. That thought convinced me to suck it up and go ahead anyway. If he screwed up bad enough, Eve might need some support. I'd seen him break plenty of hearts before, and I would rather not see Eve be next on that list.

Ten minutes after I told him we needed to leave, Corey hauled his ass downstairs and out to my waiting car. I'd left it running because of the cold December weather, silently counting up the cost of the gas I was wasting. "You're late," I told him tersely when he pulled the passenger door closed.

"Which is why you planned for us to get to the airport an hour early anyway," he pointed out, completely accurately. "We're fine, bro. Chill."

That could be Corey's motto in life, but it didn't work for me. While Corey coasted through life, relying on his charm and good looks to get him through, I had no such assets. I worked hard for everything I had, relying on my intelligence to do the heavy lifting. People might not like me the way they liked Corey, but they had to respect me. I planned everything in advance, leaving nothing to chance. How the two of us ended up as best friends remained a mystery to everyone, including us. He drove me crazy, but he also pulled me out of myself, making me take risks I never would have otherwise.

Risks like this trip, for one. I had no control over anything for the next ten days, and that both terrified and exhilarated me. Anything might be possible, including a chance to really get to know Eve Stamer, so long as I could get her out of Corey's greedy grasp.

Despite Corey's tardiness, we were the first of the group at the airport, and he took a seat across from me in the waiting area once we were through the security checks, leaning back and placing a hat over his face. "Wake me up when someone interesting gets here."

My eyes rolled so hard that my glasses slipped down my nose. Seriously, what did I see in this jerk?

Thankfully, only a few minutes passed until the next people arrived, including the most interesting person I could think of: Eve Stamer herself. She'd pulled her red hair back in a messy bun above the cashmere turtleneck she wore over her skinny jeans and brown boots, looking like she'd just stepped off the pages of a magazine, as usual. My pulse immediately increased, as it did every time I laid eyes on her.

"I told you we were going to be too early," she complained, her gaze completely skipping over me as she looked around. "There's nobody else here."

"Aaron's here," another voice pointed out. I hadn't noticed Noelle until she spoke, but of course she would have been there. She and Eve were inseparable.

In contrast to Eve's casual elegance, Noelle always looked like she tried too hard. Though her brown hair naturally curled, she always tried to straighten it, making it frizzy instead. Her makeup looked too heavy for this time of day and she seemed uncomfortable in the clothes she'd chosen, pulling at the fabric over her stomach, just like she had in that sweater dress at the party the other day.

"I think that's Corey under the hat," Noelle added. Interest immediately sparked in Eve's eyes as she walked over and took the seat next to him, ignoring me entirely.

"Are you hiding from me?" she asked, poking him in the ribs.

"Why don't you come and hide with me?" He lifted his hat enough that he could pull her close for a kiss before putting the hat back in place, leaving the rest to our imaginations.

Unfortunately, I had a pretty damn good imagination.

Noelle looked just about as thrilled with the new situation between our friends as I did, grimacing as she took a seat across from them, leaving a few empty seats between us. "Hey, Aaron."

"Hey." Aside from arguing with each other in debate club or in the classes we had together or when we competed for student body president, Noelle and I had never really had a proper conversation. I knew nothing about her on a personal level and she knew nothing about me.

Luckily, the rest of the group started trickling in so our awkward small talk only lasted a few minutes. My relief over that was short-lived, though, as Corey pulled me to one side when we all stood up to board the plane. "Can you switch places with Eve for the flight?"

He couldn't be serious. "It's a five-hour flight, Corey. I don't want to sit next to someone I don't know."

"You know her," he assured me. "It's Nolie... whatever her name is. Eve's friend."

The self-centred bastard couldn't even remember the name of the girl he'd helped me campaign against, the one I'd complained about multiple times. When I raised my eyebrows in disbelief, he groaned.

"Come on, just watch a movie or whatever, you don't have to talk to her. I promise I'll make it worth your while. Any girl you want on this trip, I'll put in a good word for you."

The only girl I wanted, he'd already claimed for himself, but I gave in anyway, knowing he would wear me down until I did. I gave him the cold shoulder as we boarded the plane, jostling with all the other people travelling before the holidays, everyone carrying their winter coats along with their carry-on bags. By the time we reached them, Noelle and Eve were already getting settled in their seats.

"How about you come and sit next to me instead?" Corey asked Eve, giving her the smile that no girl seemed able to resist. "Aaron wants to sit with Nol... with your friend."

At least he skipped over mangling her name, but putting the blame on me for the seat switch was a stretch and he knew it. Noelle looked ready to protest, but she didn't have a chance; Eve had already got to her feet. "That sounds great. See you guys there!" she exclaimed as she headed a few rows back to sit next to Corey instead, taking all my hopes with her.

With a sigh, I dropped into Eve's abandoned seat. "Sorry," I apologized to Noelle. "I had no say in this either, so you don't have to pretend to be happy about it. You don't need to talk to me or anything."

"Yeah, thanks," she mumbled, shoving some earbuds in before turning to look out the window, intent on ignoring me already.

Five hours had never seemed so long.

~Noelle~

Eve and I rarely fought, but right now, things were tense between us. Ever since the party, she'd done nothing but gush about Corey and I couldn't take much more of it.

"You always said you didn't understand his appeal," I reminded her the morning after the party as we lounged around in our shared dorm room. Sitting cross-legged on my bed, I did my best to keep my voice level so as not to betray my level of investment in this conversation. "Every time another girl talked about him, you said you couldn't see the big deal."

That had been the other reason I never told Eve about my crush. Mostly, I wanted to avoid the crippling humiliation I would have suffered if Corey ever found out about it and didn't return my feelings, but also, I knew Eve wouldn't have approved. She would have told me I could do better, though where she got that idea from, I couldn't guess. Aside from Eve, the only people who had ever considered me a catch were my parents, and they didn't count. Everyone else saw me only as Eve's less attractive friend or the plainer of the two Hanmer girls.

"Oh, I still don't think he's anyone I could be serious with," she assured me. "The guy's all style and no substance, but right now, that's kind of what I want, you know? It's just a bit of fun. We're almost done with college, this is our last chance to just be young and stupid. In just a few months, we'll have real jobs and big decisions to make. Why not enjoy ourselves while we can? And I can assure you, I enjoyed it."

Hearing the details of exactly what happened between her and Corey might just have made me sick, so I jumped on the first part of what she'd said instead, about how this wouldn't be a serious relationship. "So, this is just a one-time thing?"

The idea of Eve and Corey together at all still stung, but I could have dealt with a drunken hookup at a party.

Unfortunately, Eve shook her head, a satisfied smile playing on her lips. "He's asked me to come over tonight, and then we've got that trip coming up. It'd be fun to have someone to do couples things with."

My heart sank even further. Ever since the trip to Leavenworth had first been mentioned, I had imagined Corey and I together: ice skating hand-in-hand, going on the sleigh ride, having a snowball fight, kissing in front of the fire, making gingerbread together. It would be the perfect Christmas romance, and now, Eve would get to live out my dream with a guy that she didn't even really like that much.

If I told her how I felt, she would probably back off, but realistically, what claim did I have on him? He'd never given me any indication he might be interested in me, and for all I knew, he really liked Eve. What right did I have to interfere?

Over the next couple of days, I did my best to accept things the way they were, but Eve noticed my lack of enthusiasm anyway. When she asked me why I seemed upset and I tried to insist otherwise, that only made things worse. She informed me bluntly that she had been looking forward to this trip all term and wouldn't let me ruin it by pouting the whole time, so I should either tell her what was bothering me or get over it.

And now, she abandoned me on the plane, leaving me with Aaron freaking Speelman instead. Would it be too late to just get off the plane and stay home? Right now, that sounded preferable to being stuck with Corey's annoying best friend for the whole trip while *my* best friend made out with the guy I'd always wanted.

Aaron said I didn't have to talk to him, and I had no intention of it. Instead, I put my earbuds in and looked out the window at the grey December sky above the Newark runway, trying not to cry in frustration. Ten days of this I had to get through, ten days that I could have just been home with my family enjoying the Christmas season instead of feeling like the third wheel in a relationship that I would prefer to see crash and burn.

Aaron pulled out his laptop next to me as soon as the plane had levelled out in the air, and his typing only made me more irritated. He had actually brought along work to do on this trip, while I had purposefully left all mine behind, trying to focus on having a good time instead. Now, that seemed like a ridiculous pipe dream.

Another half hour passed in silence during which I glanced over at his screen every now and then. The paper he was working on had been assigned for a philosophy class we were both in, one that I had only begun making notes for. In spite of myself, I had to admit I found his argument rather compelling. It certainly beat the self-pitying thoughts in my head, and before long, I found myself caught up in it.

"You misused that phrase." I hadn't meant to speak the words out loud, but apparently, I did, since Aaron glanced over at me, his eyes narrowed behind his black, thick-framed glasses.

"Excuse me?"

Since I couldn't pretend I hadn't said it, I repeated myself, pointing at his screen. "Here, you said 'a priori' when you meant 'a posteriori'. Personally, I wouldn't use either though. It makes you sound pretentious."

"I don't remember asking for your opinion," he muttered under his breath, but he scrolled up and deleted the words anyway. "You've got nothing better to do than read over my shoulder?"

"Not really. Eve and I were planning on getting drunk on the flight so I didn't bring anything else to do."

His jaw tightened for no reason I could think of. "Well, you've got a call button on your seat. Don't let me stop you."

"It's not the same on my own," I pointed out. "Drinking by myself is just sad."

"So, if I have a glass of wine, you'll have one too and stop pouting?" His eyes were still on the computer screen rather than on me, but I could imagine the condescending look in them anyway. It didn't help that he'd used exactly the same word Eve had used to describe my behaviour.

"I'm not pouting. I'm stating a fact."

"No, you're pouting." He closed the laptop lid and turned to face me. I'd never been this close to him before, close enough to really see his eyes behind his glasses. They were actually a rather interesting shade of hazel, and for just a second, I wondered what he would look like without the glasses on. "Red or white?"

"What?" The question made no sense to me, and his jaw clenched again.

"Wine," he said slowly, as if speaking to a child. "You wanted a drink. Do you want red or white wine?"

"Oh. Red, please." I couldn't tell if something had upset him too or if he was always like this, but drinking with him sounded better than drinking on my own, so I answered him as graciously as possible.

He flagged down a flight attendant and ordered us both a drink, paying for it even though I tried to insist I could cover my own. He could be surprisingly firm when he wanted to be. "Cheers," he gritted through his teeth as he raised his glass.

I followed suit, draining my glass quickly in the hopes that the alcohol would help. Aaron's eyebrows raised as he watched me swallow it all down, but he kept his mouth shut.

In the silence that lingered afterwards, I spoke instead. "Why did you bring your laptop along?" I asked, pointing at the computer that still sat on his table. "We're supposed to be on vacation."

"Not every minute of the day will be filled," he replied in that calm, analytical way of his that always got under my skin. "I might as well be productive when there's nothing else to do."

"You could just, I don't know, talk to people." I shrugged as I raised my glass again, trying to get every last drop out.

"People like you who would rather ignore me?"

He had a point, but I pursed my lips at him anyway. "I wouldn't have ignored you if you'd chosen to sit next to me, but you're only here because you were forced into it, same as me."

He huffed into his glass, neither confirming nor denying that. When he'd finished his wine too, he held the glass up. "Another one?"

"Please." The more, the better.

Aaron got us both another drink, and another one after that. With each one, we talked a little more. We complained about people who were chronically late and the fact that no one had any kind of itinerary for this trip we were on. We laughed about the way our philosophy professor always accidentally stapled his sweater to the papers he brought to class, and we talked about the limited power of the student body government.

He actually could be somewhat interesting to talk to, at least with alcohol involved. Clearly, I started to feel far too comfortable, because when Eve walked past on her way to the restroom, giving us a wave as she went by without bothering to stop and say hi, my eyes narrowed after her and Aaron immediately noticed.

"Is something going on between you two? Are you fighting?"

I shook my head slowly. "We don't fight, exactly, but I can't say I'm thrilled about her and Corey together."

"You and me both," I thought he muttered under his breath, though the wine might have made me imagine it.

"What?"

He quickly shook his head. "Nothing. What's your problem with Eve and Corey? You think he's going to hurt her?"

I snorted in a very unladylike way. I had no concerns about that at all. If anyone ended up getting hurt, my money would be on Corey. "I just don't think it'll work out. They're not right for each other."

I tried to keep things vague but Aaron wouldn't be put off. He kept asking questions. "Because he's a player?"

I wouldn't use that word for him. He might date a lot, but it just meant he hadn't found the right girl yet. "He's perfect," I thought.

At least, I *thought* I thought it, but as Aaron's eyes grew wider behind his glasses, my heart began to race.

Oh, shit. Did I really just say that out loud? To Corey's best friend?

How in the world could I talk my way out of that?

Chapter Two

The Plan

~Aaron~

A few drinks helped to loosen Noelle up and, surprisingly, we were actually having a decent conversation until Eve walked by. Her hand brushed against my shoulder as she walked down the aisle on her way to the restroom, and when she turned and gave me a smile and a wave, my whole body lit up like a shot of electricity had run through me.

Frustration and lust mingled together as I watched her go. I'd never had a crush before. Normally, I wouldn't waste my time. If people didn't like me, that was their loss, and I certainly didn't feel like I had to go out of my way to impress anyone. Maybe that partly explained why Corey liked me, since I never kissed up to him like most people did.

And yet, with Eve, I felt drawn to her anyway. Maybe it had to do with the way she didn't seem to care what anyone else thought either. Whatever the reason, even though she barely knew I existed, I wanted her anyway. We would work well together, I just had a feeling. I only needed a chance to show her how good it could be.

When I turned back to Noelle, the glower on her face as she watched her friend go by took me by surprise and I couldn't help asking her about it. Her confession that the relationship between Eve and Corey bothered her surprised me far less; Corey had a reputation for loving and leaving, and I wouldn't want him dating my best friend either, even if he *was* my best friend.

But that didn't seem to be where Noelle's concern stemmed from, and when she called him 'perfect', I suddenly saw the situation with complete clarity.

"You have a thing for Corey?"

Her eyes went almost comically wide before she looked down at her wine glass with an accusing glare, as if it had said the words instead of her. "What? No. That's crazy."

"Noelle, you just said he's perfect. That's not a normal thing to say about someone if you don't have feelings for them."

"I'm drunk," she claimed next. "I don't even know what we're talking about."

She couldn't lie to save her life. "You're half-drunk at best. You were arguing with me pretty coherently about grammar a moment ago." A red flush crept up her cheeks that had nothing to do with the wine, and I tried another angle. "Listen, it doesn't matter to me whether you like him or not. I'm not going to tell him anything."

Those seemed to be the magic words and she looked back up at me hopefully. Her blue eyes were actually kind of pretty this close up, I couldn't help noticing. "You won't say anything?"

I snorted like she had just a moment ago. "Trust me, you're not the first girl who's confessed her undying love for Corey Davison to me and you won't be the last. Corey hardly needs another ego boost and I have no interest in giving him one. Does Eve know you like him?"

Corey knew how I felt about Eve and had gone after her anyway but Eve had never struck me as that kind of person. Noelle quickly confirmed that impression. "No, she doesn't know. Don't tell her either, please."

It hadn't crossed my mind, but I did have another idea, one that picked up steam as the pieces began to fall into place in my head, my eyes still on the woman in front of me. We didn't know each other well, but at the moment, it seemed we both had the same goal. We might be able to help each other out if we could get on the same page.

"Look, Noelle, you and I haven't always gotten along, but we can agree we're both pretty smart, right?"

Her confusion at the apparent change in topic showed in the way her eyebrows drew together, her blue eyes straining to focus on me under the influence of the alcohol. "What does that have to do with anything?"

"Just stay with me," I requested drily. "One thing at a time. You and I are both smart, right?"

"Sure," she agreed warily, suspicious of where I might be going with this.

"And Corey and Eve are never going to last, we both know that too."

Noelle nodded slowly. "Not likely. She's not serious about him."

My heart leapt at that fantastic news, and it would make the rest of what I wanted to propose more palatable. "On top of that, who knows Eve and Corey better than we do? No one."

Her confusion grew deeper. "I still don't understand."

"That's because I haven't got to the point yet and you're half-drunk, as you mentioned." She made a face at me that made me smile. When she forgot about trying to impress anyone, she could actually be kind of cute. However, I put that thought aside to get down to business. "We know they aren't right for each other and we know they're going to break up sooner or later, so what do you say we work together and give them a nudge in that direction sooner rather than later?"

Noelle finally understood my proposition, but her initial response was to shake her head. "Eve's my best friend. I can't hurt her like that."

Did she really think I wanted that? "I'm not talking about hurting anyone. You just said yourself she's not serious about him. If their eventual breakup happens now, Corey will be looking for someone to spend the rest of the trip with. He doesn't really like being alone. You can step in and save the day and have the best trip of your life."

"But then Eve would be all alone..." Noelle started to say, just before her eyes widened in surprise as she made the last connection. "Wait, this isn't just about me, is it? You like Eve!"

"Keep your voice down." A quick glance around told me no one had heard her over the whirring of the plane, thankfully, but we couldn't be too careful. "Yes, I like Eve, alright? And I know Corey isn't serious about her either. He's never serious about anything. I'm glad she's not going to get her heart broken, but it seems like they're wasting time together when it's not going anywhere. It would be more efficient..."

"...if they broke up now, and then you have the best trip of your life too," Noelle finished for me, eyeing me critically, as if truly seeing me for the first time. "I didn't have you pegged as the underhanded, scheming type."

"And I never had you pegged for another Corey fangirl. We've all got our dark sides."

A surprised laugh bubbled out of her mouth, along with a hiccup caused by the wine. She covered her mouth with her hand, which caused her to snort, and I found myself smiling once again, against my will. She had an awkwardly adorable kind of vibe that Corey would go for, at least temporarily. As long as Noelle only wanted some fun, she could have a good time with him and I could get my shot with Eve, just as I'd been imagining. It couldn't be more perfect, so long as Noelle agreed.

"I'm not talking about anything crazy," I assured her. "Just finding ways to keep them apart or cause little arguments. On my own, it would be tricky, but if you're working with me..."

Once again, she finished my sentence, following along with me perfectly. "...we stand a far better chance of success." We shared a brief smile before Noelle sighed. "I don't know, Aaron. It still feels sneaky."

Why did being sneaky have to be a bad thing? "It's about being proactive. I'll bet you've never just gone after what you want, unapologetically, in your whole life. And I bet Eve has."

Noelle took that as exactly the challenge I meant it to be. "I've done plenty of proactive, sneaky things. Things you can't even imagine."

I had very strong doubts about that and I told her so, leaning closer so I could lower my voice, speaking almost directly into her ear. "I don't think so, Noelle. I have a pretty good imagination, and deep down, you're a good girl at heart. However, that's exactly why this will work. Eve will never expect it from you."

A shiver ran down her spine as I pulled away, making my own body react with a rush of endorphins. Causing that kind of reaction in a woman always turned me on. It seemed that maybe Noelle liked it too, which would be interesting if I weren't so completely focused on Eve. I expected that same reaction from her when I finally got a chance to make my move. I'd imagined it so many times.

So, for the time being, I just filed that little piece of information about Noelle Hanmer in the back of my mind while I raised my eyebrows at her expectantly, awaiting her reply.

Noelle swallowed as her eyes searched mine, blue eyes that seemed more striking the longer I looked at them. "What exactly would you want me to do?"

~Noelle~

The way my body reacted to Aaron calling me a 'good girl' took me completely by surprise. I didn't know if the words themselves were responsible or the way he whispered them to me, his voice deep and surprisingly authoritative in my ear, but whatever the reason, it set off an unexpected series of tingles through my body.

Nobody had ever said anything like that to me, not in that way, and I had to admit I rather liked it for reasons I couldn't entirely explain.

If only Corey were the one saying it to me instead.

Since Aaron had offered to help me get closer to that goal, I did my best to regain my composure as I asked him exactly what he had in mind.

"We can start with sowing a few seeds of doubt," Aaron suggested, pushing his glasses back up his nose. They must have come loose when he leaned over to whisper to me. "Eve will ask you what we talked about on the flight, right?"

Normally, I would say yes, but she'd been so wrapped up in Corey lately, it might not even cross her mind. She certainly hadn't thought about me at all on this flight so far. "Probably," I agreed anyway. "What do you want me to say?"

"Just tell her Corey convinced me to come on this trip by going on about all the hot girls who would be here. He said there were three that he hadn't fucked yet that he'd be willing to take a crack at."

Had he included me in that list of girls, or had Aaron just invented the whole thing? The second option seemed more likely, and my stomach twisted at the idea of spreading rumours about Corey. "What if she tells him I said that and he gets mad at me for lying?"

"It's not a lie," Aaron told me drily. "He honestly said that. Truthfully, I don't know what you see in the guy."

"He's your best friend," I pointed out. "You must think he has some good qualities."

"The qualities I like as a friend aren't qualities that would make him a good boyfriend. There's a difference."

"I still don't think you should be putting your friend down like that. I'm not bad-mouthing Eve." Nobody *ever* had anything bad to say about Eve. Sometimes, her perfection could be just a tiny bit frustrating. She never did anything to make me feel like she saw herself as better than me, but the rest of the world made it pretty clear.

"I'm not bad-mouthing anyone," Aaron replied, his jaw clenching. "I'm repeating what he told me word-for-word. If you think that makes him look bad, that's on him, not me."

He made a valid point, I supposed. Besides, if Corey really had said it, he probably did so in a much more charming way. Aaron's delivery did him no favours.

"What are you going to tell Corey, then?" I asked, steering us back towards the game plan.

"That's what you're supposed to tell me. I'd rather not lie, so what has Eve said that Corey wouldn't appreciate?"

Despite Aaron's assurances, the idea of sharing things Eve said to me in confidence still felt wrong. And yet, Eve's own advice to me had always been that I shouldn't wait for permission all the time. "If you do it confidently enough, you can get away with just about anything," she would tell me after charming her way into a better table at a restaurant, a higher grade or a better deal on her new car. "Don't give them a chance to say no."

Did that apply to going after the guy I wanted, even if she'd already kind of claimed him? No one would expect that of me, but maybe that could be a good thing. Maybe I needed to be a little less like me if I ever wanted to get Corey's attention. Being myself hadn't done me any good so far.

Aaron's hazel eyes watched me intently as I debated what to share, his fingers tapping nervously against the closed lid of his laptop. He must really like Eve, and an unexpected wave of sympathy washed over me. Would she ever go for a guy like him? His lack of concern over his appearance and social awkwardness made it seem unlikely, and leading him on didn't seem fair, but trying to find a kind way to say that could be difficult. He'd actually been quite nice to me during our conversation, all things considered. His comments suggested he thought I could do better than Corey, not the other way around, even if only because he thought Corey made a rotten boyfriend in the first place.

And besides, I couldn't speak for Eve. Who could say? Maybe she'd see something in Aaron that I'd missed. I really didn't know him that well.

Making up my mind, I tentatively told him some of what she'd said. "Before they hooked up, she always said she couldn't understand why everyone liked him so much. It confused her that everyone made a big deal over him."

Aaron's lips pursed in disapproval at my words. "That doesn't really help. He'll only be flattered that she's changed her mind now."

Yet again, he had a point, and for some reason, I didn't want to let him down. That look of disappointment affected me almost as much as him calling me a good girl did, just in a different way. In a bid to please him instead, I blurted out something else without fully thinking it through. "Well, after they slept together, she said he was all style and no substance and that she couldn't be serious with someone like him."

Aaron's eyebrows raised, letting me know he found that much more interesting, as I tried to ignore the uncomfortable churning in my stomach. I'd never betrayed Eve's trust like this before. What would she think if she ever found out?

"That could work," Aaron mused. "He's sensitive about people thinking he's stupid."

That only made me feel worse, and I hurried to correct him. "She never called him stupid."

"Then why couldn't she be serious with him?" Aaron pressed curiously.

I tried to explain it the best I could. "It's just that Eve comes from a very successful family and she's going to have a high-powered job in the family business after she graduates. Everyone expects her to end up with someone brilliant and successful and gorgeous and rich, the whole package. There are a lot of expectations, basically, and she's under a lot of pressure."

Until I laid it out like that, I hadn't fully appreciated the difficulty of Eve's position. There were plenty of advantages to being a Stamer, but demands also came with it. Had she been referring to that when she talked about having some fun before we graduated? Maybe the pressure to find the perfect partner had started to weigh on her?

Eve's brother, Noah, had ended up with my sister, Olivia, which seemed weird to me since I'd always thought of Noah as a big brother. Apparently, Olivia saw him differently, and he knew that Olivia really liked him for himself since they'd known each other forever. Eve had no childhood friend to fall back on. She found herself surrounded by people who wanted her not just for her beauty but for her wealth and connections too. In light of that, a fling with a handsome but not-too-serious hockey player looked pretty appealing.

And there I was, trying to break them up so I could be with him instead. What kind of awful person did that make me?

"Okay, so she just meant he's not someone who would fit into her world?" Aaron clarified. "I can still work with that, and don't worry, I won't make you look bad for telling me about it. I can spin it so it seems like you're just worried about them both."

"I *am* just worried about them both," I protested. "There's no spin involved. They're not right for each other, that's what I said at the start."

"Noelle, we're on the same team," he reminded me. "I agree they're not right for each other, and I don't want them to get hurt either. Trust me. I know how to talk to Corey. By the time I'm done, he'll think you're really sweet for being concerned about him."

That *did* sound pretty good. "I'll put in a good word for you with Eve too," I promised. "I can tell her I enjoyed talking to you. It's not completely a lie either."

"Gee, thanks." He rolled his eyes in such a sarcastic way that I had to blush.

"Sorry. I didn't mean it like that. This is why I always practice so much before a debate. When I don't, sometimes things don't come out exactly as I mean them."

"I've noticed." His expression remained completely deadpan. "But honestly, you shouldn't care so much about what everyone else thinks. There's nothing wrong with you just as you are."

That might have been one of the nicest things anyone had ever said to me, and to have it come out of Aaron's mouth truly surprised me. Maybe I'd never given him enough credit before. Clearing my throat, I brought us back to the point once more. "So, we sow this seed of doubt about their compatibility, as you said. Then what?"

At last, he cracked a smile, showing off a rather cute dimple I'd never noticed before. "Then, we get creative."

~Aaron~

By the time the pilot announced we'd begun our descent to Seattle, Noelle and I had a plan for the day. We would let slip the pieces of information we'd agreed on, we'd do our best to keep our friends apart as we all got settled into our accommodation, and at the end of the day, we'd regroup and decide what further action would be needed. Hopefully, if Eve and Corey weren't really serious about each other, a little nudge would be all it took and we'd have the full ten days of the trip to try to bring about the pairings that made much more sense. With Noelle talking me up to Eve and me doing the same for her with Corey, it honestly felt like we couldn't fail.

When it came down to it, Noelle could be reasonably attractive, and we'd actually had some fun together on the flight. Corey would like her too, once he got to know her, and I already felt completely convinced that Eve and I would be compatible if she gave me a chance. Everyone would have a great time just as soon as we got Corey and Eve apart.

With Noelle's number in my phone and mine in hers, I whispered goodbye to her as we got off the plane. "You're smart and resourceful, Noelle. I know you'll do this well."

Just as she had when I called her a good girl on the plane, Noelle blushed at the praise, which intrigued me yet again. Corey could use that to his advantage if he wanted to show her a good time, and yet, the idea of sharing that information with him held no appeal for me. For now, I would hang onto it for myself.

There were a few ways to get to Leavenworth from Seattle, but as several of our group were swimming in money, we had chosen to hire private chauffeured vehicles for the two-hour drive. When I protested that I couldn't afford that on top of the flight, Corey kicked in my share. He had always been generous, never begrudging the odd treat or keeping track of who owed him what.

As I told Noelle, he did have *some* good qualities. I just wouldn't want to date him.

Each of the SUVs held five passengers, and I cornered Corey as we went to wait for our bags. "You ditched me for the whole flight, jerk. Are you going to insist on driving down with Eve too?"

I expected him to put up a fight but the argument never came. He apologized instead. "You're right, I shouldn't have forced you into it. I'm sorry. You survived, at least."

His words took me by such surprise that the rest of my planned admonishment went out the window, leaving me unsure what to say next. I managed to stutter out a reply, sticking to my plan to build Noelle up whenever I could. "Yeah, well, it actually ended up being okay. Noelle's pretty cool, actually. You guys would probably hit it off, she knows all about hockey."

I picked up that tidbit from her on the flight. She said her dad followed the game closely and taught her everything about it. She regularly went to watch Corey play and knew all about his college career, much more than I did.

"Yeah, maybe," Corey replied noncommittally before grabbing his suitcase off the conveyor belt as if it weighed nothing. "But listen, I'm not going with Eve now. We're going to drive up with some of the other guys, I want to make some plans for the week."

That sounded perfect, both some time apart from the girls and the part about making plans. Once everyone had their bags, we all split up into our separate vehicles, Eve and Noelle getting into a car with some of the other girls while Corey and I grabbed a spot with some of the other guys. Once we were settled inside, with me and Corey in the middle row while the other three guys took up the back seat, I pulled out my phone so I could make notes or help research things. However, it quickly became apparent that the types of plans Corey meant weren't what I'd been imagining at all.

Rather than talking about outings or schedules, he wanted to figure out how much booze we needed and which varieties, and come up with a system for alerting each other when the sleeping arrangements required a last-minute adjustment.

"Like tonight, for example," he told us all with a grin, throwing a wink my way. "Aaron, you're going to have to find another bed. You might as well bunk up with Eve's friend, that'd be easiest."

I really should have seen that coming. The chalet we'd rented had ten bedrooms, which meant two people per room. Corey and I were sharing but it had always been on the understanding that if either of us hooked up with someone, the other would find another place to crash. Of course, when we made that arrangement, I'd been hoping to claim the room on behalf of me and Eve, but since Corey suggested that I should sleep in Noelle's room, it must have meant he already had plans with Eve himself.

"There are a bunch of couches in the rec room downstairs," one of the other guys, Charlie, reminded us. "That could be the backup space. Anyone who gets kicked out of their room can set up there."

"That sounds more reasonable," I agreed, shooting Corey a dirty look. "You can't just expect a girl to let a random guy sleep with her."

The rooms all had king-sized beds, so whoever shared a room would also be sharing the bed.

"You mean *you* can't," he teased while the other guys laughed. "I'm pretty sure any girl on this trip would let me get in bed with her. Maybe I can put it to the test."

The other guys all egged him on while I grimaced. Those were exactly the kind of comments that made me think Eve meant nothing more than a fling to him in the first place, and I jumped on the chance to bring it up, though probably not as elegantly as I could have. "It's a good thing you're not too hung up on Eve Stamer since she's not serious about you either."

That brought the laughter to an uneasy halt as Corey's brows furrowed. "What do you mean?"

I did my best to appear casual, giving a shrug. "Just something her friend, Noelle, mentioned on the flight. She asked if you were looking for something long-term with Eve, and when I said no, she said that Eve just saw you as casual too. Noelle doesn't want you to get your hopes up. She's really sweet."

He completely ignored the part about Noelle and gave me an almost hurt look instead. "Why would you say I'm not serious about Eve?"

"Because it's true? You're literally talking about getting into bed with every girl on this trip."

"It's a joke, Aaron." An uncharacteristic scowl darkened his face before he turned back to the other guys. "Anyone want to take bets on whether Aaron can go the whole ten days without getting laid? With all the booze and the girls we've brought along, it won't be easy, but if anyone can do it, he can."

I just rolled my eyes as the other guys laughed. Obviously, I'd struck a nerve, so he put me down to make himself feel better. I understood his way of operating but it still stung, especially when he knew exactly how much I'd been looking forward to getting to know Eve on this trip. That made it easier to push down any guilt that might have tried to poke its way to the surface over what Noelle and I were doing.

Corey didn't deserve Eve, and before long, she would see it too.

~Noelle~

The other girls in our car were all over Eve as soon as we were out on the highway towards Leavenworth, asking for details about the situation between her and Corey.

"He's so fucking hot," Sarah sighed. "Please tell me he looks just as good naked?"

"Better," Eve assured her, grinning as I grimaced.

"I got a glimpse of him in the locker room once when I went to visit Sam," one of the other girls, Florence, piped up. Her boyfriend played on the hockey team with Corey and had gone in the car with Corey and Aaron. "Not that I was specifically looking, but *damn*. You could bounce a quarter off that ass."

I could have guessed that, but unexpectedly, my mind flashed back to the image of Aaron's ass in front of me as we walked up the stairs at the party a few days ago, looking for Eve. It looked surprisingly firm too, I had to admit, but why would I be thinking about Aaron when the conversation already centred on my favourite subject?

Maybe because I would rather not hear Eve's take on the whole situation, which she gave now. "You've got that right. He is hard in *all* the right places."

The other girls laughed as I tried my best to smile.

"But is he actually any good?" Sabrina asked, leaning forward conspiratorially. "Sometimes, when they're that hot, they don't think they have to actually do anything. They expect us to be grateful just because they got naked."

"Sounds like you're speaking from experience," I commented, hoping to change the subject, and the girls all laughed again.

Unfortunately, Eve returned to the topic at hand, not letting herself be distracted. "I had some concerns about that too, honestly. I've had a few duds before, but Corey's not like that. He cares about my enjoyment. I have never had a plane ride like that before."

The idea of exactly what they had done on the plane left a bitter taste in my mouth as the other girls all exchanged theories about exactly how far they had gone. Eve delighted in refusing to give up any further details.

"I guess he's got enough experience, he *should* know what he's doing." Those words weren't mine, surprisingly. Florence said them, and no one disagreed.

"I've rarely seen him with the same girl twice," Sarah added. "But he sure seems taken with you, Eve. Does that mean this is something serious?"

Based on what Eve told me earlier, I expected her to say no, but her answer this time sounded a lot less clear. "We're still figuring it out, but he's fun. I'm enjoying it for now and we'll see where it goes."

Frustration ran through me at the idea of the goalposts changing, and the words came out of my mouth before I could stop them. "Well, just stay realistic about it. Aaron told me that Corey already had a list of girls on this trip he wanted to sleep with."

The startled look on Eve's face sent a wave of guilt through me and I wished I could take it back, but the conversation moved on before I could try to smooth things over.

"What's the deal with Aaron, anyway?" Sabrina asked curiously, picking up on my mention of him. "He's strangely confident for a guy who doesn't have a lot going for him."

"Maybe it's a sign that *he* knows what he's doing too," Florence suggested. "I know a girl who went out with him a few years ago and she said the sex was amazing. I don't really see how, but she swore on it."

Why did hearing that make my whole body tingle?

"It would have to be to make up for the rest of the time," Sarah commented. "He's so obnoxious."

Although I had always said the same thing, for some reason, hearing someone else say it made me strangely defensive. I had to bite my tongue to keep from disagreeing with something that I ultimately agreed with, which left me feeling confused.

"What else did Aaron say?" Eve asked me, her earlier smile gone as she looked over at me with her dark, trusting eyes.

"About Corey?" I asked, trying to stall even though I knew what she meant. When she nodded, I tried my best to stick to the plan Aaron and I had come up with. "Well, just that he's a player, but we all knew that already. He only brought it up because he thought you might get hurt. When I told him you weren't serious about Corey, he felt a lot better."

"It's none of his business," Sarah declared. "But who else do we think is going to hook up on this trip? With all of us together in one house, things are going to get crazy!"

The conversation moved away from Corey and Aaron to the other men who would be there. Besides Florence's boyfriend, Sam, and one other guy, the others were all single and therefore fair game. Florence asked me if I had my eye on anyone, but I lied that I hadn't considered anyone in particular. However, I intended to keep myself open to seeing what came up.

"No pun intended," Eve interjected with a laugh. She seemed to be in better spirits as we got nearer to the town, and when we arrived in Leavenworth, we all peered out the windows of the car eagerly, exclaiming over the town's snowy, Bavarian-style charm. None of us had ever been there before and it looked even better in real life than it had in the pictures.

The house we had rented sat on the edge of town, on a large plot of its own that gave us plenty of space for outdoor activities but was still close enough that we could walk into town for anything we wanted to do there. The two-and-a-half-storey chalet looked like something out of a Swiss fairytale with its gabled roof, carved wooden bandings, bay windows and balconies, just as romantic as I'd been imagining.

Inside, it looked even better. It had recently been renovated and everything looked modern and clean while still maintaining a rustic, Alpine feel. The huge living room would be big enough for all of us to hang out in, with a fireplace and a bar on one side. The equally large kitchen with a central island had already been stocked with groceries for us, though I had my doubts about whether anyone actually had any intention of cooking while we were there. A large dining room and a library completed the main floor.

In the basement were three bedrooms and a large rec room, and the remaining seven bedrooms were upstairs. Eve and I claimed one of the upstairs rooms with its balcony, large king-sized bed and ensuite bathroom, and while the others sorted out the remaining rooms, we got to work unpacking our suitcases and changing into fresh clothes after the long flight. Because of the time difference between Washington and New York, although the flight took five hours and the drive another two, we'd only lost four hours since we departed. We still had half the day ahead of us.

"Did Aaron really say that about Corey?" Eve asked as she changed into another outfit that highlighted her body perfectly. Her red hair looked even brighter than normal against the soft white cashmere sweater and I couldn't help feeling a bit envious as I watched her get ready. Eve had an innate sense of style that I had never been able to achieve, no matter how hard I tried. "Was Corey really talking about being with other girls on this trip?"

"That's what Aaron said," I answered truthfully as I pulled a sweater out of my own bag, a pink hand-me-down from my mom that I had always loved. "And I don't think he would lie. He just seemed worried about you."

"But you hate Aaron," she reminded me, making me wince.

"I don't think I ever said I *hated* him. I just find him annoying sometimes, that's all, but we actually had an okay time on the flight."

That earned me an apologetic look. "I'm sorry about leaving you with him, Noelle. I planned to come and trade back with him halfway, but when I walked by, you guys seemed to be having a good time and I didn't want to interrupt."

She *had* walked past us, and I had no reason to think she would be lying about why. Maybe I needed to give my best friend more credit. Nothing she had done had been intentional to hurt me and I needed to stop acting like it had.

"It's fine," I assured her, and this time, I meant it. "We're here now, so let's forget about the flight and have some fun."

"Agreed." Her usual warm smile returned as she looped her arm through mine. "Just wait and see, Noelle. This is going to be the best trip ever."

Chapter Three

SPIN THE BOTTLE

~Aaron~

Corey and I ended up in one of the basement rooms, probably because he figured it would be easier to kick me out with the rec room just outside the door. Mostly underground, the room had one high window to let a bit of natural light in, and the plush carpet beneath my feet added to the feel of being in a burrow. It would be the perfect place to hole up with someone who could help to keep me warm. Someone just like Eve, I hoped.

"Are you going to be this much of an asshole for the whole trip?" I asked as I unpacked my clothes into the dresser on one side of the room. Corey simply threw his suitcase on the floor and lay down on the bed, taking up far more than half of it. Sleeping in the rec room was starting to look better by the minute compared to sharing with him.

"*I'm* the asshole?" he asked, raising his head to scowl at me. "You're the one who told Eve's best friend that I'm not serious about her before announcing to half the guys on this trip that she doesn't really care about me either. What the hell, Aaron?"

He had to be kidding. "You want to talk about 'what the hell'? What about the fact that I told you how much I liked Eve and you went off the next fucking day and slept with her?"

His expression remained hard. "So, this is some kind of payback? Because you're bitter that I made a move while you were still navel-gazing? You always do this, Aaron. You have all these big plans and then you sit on them. If you really liked her that much, you should have gone for her yourself."

The words stung, not only because of his caustic tone but because he had a point. I'd wanted so badly for everything to be perfect with Eve that I did nothing at all, waiting for the stars to align. That had always been my nature: I weighed the pros and cons and I took my time to make sure I had considered all the angles, giving myself the best chance of success. Nothing had ever been given to me simply by virtue of my birth or because of any outstanding physical attributes. Despite working out most days, I would never have the kind of body that came naturally to Corey. I didn't have his money or his connections, so I had to rely on myself, and although I had made peace with that, it still made me naturally cautious.

So yeah, I *was* bitter that he acted before I did, and that everything always seemed to come so easily to him, but it still didn't excuse the fact that he knew exactly how I'd feel when he went for her. No matter what he said, I wouldn't let him distract me from that fact.

"I planned to 'go for her' on this trip," I reminded him. "You just had to keep your dick in your pants for one more week. The fact that you couldn't is a pretty good indication of how much I mean to you as a friend."

"It's not always about you. I like her and she likes me, it's as simple as that. It's not like we're thinking about you when we're together."

"Whatever, Corey." The dresser drawer slammed shut as I finished unpacking and pushed it closed with a little too much force. "You've made your choice, but if you expect me to be happy about you and Eve, you're delusional."

36

He sat up as I headed for the door, seeming surprised that I would leave it at that. "Come on, don't be like this. There's no reason we can't both have a good time. There are other girls on this trip."

"Other girls that you told everyone else I don't have a chance with," I reminded him sarcastically. "And Eve isn't just another girl to me. She's special, and you knew that."

"She is special," he agreed, looking a tiny bit guilty for the first time. "But her friend seems nice too, Nolie... whatever her name is. It seems like you guys have a lot in common and you said she's sweet. Maybe you could have fun with her?"

It surprised me that he remembered I'd said that, but it also annoyed me that he still couldn't remember her name. I focused on the second part first.

"Her name is No-elle." I enunciated both syllables clearly for him. "Like 'The First Noel'. Like Christmas, the fucking season we're in."

"Oh." He looked genuinely surprised. "That's not so hard to remember."

"Idiot," I muttered under my breath, but not quietly enough. Corey leapt to his feet, his eyes blazing.

"What did you say?" He got in front of me remarkably quickly, glaring down at me with his extra five inches in height and a lot more muscle mass, and I couldn't help wincing in regret. That was a low blow. Having people call him dumb had always been a sore point for him, and I had enough actual reasons to be upset with him to not bring his intelligence into this.

For that reason, I backed down. "I didn't say anything," I lied, exhaling in an attempt to release some of the tension that had built up both inside me and between us. "Come on, we're both grumpy after all the travelling. Let's go unwind."

He knew what I'd said as well as I did, but thankfully, he let it go. "I need a drink," he replied instead, yanking the door open and heading upstairs while I followed behind.

Just about everyone else had already gathered together in the kitchen with a few open bottles of alcohol next to a stack of red plastic cups. The only people missing, as far as I could tell, were Eve and Noelle, and things were getting started without them. Corey and I both grabbed ourselves a drink as Sabrina made a suggestion.

"Who remembers playing Spin the Bottle?"

Groans echoed around the room, but I suspected half of them were fake. Mine certainly was. It might be juvenile, but the idea actually excited me quite a bit. Maybe the odds were only one in ten that I would get to kiss Eve, but those were better odds than I had on most days.

A bit of debate followed about whether we should eat first and what the rules would be, but we soon had it settled: we'd play a round or two now as an icebreaker, and after supper, we could decide if we wanted to keep going or do something else instead.

Eve and Noelle walked in at the end of that conversation, having changed their clothes, and all eyes in the room went to Eve. She looked perfect, as always, in her white sweater and skinny jeans, and the idea of being able to kiss her, even in front of a curious crowd, sent another shot of excitement through me.

Noelle's pink sweater looked pretty too, I noticed. It fit her well, unlike a lot of her clothes, and she actually had a great figure when she showed it off properly. Her eyes immediately moved towards Corey when one of the girls explained what we were going to do now and I had to wonder if a kiss would be enough to spark his interest. Was Noelle a good kisser?

I continued to mull that over as we all moved to the large living room. Three long couches lined the walls, facing the fireplace and bar on the fourth side. A Christmas tree had been set up in one corner, filling the room with a fresh, natural pine scent. After moving the coffee table out of the way, we had enough room for everyone to sit in a wide circle on the rug on the floor, and Sam placed an empty wine bottle on the floor between us all.

"I guess Flo and Charlie and I are sitting this one out," he said with a laugh as he gave the bottle a test spin. They were the only three people on this trip who were already in serious relationships, but Sabrina shook her head playfully.

"It's just a kiss. It shouldn't matter if you guys are secure in your relationship."

The challenge in her words couldn't be clearer, and when Sam looked at his girlfriend for her opinion, she shrugged. "It's okay with me if it's okay with you."

No way in hell would I kiss another girl in front of my girlfriend, or want to see her kissing someone else, but to each their own, I supposed. When they all agreed they were in too, Sabrina asked who wanted to go first.

"Me," Corey immediately volunteered, and I noticed how all the girls in the circle immediately sat up straighter, hoping they'd be the one chosen. He really could have had his pick, it seemed.

He gave the bottle a firm spin and it felt like it spun around forever before coming to a stop pointing right at... me.

The room erupted into laughter as Corey and I side-eyed each other. "In your dreams," I teased him before he got a chance to say it first, and thankfully, he laughed along with everyone else.

"Let's add a rule where you get to choose the gender ahead of time," Corey suggested. "Unless you're happy either way."

Everyone quickly agreed, and he spun again. This time it landed on Katie, a pretty girl whose mother had made a fortune in some kind of makeup products. Corey gave her a wink and beckoned her over to him with a curl of his finger. Her cheeks flushing, Katie got up and came to kneel beside him. His arms wrapped around her waist as their lips connected, and I quickly glanced around the room to gauge people's reactions.

Noelle couldn't look more jealous with her lips pursed unhappily, but Eve proved harder to read. She watched the whole thing with no clear emotion on her face, not even when Corey whispered something into Katie's ear before she stood back up, returning to her place in the circle with cheeks redder than ever. That gave me an idea; words had always been my favourite method of seduction and if I got lucky enough to land on Eve, I could test out her response.

Charlie went next, then Sabrina, who'd suggested the game in the first place. Her spin landed on Corey, and once again, he made her go to him. Just as before,

Noelle looked like she'd tasted something sour while Eve remained completely impassive.

My turn came next, and although I'd never been a religious person, at that moment, I prayed to any and all forces that might be at work in the universe to point the damn bottle in the direction I wanted. Holding my breath, I released it and watched as the bottle began to slow as it got closer to Eve.

I had just started to think this might actually happen when the bottle inched just past her to point at the person sitting next to her instead: Noelle.

~Noelle~

As the bottle slowed down just before reaching Eve, I thought Aaron must have fixed it somehow. What were the odds it would land on the one person in the room out of twenty he wanted to kiss most? He would have to teach me how he'd done that so I could do the same.

But even as the thought crossed my mind, the bottle kept going, rotating just a tiny bit further before coming to a stop in my direction. Everyone turned to look at me curiously, sending a flush through my body from the unaccustomed attention. Having a beautiful older sister and a gorgeous best friend, I'd quickly learned that the attention would always go to them first, and any that came to me afterwards would be relatively muted. As a result, I shied away from the limelight, not wanting to invite any extra comparisons besides the ones already being made.

"It's kind of pointing between us," Eve whispered to me. "Do you want me to take it?"

Knowing my feelings about Aaron, at least before that day, she only wanted to help me out, but we had to be honest: the bottle clearly pointed at me. Even if

Aaron would have preferred to kiss Eve, the game still had rules. If I went along with her claim, I'd probably be labelled a coward or a cheater, and I didn't want Corey thinking of me as either of those things. I'd just have to kiss Aaron, like it or not, and as he got to his feet to come to me, unlike Corey who made the girls go to him, my heart began to beat faster.

All the eyes on me were making me nervous, I told myself. That explained my increased heart rate and nothing else.

Not knowing where to look as he kneeled down beside me, I glanced over at Corey to find him watching me curiously. He looked directly at me so rarely that I smiled at him instinctively, and to my surprise and delight, he actually smiled back.

"You might have to look at me for this to work." Aaron's voice vibrated low and deep next to my ear, sending a shiver down my spine as I remembered the way he whispered to me on the plane. "I won't bite, unless you want me to."

He sounded so sure of himself that the things the girls had said during the drive here came rushing back to me. *Maybe it's a sign he knows what he's doing?* It looked like I would soon find out. A warm hand cupped my cheek as he tilted my head back with just the right amount of force, and then his lips were on mine.

I wouldn't say I'd kissed a *lot* of guys before, but I'd kissed some. I'd slept with a couple of them too, but I'd never kissed anyone in front of a crowd before. That was my sister's scene, not mine.

But as soon as Aaron kissed me, his lips warm, his hand still touching my cheek and his surprisingly sexy cologne overwhelming my senses, I forgot about everyone else in the room. Even remembering to breathe took some effort as Aaron's mouth moved against mine, confident but inviting, his tongue playfully teasing along the edge of my lips.

It probably lasted only a few seconds, no longer than any of the other kisses we'd watched so far, but when he pulled back, it took me a second to remember where we were. That feeling of unreality only got stronger when his lips brushed against my ear again before he stood up and he whispered to me once more: "You've got perfect lips for kissing."

Holy fuck. Did he really just say that? My body erupted in tingles as I looked up at him in startled surprise, but he had already turned away, walking back around the circle and returning to his spot while the game moved on to the next player.

The way my body reacted mimicked my earlier response on the plane when he called me a good girl, and I didn't understand it at all. I'd never reacted like this to mere words from anyone. Did he know some secret code that turned me on? Did he say it to toy with me? What did it mean?

I would have to try to figure it out later. As the game continued, one of the other guys, James, also landed on me. Imagining himself as big a prize as Corey, he beckoned me over to him and I begrudgingly got to my feet. When Corey did it, the gesture oozed charm, but with James, it just seemed arrogant. The kiss didn't come close to Aaron's, but I couldn't really complain either. I'd definitely had worse. I'd also never kissed two guys in one night before, and I still hadn't had my own turn yet. This trip seemed to be shaping up to be full of new experiences already.

Eve's turn came just before mine and she looked around the room with a confident smile, sure that anyone the bottle landed on would be thrilled with their luck. It landed on Sarah first, who declined the offer despite the urging of all the men in the room, while the rest of us girls all rolled our eyes at their enthusiasm. They wouldn't kiss each other but they wanted us to: how typical.

When Eve spun the bottle again, it landed directly on Aaron.

His lips twitched as he tried not to show his pleasure at this turn of events, and an odd feeling bubbled up in my stomach. It almost felt like jealousy, but that would be crazy. I *wanted* Eve and Aaron to get together so Corey would be available for me. Everything I'd done since the plane had been with that in mind.

Getting up again to come to her, Aaron knelt down on the other side of Eve rather than between us, and he put his hand on her cheek just as he had on mine. I could almost feel it there again as I watched them. Since I would rather not watch them kiss, I looked over at Corey instead and the scowl on his face took me completely by surprise. I'd never really seen him looking unhappy before; he always seemed so confident and easygoing. Did he really like Eve so much that her kissing someone else even as part of a game upset him that much?

I turned back just in time to see Aaron pull back from the kiss and, just as he had with me, he seemed to pause next to Eve's ear. It crossed my mind that he might be telling her the same thing he told me, and once again, that odd, gnawing feeling pulled at my stomach. I thought that compliment had been sincere and specific to me; the idea that he said it to Eve too made it feel a whole lot less special.

My emotions and my thoughts were all over the place, but I couldn't process any of it before everyone turned to me as the next person in the circle. *Please land on Corey*, I begged the universe, but as usual, luck gave me a wide berth. The bottle landed instead on Sam, Florence's boyfriend, and we both got up, meeting each other halfway for a quick, awkward kiss that made a complete mockery of my turn.

The rest of the circle completed their turns before Florence announced that she might die of starvation unless we ate soon, and most of the rest of the group seemed to agree. By general consensus, we agreed to pick the game up after supper. A few suggestions were tossed around about how to spice things up, which sounded both scary and exciting, but I tried not to panic before anything had been set in stone. For now, I got to my feet and followed Eve into the kitchen.

After a bit of discussion, we all agreed the girls would put supper together while the guys went into town and picked up more alcohol. As soon as they were gone, we all began comparing notes about the kisses that had just taken place, naturally.

Eve had ended up kissing two guys and when Sabrina asked her to compare them, she gave an honest assessment. "Caleb had way too much sucking going on. I don't mind once we're into it, but straight off the bat is excessive."

I felt a bit bad for him as the other girls all laughed, but I also knew the guys were probably being just as blunt about us, if not more so. What would they say about me, I wondered? Would Aaron stick to what he'd told me privately or had he just been flattering me?

"What about Aaron?" Sabrina asked curiously, and I found myself holding my breath as I waited for Eve's reply.

"His kiss was… surprisingly good," Eve admitted. "But what he said to me afterwards kind of ruined it."

Ruined it? If he'd told her the same thing he told me, I couldn't see how that would be possible.

Of course, the girls all pounced on that. "What did he say?" Katie demanded as the others all echoed her request.

Eve shrugged, looking almost sorry that she'd brought it up. "He probably didn't want it shared."

"Then you shouldn't have mentioned it," Sabrina pointed out, completely accurately. "Now you have to tell us!"

They badgered her a while longer before Eve gave in. "He just said I should be proud of the way I kiss. That's weird, isn't it?"

Personally, I would be thrilled if anyone said that to me, especially in that deep, rather sexy way Aaron had of speaking when he whispered directly to me. It probably sounded a lot hotter coming from him than Eve had made it sound.

It seemed my feelings on the subject were in the minority, though, since everyone else agreed it had been a strange thing to say. When they asked me if I agreed with Eve about Aaron's kiss, I simply told them I enjoyed the kiss and left out what he said to me afterwards. It felt personal and private anyway, and at least now I knew that he hadn't said exactly the same thing to Eve. He told her she kissed well, but my lips were *perfect* for kissing. Perfect meant better than good, I felt pretty certain.

Why I should care so much what Aaron thought baffled me, but the words meant something to me anyway. I tucked them away safely in my memory where I could think back on them whenever I needed a boost, and taking a deep breath, I focused back on the rest of the evening instead.

~Aaron~

The crude conversation of the men around me as we all headed to the liquor store kept intruding into my own thoughts, whether I liked it or not.

"Did you see Katie's ass in those jeans?"

"I thought Jessica was going to pop out of that shirt."

"Give me two minutes alone with her and I'd have her out of it."

A nervous energy permeated the air as the guys all jostled for position, making our way down the lighted, snowy streets of Leavenworth. Besides the streetlamps, most of the houses had Christmas lights on, making the streets sparkle, and the people I could see through the windows looked warm and cozy, emphasizing the chilliness outside. Plenty of other people lined the streets too, all caught up in their own activities. December marked the high tourist season for this Christmas town and no one paid us any special attention as we headed downtown.

They weren't missing out, since the comments being made within our group weren't anything worth overhearing. Observations about the appearances of almost all the women on the trip with us were made, along with assessments of their kissing skills, except for three of the girls: Florence, because no one would risk saying anything about her in front of her boyfriend, Sam; Eve, because no one felt entirely sure about how serious she and Corey were; and Noelle, because... well, honestly, I couldn't really say why Noelle got left out. People just seemed to forget about her, not only then, but in general.

I'd never paid her much attention in a physical way before that day either, but now, I honestly couldn't remember why not. Maybe it could be the 'ugly friend effect' in reverse. Studies showed that hanging out with less attractive friends made people look better, and it must work the opposite way too. Associating herself with someone as stunning as Eve seemed to make Noelle fade into the background, even though, objectively, she shouldn't. She had a lot of attractive features and qualities, and now, I could add the way she kissed to the top of that list.

Her nerves were apparent when I knelt down beside her, but more than that, the trust in her eyes when she looked at me really struck a chord. Whether she felt anything for me or not, and my guess would be 'not', she still had a willingness and an eagerness to please that played right into my own personal preferences.

My holy grail in the bedroom had always been a woman who got off on doing a good job and being praised for it. All of the most satisfying experiences I'd ever had with any woman had an element of praise to them. I loved giving it, loved the power and feeling of dominance it gave me, and when she loved receiving it too, fireworks could happen.

Noelle seemed to be one of those who loved it, whether she knew it or not, and once again, I suspected she didn't. The startled but clearly aroused look she gave me when I paid her a compliment made that pretty clear. Her own reaction surprised her, but she liked being told she'd done well. Maybe that explained why she always tried so damn hard.

However, when I gave Eve a similar piece of praise, personal to her, her reaction seemed closer to confusion, and my heart sank. I had been so sure we would have this in common. I'd imagined it in my head so many times that it seemed impossible it wouldn't be true. Perhaps I'd simply come on too strong and taken her by surprise. The kiss had been good but not spectacular, but what else could be expected for a first kiss in front of a roomful of other people? Maybe her thoughts were still too much with Corey to be open to anything else.

I would just have to back off and bide my time before trying again. I had no plans to give up yet, not by a long shot, but it looked like a bit more groundwork would be needed to make the moment just right.

So, when the talk turned to playing another game after dinner, my enthusiasm didn't match everyone else's. My ultimate goal involved a lot more than a quick, drunken kiss in front of a crowd. I needed to form an emotional connection with Eve first, to find out what really motivated and turned her on, and then the earth would move for us. I felt sure of it.

"We're not in high school anymore," James pointed out as the group debated how to spice things up. "Fuck Spin the Bottle. We do Seven Minutes in Heaven and things'll get a lot more interesting."

"That's still a high school game," I couldn't help pointing out.

"If that's what you think, then you're not doing it right," Alex teased. "Seven minutes in private..."

"... is all the time Alex needs," Corey interjected, setting off a round of laughter as the others all taunted and poked fun at each other.

The conversation moved on, but as we headed back to the house with our purchases, the more I thought about it, the more potential I could see in the premise. Seven minutes in private did actually hold quite a lot of potential, with 'private' being the key word. Eve and I had never been alone together that long. It wouldn't have to be anything physical; we could just talk and actually start to get to know each other properly. That could be far more useful than a simple kiss with everyone watching.

By the time we returned, the girls had some food ready and we poured out some more drinks from the bottles we'd just bought. Everyone ate and drank while standing around the kitchen, eager to move on to what came next, and when James suggested Seven Minutes in Heaven, hardly anyone protested.

Sam and Florence insisted they'd have to be paired together, naturally, but after some half-hearted objections, the girls convinced Charlie to take part despite his girlfriend being several thousand miles away. At this point, if his relationship survived the length of this trip, it would be a miracle.

"We should all pair off at once," Sabrina suggested. "No point in sitting around waiting for people to come back."

Again, everyone agreed, and someone else suggested pulling names from a hat.

"Screw that," Corey said with a laugh. "Aaron can do a random list on his phone. It'll take two seconds."

Everyone turned to me curiously and I nodded in both agreement and satisfaction. Corey knew I had an app that produced randomized results since we'd used it together before on a number of different occasions. Even better, by placing the power in my hands, Corey had given me the perfect opportunity to manipulate the results in my favour. I couldn't ask for more.

"Alright, I'll put all the men's names in, except for Sam," I announced to everyone as I pulled up the app and got to work. "Then the girls can decide who gets first dibs."

They argued between themselves for a minute while I finished entering all the names and when I looked up, Sabrina got my attention. "Me first."

With a tap of my finger, a name appeared on the screen. "James." Two more girls went before we got to Katie. When I pressed the button, my own name appeared, but since no one else could see the screen, I lied, simple as that. "Charlie."

Noelle went next, and I gave her a small nod before tapping the screen again.

The name Caleb popped up but I stuck to our plan instead. We were trying to engineer as much time as possible for us to be with the person we actually wanted to be with, and there couldn't be a better opportunity than this. "Corey."

Noelle's eyes widened in surprise, as if she hadn't been expecting it, and I almost laughed. She really was a good girl, no matter what she tried to claim.

Eve came next, right behind her, and of course, I gave my own name. She didn't look disappointed, but then, Eve had more class than that. She wouldn't have shown disappointment no matter who she got paired up with.

When everyone had a partner, it took a couple of more minutes to sort out who would go to which rooms and how we would know the seven minutes were up, but finally, the couples began to disperse. My heart racing in anticipation, I gave Eve a warm smile as I stepped closer to her. "I'm all yours, Eve. Lead the way."

Chapter Four

SEVEN MINUTES IN HEAVEN

~Noelle~

Could this really be happening? I glanced around the room, waiting for someone to tell me they'd set the whole thing up as a prank, but no one said a word. By all appearances, I was going to get to spend seven minutes alone with Corey in a situation where everyone expected us to be making out, including him. My dreams were coming true, thanks to Aaron, but when I glanced over at Eve, guilt ran through me again. Even if it still seemed likely she and Corey would break up before long, for now, they were still kind of together. How would she feel about anything happening between me and Corey, even as part of the game?

Even though it went against everything Aaron and I had agreed on, I heard myself making her an offer: "Do you want to trade? You could go with Corey and I'll go with Aaron."

I tried not to imagine how upset Aaron would be with me for messing up his plan, and I also had to ignore the little feeling of excitement that bubbled up inside me at the idea of going with Aaron instead. Kissing him again wouldn't be so bad if it were anything like our earlier kiss. On the other hand, the odds were good he might simply yell at me for the entire seven minutes.

However, I wouldn't have to worry about either of those things happening since Eve declined my offer. "No, it's fine. It's just a game."

"So, you're going to make out with Aaron? And Corey won't mind?"

She shrugged in that cool, casual way of hers. "We'll see what happens. Corey and I aren't *together* together and we're all here to have fun. It's fine."

Those were the words I needed to hear, and I gave her a smile just as Aaron came up to us with Corey close behind him. "I'm all yours, Eve," Aaron said. "Lead the way."

She gave him a curious smile. "We're not going to your room?"

"Nah, I'm taking Noelle there." Corey threw me a wink that had my stomach doing cartwheels. Apparently, I'd never heard him say my name before, because hearing it now sounded unbelievably sexy. "See you guys in seven minutes."

He headed for the basement stairs while I hurried after him, glancing back just in time to see Aaron following Eve up the main staircase. My partner-in-crime gave me a covert thumbs-up while no one else could see and I smiled back even as I started to feel like I might be sick. My legs trembled so much going down the stairs that I had to hold onto the handrail to keep my balance.

Corey and Aaron's room looked just as big as mine and Eve's, with the same king-sized bed and an ensuite bathroom. Corey flipped the light on as he walked in, leaving the door open for me. I closed it behind me, imagining we'd want some privacy even though I didn't have a clue what might happen next. Would he actually kiss me? Would it be just as spectacular as I always imagined? Could this be the moment I'd been waiting more than three years for?

"So, do you want me standing up or lying down while you suck my dick?"

The question pulled me out of my head so fast, I nearly tripped. "Wh... what?"

My cheeks turned a bright red as my gaze inadvertently dropped to his crotch, and Corey laughed in a slightly unpleasant way. "Relax, it's a joke. I'm just kidding. We're not going to do anything, obviously. Take a seat, make yourself comfortable."

He dropped onto the bed, stretching his legs out in front of him and leaning back against the headboard with his hands behind his head, looking perfectly at ease and in control as usual. Completely confused, I walked around to the other side of the bed and sat down gingerly on the edge of it. "What do you mean we're not going to do anything?"

He raised his perfect eyebrows at me. "I'm dating your friend. No matter what you've heard about me, I do have some moral standards."

Well, that was interesting, and disappointing, and not at all what Aaron had told me. Had Aaron lied to me after all? If so, he'd been very convincing.

Despite my disappointment, a tiny bit of relief wormed its way into my chest. At least I wouldn't have to worry about crossing any lines with Eve. And besides, if Corey and I *had* made out and he hated it, that might have been the end of my chances. This way, I could talk to him and have him get to know me first. Although I already knew everything about him, he'd never paid me much attention, I knew that for sure.

"People like to say stupid stuff about anyone they're jealous of," I sympathized, referring back to his comment about 'no matter what I'd heard'. "I don't care what they say."

His eyebrows somehow raised even higher and the corner of his mouth twitched. "Is that so? Is that why they say those things about you, because they're jealous?"

My mouth dropped open in dismay as my mind raced, trying to figure out what he meant. In the end, I couldn't work it out so I had to ask: "What do they say?"

Corey laughed darkly again, shaking his head. "That's what I thought. You do care."

Embarrassment rushed through me as I realized he made up the whole thing to call me out. It seemed unnecessarily mean since we hardly knew each other, but pointing that out wouldn't help my cause. He'd basically just called me oversensitive, and I didn't need to prove his point. "Alright, I do care what people think about *me*, but I don't pay attention to gossip about other people. There's a difference."

"Gossip is gossip," he muttered. "Even when it's about your best friend."

My heart sank even further as I started to realize what lay behind this attitude towards me. Just as I'd been afraid would happen, he must be angry about what I told Aaron. So much for Aaron mentioning it delicately, as he'd promised. Although, to be fair, I hadn't exactly softened the blow for Eve either.

Since I couldn't deny I'd said it, I would just have to explain myself. "If you're talking about the conversation Aaron and I had on the plane, there are two things you should know: first, we had quite a lot to drink, and second, I only mentioned it because I don't want you to get hurt if you think what's happening with Eve is something serious. Just because you're popular doesn't mean you don't have feelings, even if people sometimes think that's true."

"And how would *you* know about that?" Again, his question felt almost cruel, but it helped to focus me. As someone who joined the debate club for fun, I never shied away from an argument, and I soon had my response ready.

"I'm friends with one of the most popular girls at college. I've seen first-hand the way people think they can say whatever they want about her and it doesn't matter because she's rich or beautiful, but it hurts her just as much as it would for anyone. She's a real person, and I bet somewhere behind this hissy fit you're throwing, you are too."

Corey's eyes widened at the last part, and my heart pounded in disbelief at what I'd just said. Had I just blown it? My first chance to have a conversation with him and I insulted him to his face. He would kick me out and never speak to me again, I felt certain, even though he bore some of the blame for starting it.

However, he didn't ask me to leave. Instead, after staring at me in surprise for a minute, he began to laugh again, much more genuinely this time, the hard edge gone from his voice. "Well, Noelle, looks like you've got some backbone after all."

"Whoever said I don't doesn't know me very well." I flashed him a quick, tentative smile before a thought occurred to me which made my stomach twist all over again. My insides were definitely getting a workout. "Wait, did Eve say that?"

Who else would Corey be talking to about me? Possibly Aaron, but Aaron promised to sing my praises. Besides, Aaron and I had butted heads so many times, I couldn't imagine him saying I lacked a backbone anyway.

"You don't care about gossip, remember?"

This time, Corey's words were teasing rather than mean-spirited, but they also made it clear he had no intention of answering me. Did that mean Eve *had* said it? Why would she? Or had Corey just made this up too?

When I didn't answer him, Corey glanced down at his watch and sighed. "We've still got four minutes. What do you want to talk about? Aaron told me you like hockey."

I could definitely hold my own in a conversation about hockey and I sent Aaron a silent thanks in my head. It seemed he was keeping up his end of the bargain, talking me up to Corey and setting us up together too. "I do. I'm at most of the games. You guys are having a great season but your goaltending is letting you down. The coach should play Robertson more. I know he's a freshman but he's quicker than Johnson."

Real interest sparked in Corey's eyes for the first time since we got to his room. "That's what I said. It shouldn't matter who's been waiting longer for their chance to start, it's who performs best."

Though he couldn't have known it, that almost felt like a dig at me: no matter how long I'd been waiting for a chance with him, it made no difference when Eve turned his head. However, I had no plans to give up that easily. "Speaking of quicker, your breakaways look even faster this year. Have you been working on something new?"

"Yeah, I have, actually."

He seemed to be flattered as he explained his new workout routine to me, and by the time his alarm beeped to tell us the seven minutes were up, he'd promised to show me a couple of things when we all went to the ice rink in town sometime in the next few days.

As we stood up to return to the party, Corey put a hand on my arm. "Hey, I'm sorry I acted like a jerk off the bat. I'm upset about a couple of things and I took it out on you. That's not cool."

I did my best to mimic Eve's elegant shrug. "That's okay. I enjoyed talking to you anyway."

"Yeah, I enjoyed it too." He sounded almost surprised. "We should do it again sometime." *Yes!* I had hoped for exactly this outcome... until he added one more thing. "Maybe we can double date tomorrow, me and Eve and you and Aaron?"

No! I tried to keep the smile on my face even though inside I felt like screaming. "Yeah, maybe. That could be fun."

He walked past me up the stairs as I squeezed my eyes shut in frustration. So close, and yet so very far. Hopefully, Aaron had a bit more luck with Eve, because if we were relying solely on me, the chances that this plan would pay off were looking very slim indeed.

~**Aaron**~

The look on Noelle's face before heading downstairs with Corey made me smile. Part excitement and part terror, she seemed to realize she'd be walking straight into the lion's den but she couldn't look happier about it. They wouldn't actually fuck in seven minutes, but Corey wouldn't let the time go to waste either. As soon as he got Noelle alone and close up, he'd see just how cute she actually was and he'd take advantage of that.

And once he got a taste of those sweet lips of hers, he'd be hooked. I did my best to ignore the weird twinge of discomfort in my stomach brought on by that thought.

When it came to me and Eve, though, I didn't plan to make any kind of move at all, not in that way. I'd already kissed Eve earlier during the game and it hadn't been quite as amazing as I'd imagined, but I had a theory about why not. We needed an emotional and intellectual connection first so that the next time we kissed, it would be much more exciting.

"Sorry for the mess," Eve apologized once we got to her room. She let me in and closed the door behind us, looking fully at ease as she waved a hand over the clothes strewn across one side of the room. "If I'd known I'd be bringing anyone else in here, I would have cleaned up first. Noelle's used to me by now."

So, the tidy half of the room must have been Noelle's side. No shock there given how fastidious she seemed in other ways, but Eve's disorganization surprised me. She always looked so put-together, I assumed that would have carried over to other parts of her life too.

I could live with a little messiness, though. "Don't worry about it. Our room looks a lot worse."

It did, but only because of Corey. My side looked just as neat as Noelle's, to be honest. I wondered if Eve would guess that, but she let the comment slide, moving on to ask me straight out about my intentions.

"So, what did you have in mind? How worried should I be right now?"

Her teasing made me smile, as did her confidence. She trusted that I would want to do something with her, but she would also have no problem turning me down if I suggested anything too forward. Luckily, I had no plans to make her uncomfortable. "You've got nothing to worry about. I enjoyed our kiss earlier but I'd like to just talk to you now."

"Oh." Eve looked surprised, and perhaps even a tiny bit disappointed as we both took a seat on the bed. "What do you want to talk about?"

"Well, you, mostly. We've hung out in the same group of people for more than three years but we've never really had a conversation. I guess I'm curious about the real Eve Stamer."

"What does that mean?" She watched me warily as she waited for my answer, as if it might be a trap.

"Let's start with something basic. What made you pick Leavenworth for this trip?"

Instantly, her eyes lit up, letting me know I'd chosen the right question. "My mom is crazy about Christmas and she always made it a really special time of year for us. I have so many great memories of Christmas growing up, and being in a place like this just makes me feel warm and cozy and comfortable. The Danish have a word for it: they call it hygge, and that's what Leavenworth feels like to me. It's all hyggely."

We both laughed at the made-up word. Her laugh was cute, but maybe not quite as infectious as Noelle's, I couldn't help thinking. "It sounds like your mom is pretty great. What about your dad?"

"When it comes to Christmas or in general?".

"Both." I wanted to know everything.

Eve thought it over for a moment. "Well, he loves Christmas too though he'd never admit it. He's much more controlled and less demonstrative than my mom, but he feels things just as deeply even if he doesn't show it. He loves my mom and he loves me and my brother too. I've got a pretty great family, all in all. I can't complain."

It certainly sounded that way. "And your brother? What's he like?"

Eve leaned back, her hands resting on the mattress behind her, looking more relaxed and comfortable by the second. "Noah's like my dad in a lot of ways. Very reserved in public, he likes to keep his private business private, but he's very confident and sure of himself too. He's engaged to Noelle's sister, Olivia. I don't know if you knew that."

I knew she had a brother, but everything else she'd shared, I hadn't known. "I had no idea. Your whole families are close then, not just you and Noelle?"

Eve nodded vigorously. "That's an understatement. My mom and Noelle's mom were best friends before my mom and dad met, and so were my dad and Noelle's dad. Honestly, Noah and Olivia getting together feels a little incestuous to me, we're practically family!"

The closeness she and Noelle obviously had made a lot more sense in that context, and her laugh made it clear she was joking about her brother and his fiancée. She seemed happy with the way things had worked out.

"And what about your family business? Does your mom work for Stamer Hotels too?"

"In a way. She's an architect and she has her own design firm that looks after all kinds of projects, but personally, she hasn't designed for anyone other than my dad for years. I think he's too possessive to let her work for anyone else."

I could relate to that. When I found something special, I wanted to keep it for myself too. Maybe Eve's dad would be someone I would get along well with. "And you're going to work there after graduation?"

For the first time since the conversation started, a conflicted look clouded Eve's face. "Yeah, it looks that way. But that's enough about me. We're going to run out of time and I haven't got to ask a question yet. What's your family like?"

Obviously, I'd touched upon a slightly sore spot and I wanted to know more about it, but she was right that our seven minutes wouldn't last forever so I accepted the change of subject. "My family's far less impressive, I'm afraid. My dad's a veteran now but he was active during my childhood so he would often be away. When he came back for good, my mom had gotten too used to living on her own and they clashed a lot. Eventually, they split up. She's remarried now."

Eve followed along carefully, listening with interest. "What about your dad?"

I assume she wanted to know if he'd remarried too, so I answered that and threw in some extra information. "He's got a new girlfriend every few months and a couple of kids with some of them. We don't really have a lot in common, but he makes an effort. We get together as often as we can."

"How many brothers or sisters do you have?"

I didn't have a straightforward answer to that. "I've got one full sister and two half-brothers and a half-sister, I think. There could be more."

Eve exhaled loudly, blowing the air out through her lips so that they vibrated. "Well, shit. I wish you'd gone first before I went on about my family."

Her blunt self-criticism made me laugh. "I don't think there are many families that could hold a candle to yours, but you don't need to feel bad for me. Mine's okay. My mom and dad are both in my life and they care about me, so it could be a lot worse."

In a way, growing up without a steady father figure and then dealing with my parents' divorce had forced me to become more self-sufficient at an early age. My work ethic probably stemmed from that, as did my tendency to not really care what other people thought about me. I'd dealt with much bigger problems than being popular or not, so I only really paid attention to the opinions I cared about which, at the moment, included Eve's. With that in mind, I brought the conversation back around to her.

"Besides, just because someone has a great family doesn't mean their life is easy all the time."

Her lips curled into an appreciative smile. "Not everyone understands that."

I smiled back at her and for just a moment, it felt like we had a brief connection before Eve glanced down at her watch.

"We've only got a minute left. You don't want to kiss me at least once so you can brag about it to your friends?"

The fact that she knew and accepted that kind of conversation went on made me wince. "That's not really my style. Besides, everyone already saw us kiss downstairs. They can use their imaginations this time around."

Eve seemed to like that idea. "Well, thanks. This was nice, actually."

"Actually?" I raised my eyebrows at the qualifier, and Eve laughed.

"Sorry, that sounded rude. I didn't mean you in general, I just thought that whoever I ended up with would try to push their luck. I appreciate that you were different."

"The week's still young, Eve. Don't give me too much credit yet."

She laughed again and we both headed back downstairs with smiles on our faces, mine a bit bigger than hers. That couldn't have gone much better. Hopefully, Noelle had laid some similar groundwork and we'd be with the people we wanted to be with in no time at all.

Yet, to my surprise, I found myself looking forward to catching up with Noelle almost as much as I had looked forward to speaking to Eve in the first place. The day certainly hadn't turned out anything like I expected it to when I woke up that morning, and I couldn't begin to guess what the rest of the week might bring.

~Noelle~

No further rounds of Seven Minutes in Heaven were played that evening. It seemed other people's experiences had been just as disappointing as mine, and no one wanted to waste any more time on pairings that weren't going anywhere. One couple stayed away for an extra ten minutes on top of the original seven, leading to hoots and whistles from the rest of the group when they finally showed up, but they seemed to be an exception. For the rest, I suspected people were wary of hooking up too early and ending up stuck with that person for the rest of the week.

Or maybe they were just keeping their cards close to their chests. Aaron and Eve both seemed to be in a good mood when they returned from our room and another unexpected wave of jealousy washed over me at the thought that things had gotten hot and heavy between them. What was I even jealous about? That Aaron had better luck than I did, or that Eve got to hear him whispering hot and seductive things like he'd done to me earlier? Did I want them to get together or not? My mind said one thing and my body said another, and my heart seemed to be caught somewhere in the middle. The whole thing left me feeling very confused.

After my slip on the plane, I took the alcohol slower that night, not wanting to blurt out anything else that I shouldn't, and the long day started to wear on me. It might have only been nine o'clock in Washington, but it was midnight back in New York, and without the prospect of anything further happening with Corey that evening or the assistance of the alcohol to keep me going, my bed started to sound pretty good.

"I think I'm going to head upstairs," I whispered to Eve. "I'll see you when you get up there."

She gave me a quick hug as she whispered back to me. "I might spend the night with Corey, so don't worry if I'm not there."

Shit. I supposed expecting our plan to be working already would be unrealistic, but a bitter taste filled my mouth anyway. Especially since I could picture Corey in his room now, lying back on his bed while Eve...

Nope, I definitely didn't need to imagine that. Pushing the mental picture down, I nodded and got to my feet, glancing around the room to see if anyone else noticed me getting up. Corey seemed to be caught up in a conversation with a couple of the other guys but Aaron looked over in my direction. I nodded once at him in what I hoped felt like a friendly, supportive way before heading up the stairs.

Alone in my room, I pulled out one of the pajama sets I'd brought along for the trip. Ever the optimist, I'd brought a few sexier sets in case I did somehow manage to get lucky, but I also brought some comfortable pairs for lounging around and the far more likely scenario that I ended up sleeping alone. I pulled one of those out now. The fuzzy pants were red with snowflakes on them and the red and white striped top had a checklist on the front. The options 'naughty' and 'nice' were left blank, while the box checked read: 'I tried'.

Eve had an almost matching pair except that hers said 'Does nice-ish count?' on the front. Ever since we were little girls, we'd always had matching Christmas pajamas. Our moms used to buy them for us and now, we carried on that tradition on our own.

Despite my fatigue, I took my bedtime routine as seriously as always, scrubbing my face clear from my makeup before exfoliating and moisturizing. I brushed out my hair and pulled it back into a loose ponytail to keep it off my face while I slept, brushed and flossed my teeth, and rubbed lotion into my hands and feet. In my case, nature needed all the help it could get so I never neglected it. When I felt satisfied I'd done all I could, I turned off the light and headed for bed, but no sooner had I crawled in when a knock sounded at the door, making me frown.

Eve wouldn't knock, so who else would be there? Maybe someone had the wrong door?

"This is Eve and Noelle's room," I called out, not really wanting to get up now that I'd made myself comfortable, but to my surprise, the door swung open, and I yelped as I sat back up. "I didn't say to come in."

"Relax, it's just me."

The light from the hall backlit the man in the doorway, making it impossible to make out his face, but I knew exactly who the silhouette belonged to anyway.

"Aaron? What are you doing here?" My heart, already sped up a bit from the unexpected intrusion, kicked into an even higher gear.

"I want to talk to you. Have you got a lamp there or something? I don't want to hurt your eyes by turning the main light on." That was unexpectedly thoughtful, and I reached over to flip the switch on the bedside lamp. As soon as the light turned on, Aaron closed the door behind him and walked towards me. "You weren't sleeping, were you?"

"No," I assured him. "I just got into bed. What's up?"

The bed sank beneath his weight as he sat down on the edge next to me and I quickly shuffled further over to give him more space. In the soft light of the lamp, he gave me an almost confused look. "You look good like this, Noelle."

His surprise made it sound like an insult, and I returned his gaze suspiciously. "In the dim light, you mean?"

"What?" He looked even more confused for a second before shaking his head. "No, I didn't mean it like that. I just mean this more natural look, without all the makeup. It really suits you. I can see your eyes better, for one thing."

That made no sense to me since I had designed my eye makeup based on all the videos I'd watched about how to make them stand out more, but it did remind me about what I'd been wondering on the plane about *his* eyes. "Do you ever wear contacts?"

He answered me as bluntly as usual. "No. I tried, but my eyes are a funny shape, apparently, so the contacts were uncomfortable. I had to stop playing any sports that I couldn't do without my glasses on."

He used to be an athlete? Maybe that explained the hints of a toned body that I'd seen hiding beneath the unflattering clothes he usually wore.

"Can I see what you look like without them?"

Maybe I drank more than I realized. My boldness in asking surprised me as much as him, but he didn't argue with me. Aaron pulled the thick black-framed glasses from his face, blinking as he turned to face me. "Satisfied?"

Perhaps the lamp light really did provide a flattering angle, or maybe I was feeling the effects of the time change or the alcohol, or both, but at that moment, Aaron Speelman actually looked pretty damn sexy. His hazel eyes looked bigger without the glasses on, his eyelashes long and thick, and it completely changed the proportions and symmetry of his face. Somehow, even though his eyes stood out more, his lips also somehow managed to look more appealing.

"Uh, yeah," I managed to stutter. "You look good too. It's a shame you can't go without your glasses more often."

Too late, I realized what a backhanded compliment that sounded like, but Aaron noticed it right away. His lips tightened as he shoved his glasses back on. "Well, it is what it is. Anyway, I've been kicked out of my room because Eve's in there with Corey. What happened between you and Corey?"

So, they were spending the night together after all. I waited for the disappointment to hit me but although it did come, it missed its usual bite while Aaron sat next to me.

I told him about the conversation I had with Corey, and Aaron's brow furrowed as he listened to me. "Something's going on with him," he mused. "He can be a jerk to me at times but he doesn't usually act that way with other people."

"Maybe he knows what we're up to?" I suggested, the thought making my stomach twist, but Aaron shook his head.

"No, I don't think that's it. There's something else, I just don't know what." He told me about the conversation he had with Eve, and the fact that they hadn't kissed either made me much happier than it should have.

"Corey suggested the four of us go out together sometime," I told him. "What do you think about that?"

"I think that could work," Aaron said slowly, turning the idea over in his head. "It'll give them a chance to directly compare us to their current partners. You get Corey talking about hockey again and Eve won't be able to get a word in edgewise."

It sounded risky to try to flirt with Corey right in front of Eve, but if Aaron thought it would work, I wouldn't argue. Even if things went wrong, we'd still have each other to fall back on.

"Alright, I'll let you get some sleep then," Aaron said, getting back to his feet. "Good night, Noelle."

"Wait." The word burst out of my mouth and he stopped immediately. "Where are you sleeping tonight if Eve is in your room?"

His eyebrows raised curiously. "In the rec room in the basement. Why?"

I had no idea why I asked, honestly, but Aaron seemed to have a theory as his lips curled into a teasing smile.

"Are you asking me to sleep with you, Noelle?"

Chapter Five

OVERHEARD

~Aaron~

I didn't expect Noelle to say yes. The startled look in her eyes when I asked if she wanted me to stay made it clear she hadn't meant it that way. Maybe her question about where I planned to spend the night had been an attempt at polite conversation, although politeness hadn't really factored into our dynamic so far. With our temporary alliance built on a slightly underhanded foundation, basic civility hadn't been much of a concern.

So, her reply came completely out of left field, at least to me. "Well, it looks like I'm going to be alone in here all night and the bed is huge. There's room for you if you want a more comfortable place to sleep than the rec room."

People rarely surprised me, but Noelle had managed it, starting with the way she looked right now. I meant it when I said this more natural look suited her. Sitting there in her pajamas with no makeup and her hair pulled back, she actually looked far more appealing than I'd ever seen her before. When I sat down next to her with those enticing blue eyes looking over at me, I couldn't help remembering the way she'd reacted to my words earlier and the look in her eyes then.

When she asked me to take my glasses off, giving me a hint that she might also be looking at me in a new light, I had to wonder how she might respond if things got more heated between us.

Those were crazy thoughts, though. I wanted Eve, and I shouldn't need to remind myself of it. For the first time, I'd actually made some progress towards that goal. Messing around with Noelle, no matter how enjoyable it might be in the short term, would only hurt me in the long run. I had to keep my eyes on the prize and so I stood up to leave before things could get out of hand.

Then she went and offered me a spot in her bed, and fuck it all if I wasn't tempted.

"You aren't worried I'd try something?" I asked her, partly teasing and partly to place the decision back in her hands. It would be so much easier if she just told me to go.

Instead, she gave me an incredulous look. "Do I need to be worried about that? The fact that you're bringing it up is a pretty good sign I don't."

She had me there. We'd discussed that very tactic of deflection during our debating sessions before. "How will it look to everyone else if they see me coming out of your room in the morning?" I tried instead.

Noelle simply shrugged. "They can think what they want. If Eve asks me about it, I'll tell her the truth. Stop stalling and make up your mind. I'm tired."

Her bluntness and uncharacteristic confidence made me smile, and I couldn't help thinking she should be that sure of herself more often. To tell the truth, her bed did look a hell of a lot more comfortable than the sofa in the rec room where I'd probably be joined by a handful of other guys whose snoring would keep me up half the night.

One small problem remained. "My pajamas are in my room, which is currently off-limits. I had planned to sleep in my underwear."

Noelle's eyes widened for just a second before she shrugged again, less confidently this time, though she tried to pretend otherwise. "Whatever you do on your side of the bed is your own business."

If she honestly felt that way, then maybe it wouldn't hurt. My excuses had all run out. We were both adults, and friends, sort of. It would be fine. "Alright. Turn the light off, then."

Noelle obeyed, turning the light off and lying down so that she faced the outside of the bed, away from 'my side', as she called it. Enough light still came in through the curtained windows that I could make my way over to the opposite side of the bed without running into anything, and I quickly stripped off my clothes, folding them in the dark and placing them on the bedside table before laying my glasses down on top of them. That made it harder to see in the darkness, but I managed to grope my way beneath the covers and make myself comfortable, sinking down gratefully into the soft mattress.

"Good night, Noelle."

"G'night," came the muffled reply, her face still turned away from me.

Sleep came relatively easily, but unfortunately, due to the time difference and jet lag, I woke up long before sunrise. I couldn't tell the time without my glasses on but with the house still dark and quiet and Noelle still sleeping soundly beside me, I guessed it must still be early.

As I lay there trying to go back to sleep, my mind wandered again to the girl in the bed next to me. I felt I knew her so much better than I had a day ago, and yet, there were still a lot of things I didn't understand. Why would such a smart, pretty girl be so insecure? How did she manage to present herself as less appealing than she actually was in almost every circumstance? And what did she see in a guy like Corey anyway?

He had to be the centre of attention at all times and that wouldn't do Noelle any favours. She already spent most of her time in the shadow cast by Eve's spotlight. She needed someone who would make her shine instead, someone who would appreciate her and give her the approval she seemed to crave. Someone who enjoyed making their partner feel special, who got off on it.

Someone like me.

I shut my eyes against that thought as soon as it entered my head. Nothing about this train of thought could be considered helpful, especially not when I currently lay only a matter of inches from the girl on my mind.

Sure enough, as soon as *that* thought crossed my mind, my body began to wake up all on its own and I stifled a groan of frustration. Trying to think about something else only brought me back to the very thing I wanted to avoid, and my mind flooded with images of Noelle shivering against my words, following my instructions to earn my praise, and eventually, I knew if I wanted to have any chance of going back to sleep, I would have to do something about it.

Shoving my glasses on in the darkness, I could just make out the path to the ensuite bathroom and I moved as quietly as possible through the dark room. Inside, the bathroom felt even darker, but turning the light on might wake Noelle. I simply closed the door instead and tried to turn the lock, but it didn't seem to be latching. Frowning, I tried three different times, the clicking sounds getting louder until I had to give up. Any more noise and I would definitely wake her up, and at this point, getting to the finish line wouldn't take very long anyway.

Pressing my lips tightly together to hold in any sounds that might try to escape, I pulled down my underwear to free my dick, already stiff with need. My hand wrapped around its length as I choked another groan in the back of my throat. Fuck, it had been a long time since I'd been this turned on by only my imagination. It felt a little cheap and dirty to be doing this so close to her, but I had passed the point of no return. Besides, Noelle would never need to know.

There was nothing drawn out about it. I spit into one hand while grappling around in the dark with the other until I found some toilet paper to finish into. Classy as fuck, naturally, but I no longer cared. With my eyes closed, I began to pump myself hard, Noelle's face appearing behind the back of my eyelids, wearing that startled, aroused look she had after I kissed her during Spin the Bottle.

"Fuck." I couldn't help gasping the word as my orgasm built hard and fast, grunting as quietly as I could as my hand went faster, the friction almost painful but too good to stop. "Damn it, Noelle."

Saying her name out loud gave me the push I needed and I came hard into my other hand, exhaling in relief more than anything as my arousal finally found its release. Now, I could go back to sleep.

Inhaling deeply to catch my breath, I threw the toilet paper into the toilet, pulled my underwear back up and washed my hands before opening the door.

Or at least, I *should* have had to open the door. Although I hadn't been able to lock it, I knew for sure that I had closed it, but when I went to grab the handle, it pulled right open, as if it hadn't been closed at all.

~**Noelle**~

A strange, clicking noise woke me from my pleasant sleep. In my dream, I'd been home for Christmas with my family, all of us gathered around the tree. The lights twinkled as the mouthwatering smell of fresh cinnamon buns and the soothing, familiar melodies of Christmas carols filled the air. My mom and dad sat next to each other in their matching Christmas sweaters, my dad beaming with Christmas cheer and my mom affectionately indulgent. Noah and Olivia were cuddled up together, unable to keep their hands off each other as usual, and, surprisingly, someone's arm rested around my shoulders too. The warmth of his body and the enticing smell of cologne filled me with satisfaction even though I couldn't see his face. Despite the mystery of my companion's identity, I had never felt so blissfully comfortable in my own skin, feeling so entirely like I belonged.

After that, blinking in disorientation into the darkness of the unfamiliar room in Leavenworth felt like quite a letdown.

The clock next to me read 3:12, far too early to be getting up, so I closed my eyes again, hoping to go straight back to the dream I'd been pulled out of all too soon. Unfortunately, my bladder had other ideas. With a sigh, I slipped out of the covers, trying not to disturb Aaron on the other side of the bed as I made my way to the bathroom door.

However, when I reached it, I paused for a moment in confusion. Why was the door closed? I could have sworn I'd left it open after getting ready for bed, and Aaron hadn't used the bathroom before he got into bed. Maybe he'd already been up and left it closed afterwards? No light shone from beneath the door, making it seem empty, but I glanced back over to the bed to be sure anyway. That didn't help; in the darkness, I couldn't see much of anything at all.

It would be locked if Aaron were in there, I reasoned, so as gently and quietly as I could, I pulled the handle down. Since it gave straight away, I pushed it open a little, and that was when I heard him.

"Fuck."

The word sounded strained, almost as if he were in pain and I immediately froze. Did he need help? Should I say something? The laboured breathing I could hear through the slight crack of the open door sounded unnatural, but if I were unwell in the middle of the night, I wouldn't necessarily want a stranger barging in on me.

"Damn it, Noelle."

Oh, shit. He must have seen me or heard the door and now he would think I had been spying on him or being some kind of creep. I had my mouth open to apologize for intruding when he exhaled, grunting and groaning quietly in a way that didn't really sound painful at all. No other words followed, and it almost sounded like...

Oh my God.

Letting go of the door handle, I raced back to the bed, my bare feet sinking into the carpet with each step, my heart pounding and every nerve in my body tingling as I pulled the covers back up around me, trying to look as if I had never gotten out of bed at all.

Did that really just happen? Maybe my dream had just taken a very odd turn, but it felt too real for a dream. Unless I was completely off base, it sounded very much like Aaron Speelman had just gotten off while thinking about *me*.

That *should* be creepy. I should be horrified, but as I lay there, my mind and heart racing, I had to admit that what I felt couldn't be called horror at all. I almost felt... excited.

A moment later, the toilet flushed and I heard the tap turn on and off, none of which helped the situation with my bladder. Since I couldn't do anything about it, I pressed my legs tighter together, which didn't help my *other* problem, the arousal starting to take over my body. Part of it came from being flattered that of all the girls he could have been thinking about, anyone in the world including Eve, he had me on his mind. He said *my* name as he came.

The other part of my stimulation had to do with picturing his body in a way I never had before. What did he look like naked? I already knew he looked better without his glasses on; maybe the same would be true for the rest of his clothes too?

After the tap turned off, nothing else happened for a moment. Lying there, my heart beating wildly in the silence, I realized, too late, that I hadn't fully closed the door. Would he notice?

Of course he would *notice*, I quickly admonished myself. The real question was: would he realize what had happened?

Before long, I heard him moving back through the room, getting back to his side of the bed, the mattress moving beneath me as he lay back down. Could he hear how loud my heart pounded right now? Did he know what thoughts were in my head?

"Noelle?" Aaron whispered my name into the darkness, very quietly, obviously not trying to wake me but to gauge if I *was* awake, and I kept my lips pressed tightly together, not even daring to breathe.

It would be far better to pretend I hadn't heard anything. Maybe he'd assume he just hadn't closed the door fully, or that it had somehow sprung open on its own. After all, we were in an unfamiliar place in the middle of the night. Why the hell hadn't he locked the door anyway?

After a moment, he seemed to accept that no response would be coming, and he must have rolled over since the mattress moved again. Not long afterwards, his breathing evened out while my heart continued to race. Eventually, I did manage to sneak out of bed to use the bathroom, and finally, an hour later, with images of Aaron's naked body still in my head, I managed to fall back asleep.

"Hey, sleepy-head!"

The greeting took me by surprise as someone poked my shoulder, and when I tried to open my eyes, the brightness made me wince.

"Eve?" I sat up, still squinting as my best friend grinned at me. As subtly as possible, I glanced over at the other side of the bed, looking for Aaron. Not only was the bed empty, it looked like no one had ever been there at all, leaving me more confused than ever.

Had I dreamt the whole thing? Surely, my imagination wasn't that good.

"Are you feeling okay?" Eve continued smiling at me, but concern flickered in her eyes too. "I'm never up before you. It's almost nine."

"Uh, yeah, I'm fine." I rubbed my face with my hands, trying to wake myself up fully. "I woke up during the night, it must have been the jet lag."

"I thought that might be it." Her expression cleared in relief. "It's so dark in the basement, I slept like a log. We should have taken a room down there."

"With all the smelly, sweaty men? No, thank you."

Eve's sparkling laugh filled the room. "It's not always a bad thing when they're smelly and sweaty." Her wink made my stomach sink as I remembered exactly who she had spent the night with. And then, before I could stop it, my mind brought up the image it had spent half the night creating: Aaron working up his own sweat in the bathroom. My eyes flitted to the open bathroom door, but the room beyond appeared to be just as empty as the other side of the bed.

"What's the plan?" I asked as I got out of bed myself. Eve had already gotten dressed, giving me another sign of just how late I'd slept. Nine o'clock here would be noon in New York; everybody else must already be up. My best friend looked fresh and beautiful, as always, in jeans and a red and white sweater that complemented her red hair perfectly.

"We're going to the reindeer farm!" she announced gleefully. "I booked it ages ago, I just kept it quiet because no one wanted to be on a schedule. They all think I just did it this morning. We have to be there in an hour and it's a mile walk, so hurry and get ready."

"What?!" Doing the math in my head, I knew I would never get through my whole routine in that time. "Eve, why didn't you wake me sooner?"

"You looked so cute snoring there," she teased. "And I thought you'd wake up on your own while I got ready. Don't worry, everybody's dressed casually, just throw some clothes on, brush your hair and you'll be fine."

She would be fine like that. I needed a bit more work, but I would just have to make the best of it as I sprang out of bed and got started.

"Is everyone else ready?" I asked, pulling out my clothes and starting to change. Eve and I weren't shy around each other so I whipped my pajamas off in front of her.

"Yup. They're just having breakfast."

"Did you... uh, did you see Aaron?" She hadn't mentioned anything about knowing that he spent the night here with me, but did that mean she didn't know?

"Yeah, he's down there too. Why?"

Why indeed? I tried to come up with a reasonable excuse for asking. "I wondered how things went between you two during the game last night."

We hadn't had a chance to talk about it yet, but I knew from Aaron that nothing had happened, and Eve quickly confirmed it. "Same as you and Corey. We just chatted a bit."

So, Corey had told her nothing happened between us either. At least we were all on the same page.

"Aaron seems nice," she added thoughtfully. "Not as condescending as you always said."

I had said that, hadn't I? The memory made me wince. "Well, I guess it depends on the situation. I can probably be hard to deal with too when I'm passionate about something."

"Probably?" Eve arched an eyebrow at me in that teasing way of hers. "I'm surprised he hasn't completely lost it on you, the way you go up against him for everything and usually win."

"I don't usually win," I protested. Olivia had always been the overachiever in our family, not me. "I won for president, yes, but he beat me for top marks last year *and* in the debate final."

"Right. You're such an underdog." Eve rolled her eyes again. "Come on, stop wasting time! You need to eat something before we go play with the reindeer."

I had my clothes on but not enough time to straighten my hair. I pulled it part way back instead, leaving a few strands loose. Hopefully it looked intentional and not just like I hadn't had time to finish. I managed to get some foundation on and a hint of blush before Eve pulled me away, claiming we were out of time.

The kitchen buzzed with conversation and laughter as we arrived. Everyone said good morning to Eve and a few added a hello to me too. Aaron and Corey sat at the end of the kitchen island, and they both gave me curious looks as I waved, making my heart sink. Did I really look that bad? Maybe I still had time to grab some eyeshadow...

"No." Eve grabbed my arm firmly, sensing my intention even though I hadn't said a word. "Grab a granola bar to eat on the way. Time to go, everyone!"

She made the last announcement loudly enough that everyone heard and the exodus to the front door began as I shoved a granola bar and a mandarin orange into the pockets of my coat. Hopefully, we wouldn't be gone too long and I could come back and get ready properly before anyone paid me too much attention.

~**Aaron**~

Though I still didn't understand how the bathroom door had opened during the night, I had to let it go. Maybe when I tried to lock it, I accidentally pulled it back open. Maybe it hadn't been as fully closed as I thought. Since Noelle was still asleep when I got back to the bed and no one else seemed to be around, I had no other explanation.

I woke up again as the sun began to brighten the sky outside the window and glanced over at the other side of the bed, getting a view of Noelle's back. She faced away from me as she had all night and seemed to be fast asleep. Silence still filled the whole house, making me think it would be a good time to sneak out of the room without being seen, so I got up and quickly threw my clothes back on, heading downstairs to use the bathroom there since the one in Noelle's room apparently had a defective door.

A few people had already gathered in the basement rec room so I joined them there until Eve appeared from Corey's rooms. A couple of the guys made catcalls, but she silenced them with a well-placed barb: "And that's why you guys are all sitting out here alone." Her stern expression softened when her eyes moved to me, and her lips curled just a tiny bit before she headed upstairs and I went into my own room to get ready for the day.

Corey hadn't got up yet but he was awake, and he nodded at me in greeting. "Hey. Did you have a good night?"

The memory of my self-induced orgasm still lingered in my mind, as did the cause of it, but I had no intention of sharing any of that with him. "Fine. Do you know what we're doing today?"

He yawned, the covers slipping further down his body as he stretched, making it clear that once again, he had no clothes on. "Eve said something about reindeer."

Not what I expected, but sure. Why not reindeer? I put some jeans on and one of the sweaters I'd bought for this trip. I never went shopping with an occasion in mind, but this time, I'd made a conscious effort to get the kinds of things people seemed to wear on TV when they went on winter vacations. Since I hoped to impress the fashionable Eve, it couldn't hurt to make a bit of an effort.

A couple of the other guys soon joined us, everyone eager for an update on how the night had gone for everyone else. It seemed a few people had ended up in someone else's bed, like I had, though in their cases, it meant more action than I'd got. Notes were compared about the girls and I did my best to stay out of it until James brought up Noelle. Despite having spent the night with Sabrina, he seemed ready to explore his other options.

"Noelle's actually a decent kisser," he told the group, reminding me that he'd also kissed her during Spin the Bottle. "And she seems a little needy. Those kinds of girls are usually down to do any freaky shit if you pay them some attention."

"Has anyone here bagged her before?" Alex wondered and everyone shook their heads, which pleased me more than it should have.

"Maybe she's a virgin," James suggested almost gleefully, and I rolled my eyes.

"She's 21 years old with a great body and a good personality. If she's a virgin, it's because she wants to be, not because she's been waiting for *you*."

Corey's laugh encouraged the others to join in, and no one else said anything about Noelle. Once we were ready, we all headed upstairs where almost everyone else had gathered, other than Eve and Noelle. Talk turned to what we would do after the reindeer farm and someone mentioned a brewery in town which quickly got approval from the others. Why not start drinking in the middle of the day?

I kept glancing at the clock, wondering what could be keeping Eve and Noelle. When they eventually made an appearance, Eve looked as stunning as always, her sweater clinging to her in all the right places without looking like she'd made an effort, but I only glanced at her for a second before my eyes were drawn to Noelle.

She looked almost as good as she had in her bed. The heavy eye makeup had gone, letting the natural blue colour of her eyes shine through, and her hair, partly pulled back, curled naturally over her shoulders, making it look thicker than when she tried to straighten it. It seemed she'd taken my words to heart, and the effect couldn't be more enticing.

"Huh." That sound came from Corey next to me, and I turned to him to find him also staring in Noelle's direction. "It's weird how spending a bit of time with someone makes them look different."

Taking a deep breath, I resisted the urge to make any kind of snarky response. He recognized something had changed about Noelle but he couldn't put his finger on it. Clearly, he'd never paid her much attention before. I also had to fight against the odd feeling of jealousy that bubbled in my chest at the thought that he might pay more attention to her now. She wanted him to, I had to remind myself. We were doing all of this for that purpose.

Eve announced to the group that we had to get going, and everyone headed to the door without complaint, all eager to get the day started. I picked up my boots and turned around to find an empty space to put them on, and almost ran straight into Noelle who had come up behind me.

"Oh, sorry." She blushed as her chest bumped against mine. "I didn't see you there."

I let out a snort. "Really? I know I'm not six feet tall, but I'm not a hobbit either."

"You were bent over," she argued, trying to have the last word, as usual. "How tall are you, anyway?"

Why did she want to know? "Taller than you."

She narrowed her eyes at the deflection as people jostled for position around us. I had to get out of the way, so I stepped past her, but not before whispering into her ear first.

"This look really works for you, just like I said. You take instructions very well."

Her blush deepened and her pupils dilated, giving me exactly the response I anticipated. It couldn't be getting much clearer that Noelle Hanmer had a praise kink, and a million different ways I could help her explore it immediately rushed into my head. Though she didn't know it, she would make a perfect foil to my own brand of pleasure.

Those thoughts needed to stop before my new jeans got too tight, and before I lost sight of my goal for this entire trip.

"Here, Noelle, put your boots on." Eve handed them to her, looking between us curiously as she came up beside her friend. "Everything okay?"

"It's great. Good. Fine." Noelle's flustered response made me smile again as she took the boots from Eve and bent down to put them on.

"So, reindeer, huh?" I asked Eve as I pulled my own boots on. "How did you hear about this? Have you got some kind of Christmas radar?"

"Absolutely," she agreed, grinning happily. "My family went to see them in Lapland years ago, so when I heard they had a farm here, I knew we had to go."

"Do we get to ride them?" Corey wondered as he joined us too.

A lot of people would have laughed at that question, but not Noelle. She popped back up, eager to show off her knowledge on the subject. "It *is* possible to ride reindeer. There's a whole group of people in northern Mongolia who are traditionally reindeer herders and they ride them. But the ones we see today aren't for riding."

"I think you might be too heavy anyway," Eve teased Corey. "The poor reindeer wouldn't be able to stand up with you on top of him."

Corey took the jibe in good humour. "That's okay. I prefer being ridden anyway."

He gave her a wink and Eve rolled her eyes while Noelle looked away, her lips pursing in disappointment at the reminder of their intimacy.

"Don't we need to get going?" I reminded them, and Eve quickly shooed everyone out the door.

The reindeer farm was a mile out of town and given the size of our group, Eve had decided it would be easier to walk rather than get transportation. The crisp air of the December morning quickly rid us all of any last vestiges of sleepiness, and Eve and Corey walked together down the street just ahead of me and Noelle.

"So, how are you feeling after last night?" I asked Noelle under my breath, quietly enough that we wouldn't be overheard.

She looked up at me with that startled expression I had begun to find rather adorable. "What... uh, what do you mean?"

She seemed to find the question more complicated than I'd meant it to be. "Our plan? Are you still wanting to go ahead?"

"Oh. Right. I mean, yes. I do."

That response sounded even more flustered than usual, but I put it down to her still being upset over the exchange between Corey and Eve, and as it happened, we could use that slightly awkward energy to our advantage anyway. "Good, because I have an idea. I'll just need your help."

Chapter Six

ACCIDENT

~Noelle~

Somehow, even with my late start, we managed to get to the reindeer farm five minutes early, and as the group stood around in the snowy yard waiting for our guide to show up, Corey became the centre of attention, as usual. With Eve at his side and the sun shining off his perfect hair and smile, he looked every inch the big man on campus; the guy every guy wanted to be and every girl wanted to be with.

But though I glanced over at him from time to time, my eyes kept wandering to the guy on the outskirts of the group, the guy who faded into the background for most people, hidden behind his heavy-rimmed glasses. From our interactions so far that morning, I suspected Aaron had no idea that I overheard him in the bathroom and I intended to keep it that way, even though I desperately wanted to know what it meant.

Why had he been thinking about me? Did he mean it when he said he liked the way I looked? Why did it send such a thrill through me when he told me I followed instructions well?

And why, if this growing electricity between us wasn't all in my head, did he still want to go ahead with our plan to break up Corey and Eve?

That last question puzzled me most of all but he'd made it perfectly clear. He had a plan on how to maneuver us more time alone with our partners of choice. His thoughts were still clearly slanting in that direction, so despite what I'd heard the night before, anything between me and him must have been more on my side than on his. I would have to keep that in mind before I ended up developing yet another crush on someone far more interested in my best friend than in me.

The woman from the farm arrived for our tour, and after giving us the rundown on safety and what to expect, we followed her outside to go see the reindeer. My dad would love this, I couldn't help thinking, looking around the farm buildings decorated for Christmas with the snow-covered mountains in the distance and the bright blue sky overhead. Anything wholesome and fun always made me think of my dad, the sweetest man in the whole world.

Unfortunately, I wouldn't be able to tell him very much about it, since Aaron's plan involved me missing out on a lot of the tour, and as soon as we were a good distance from the house, I put that plan into action.

"Ouch!" I stumbled dramatically through the snow, tripping over my feet before righting myself and glancing quickly over in Corey's direction. His attention remained focused on Eve, and no one else spared me a glance either, carrying on as if nothing had happened.

Seriously? I bet if Eve so much as broke a nail, everyone would stop in their tracks.

Aaron's eyes were on me at least, but with a less than impressed look in them, and my cheeks flamed in embarrassment. The idea of disappointing him upset me far more than it should have, so, with determination, I tripped again, this time hitting the snow-covered ground and banging my knee much harder than I intended.

"Shit!"

That got everyone's attention, finally. They all looked around, trying to figure out what had happened, until their gazes moved downwards to where I sprawled out rather inelegantly on the cold ground.

"Noelle!" Eve got to my side first, concern in her eyes as she bent down to help me. "Are you okay?"

"I think so. I just slipped." I winced as I tried to get onto my hands and knees. That really smarted.

"What hurts?" Aaron appeared on one side of Eve as Corey came up on the other. The tour leader also arrived to see what had happened.

Though my knee actually hurt, I stuck to the story Aaron had come up with for me to use. "My ankle. I think I just twisted it. I'll be okay."

Again, I grimaced as I put pressure on my knee, which required no acting at all.

"Corey could take a look at it for you," Aaron suggested. "He's training as a sports therapist."

"That's not necessary," I said quickly. "I'm sure it's... ow!"

That cry sounded fake even to me as I attempted to put weight on my ankle.

"Could you take a look at her?" Eve's big dark eyes looked up at Corey hopefully, a look that I knew from experience could be hard to resist.

"It would be better inside," he mused, looking back towards the farmhouse. "I guess I could take her back there quickly."

The tour leader confirmed that they had a first-aid kit inside if I needed anything and people who could help. The more attention focused on him, the more Corey seemed pleased to be given the responsibility and to be the one everyone looked to for help.

Aaron's plan seemed to be working perfectly until Eve spoke again. "I'll come with you too."

"No!" The blurted-out word made them both turn to me in surprise and I quickly tried to backpedal. "I mean, I don't want you to miss out on this, Eve. You've been looking forward to it so much. I'm sure my ankle's fine. I just need to walk it off and we'll catch up to you. Please, don't worry about me."

"Are you sure?" She sounded unconvinced, but I nodded firmly.

"I'm sure. We'll be back before you know we're gone."

Corey bent down to help me to my feet, his arm strong around my waist, and my whole body flushed at his proximity. After all this time, he finally touched me, just like that. Why hadn't I ever tried this before? It seemed so simple.

"I'll keep you company until they get back," I heard Aaron say to Eve as the group set off once more towards the reindeer pens, smoothly sliding into Corey's vacated spot.

"Can you put weight on it?" Corey asked me, his voice deep next to me, the smell of his cologne almost making me light-headed.

"I think so." I took a tentative, limping step forward, wincing at the pain in my knee, and his lips pursed.

"Don't make it worse. I can carry you."

Before I could protest, if I even meant to, he swept me up in his arms like some kind of rag doll, and set off back towards the house.

"You're... uh, you're studying sports therapy?" I asked to make conversation, even though I knew the answer perfectly well. I knew an awful lot about him.

Corey nodded. "I've seen a lot of guys get hurt on the ice over the years. Some get better quickly and others don't, and I always wondered what made the difference so I decided to find out."

I had to admit I hadn't expected such a considered reason why it interested him. "So, you'll be able to tell me if I can ever play hockey again?"

He grinned, not falling into my trap. "Could you play before?" I shook my head sheepishly and he laughed, his chest rumbling against me as he did. "That's what I thought."

The person who let us back into the main building asked if we needed help but Corey waved them off, saying he had it under control. He set me down gently in a large, comfortable armchair in an empty reception room.

"I'll need to take your boot off to get a look," he explained, and even though it only involved my boot and we were in public, my heart beat faster at the idea of

Corey undressing me in any way. His big, strong hands made short work of my boot and peeled my sock down before examining my ankle with a surprisingly gentle touch. "I don't see any swelling which is good. It hurts like a bitch when you go over on it, but if you haven't sprained it, it should be okay in a couple of minutes."

His kindness and consideration made me feel terrible about lying to him in the first place, so I directed his attention to the part of me that actually hurt instead. "It's already feeling better, but my knee's throbbing. I banged it when I fell."

His lips pursed as his gaze travelled up my leg. "I can take a look at it but I think your jeans are too tight to roll up that far."

He had that right. I had chosen my skinniest pair to try to impress him. Before I could make any suggestions, however, he stood up and grabbed a blanket from one of the other chairs nearby.

"Here. Take your pants off and put this over your lap."

"Well, now I really feel like I'm at the doctor's office," I joked, making him smile even as my hands trembled. Was I really going to strip down to my underwear in front of him?

He seemed to think so as he turned his back to give me some privacy and I quickly pulled my jeans down and off before covering myself with the blanket as he suggested. When he turned back, his brow immediately furrowed in concern.

"Damn, Noelle, you must have banged it good."

I'd been so focused on my state of dress that I hadn't even looked at my knee, but now that I did, the red, swollen state of it made me wince. It looked even worse than it felt.

Corey's hands gently prodded at it, watching my reaction as he moved my leg back and forth. "Okay, I don't think you've torn anything. It's going to be sore for a while, but you should be good as new before long. You better put those jeans back on before it swells anymore or you might have to head back to the house without them."

I didn't know if that would really happen, but I wasn't about to take that chance. Hurriedly, I pulled the pants back on, wincing as the tight fabric squeezed my sore knee.

"I guess I'm missing the rest of the tour," I said when I'd buttoned myself back up, letting Corey know he could safely turn around. "You should go ahead, I don't want you to miss out too. I can wait for you guys here."

"I'm not leaving you alone," he replied in a tone that allowed no room for argument. "I'll call a taxi for us and take you back to the house so you can change into something more comfortable. We can catch up with everyone else later."

I hadn't expected this level of care from him, and as he stepped away from me to make the call and let Eve know where we were going, I had to give credit where credit was due: Aaron Speelman might just be a freaking genius.

~Aaron~

Eve seemed subdued as we listened to the guide talk about the reindeer but I didn't get a chance to say much to her until we broke into smaller groups where we were given food to feed the animals and allowed to pet and take pictures with them.

"I think it's against the law not to smile when you're standing next to a reindeer," I tried to tease her. "The Christmas police will be after you."

Her lips did curl, but only for a moment. "I'm just worried about Noelle."

I hadn't really considered that. While I knew Noelle hadn't really hurt herself, Eve thought she had, and of course she'd be concerned for her friend. "I'm sure they'll be back any minute. Why don't you send her a text if it'll help put your mind at ease?"

Nodding in agreement, Eve handed her reindeer food to me and pulled out her phone, but it only took a moment for her frown to deepen. "There's no signal."

The tour guide overheard her but misunderstood the reason for her statement. "There's wi-fi back at the farmhouse. You can upload your photos as soon as you get back there."

"I'm sure Noelle's fine," I reassured her again after the guide moved on. "She's in good hands with Corey. Here, I can take some photos for you."

Eve handed her phone over to me with a distinctive lack of enthusiasm, but once she got close to the reindeer, her mood improved. I told her some terrible jokes that made her laugh and managed to get a few pictures of her genuinely smiling. Even in the ones where she didn't smile, she still looked beautiful. It seemed impossible for her to take a bad photo.

When everyone had their fill of photos, we began walking back to the main building, but there had still been no sign of Noelle or Corey. The plan had only been for her to get them a bit of alone time, not the whole visit, and I remained in the dark until Eve's phone pinged when we got closer to the house.

Dismay flashed across her face as she read the text. "Corey took Noelle back to the house, he says her knee is pretty banged up."

What? Corey should have been able to tell she hadn't seriously hurt herself. Had Noelle really been that convincing?

Eve looked up at me in concern. "I should go check on her."

"We'll both go," I offered, an uncomfortable feeling forming in the pit of my stomach. "Let's see if we can get a taxi, it might be quicker."

The rest of the group were all planning to walk back into town to visit the brewery, so Eve and I said goodbye as we waited for the taxi to arrive.

"She's always been uncoordinated," Eve told me, her hand tapping nervously against her thigh as she kept her eyes on the drive, looking for a car. "She jokes that her sister inherited the athletic genes, and the brains too."

That didn't sound like much of a joke; it sounded like Noelle being too hard on herself. From what I'd seen, I wouldn't call her particularly clumsy, and she was definitely smart. Why did she have to make the comparison?

Trying to ignore the twisting feeling in my stomach, I turned the conversation back to Eve instead. "You're a good friend to her. In fact, you've got a bit of a mother hen vibe going on with everyone. Is that something you picked up from your own parents?"

Eve gave a small huff, the sound somewhere between amusement and disagreement. "My parents aren't exactly philanthropists. They give a lot of money to charities and go to the right parties, but all my dad has ever really cared about, besides his family, is hotels."

I hadn't expected that level of passion in her response. Apparently, I'd touched a nerve, the same as I had the night before when I asked her about working for the family business. "And you don't think hotels are a force for good in the world?" I guessed, keeping my tone light to encourage her to continue while making my interest in the conversation clear.

"Not really," she admitted, chewing her lip distractedly, her eyes still on the road. "People pay hundreds or even thousands of dollars a night to stay in a Stamer hotel, while on the street outside, someone's begging for food. It doesn't seem right."

Who knew that Eve Stamer had a social conscience? The rich-girl persona she presented to the world certainly didn't indicate one. "Have you talked to your dad about it?"

Her face contorted for just a second. "I've tried. He just points to all the money that the company donates, which wouldn't happen unless the business made money in the first place. And I know he's got a point and it's better than doing nothing, but it doesn't feel like enough."

I would have asked her more but the taxi arrived and Eve hurried over to it before I could get another word in. We sat silently for the short ride back to the house and she raced ahead of me into the house when we arrived.

"Noelle?" she called out while pulling her boots off at the door.

"Hey, Eve." Corey appeared from the living room door, his eyebrows raising in surprise when he saw me there too. "And Aaron. Noelle's fine, she's just in here."

We followed him into the living room where Noelle lay on the sofa, having changed out of her jeans and back into her pajama pants from the night before. A pillow rested beneath her knee and she had a mug of hot chocolate in her hands.

"Hey." She greeted us both with a smile. "Sorry if I worried you. I'm okay and Corey's been taking great care of me."

She certainly looked pleased with the care she'd received, and the grateful smile she gave Corey made my stomach twist again, for a different reason this time.

"What did you do to your knee?" I asked as Eve and I walked over to her. We'd agreed that she would say she twisted her ankle. Her knee had never factored into it.

"I just landed on it when I fell," she explained sheepishly. "It's not a big deal. It already feels a lot better."

"Let me see."

Noelle and Eve both seemed surprised by the order, but Noelle obeyed, pulling up the leg of her pants until I could see the bruised and swollen joint, and my blood immediately ran cold.

"Damn it, Noelle," I muttered under my breath. I hadn't wanted her to actually hurt herself.

For some reason, her cheeks turned a bright shade of pink at my words. "It... uh, it looks worse than it is. It really doesn't hurt that much."

"She's been very brave," Corey told us all with a laugh, giving Noelle a wink. He seemed in a better mood now, and the idea that Noelle must be responsible for it sat just about as well with me as the grateful look she'd given him earlier.

"Everyone else has gone to the brewery," I told him, turning to Corey and Eve. "Why don't you guys go too? I can stay here with Noelle. I've got some work I wanted to catch up on anyway."

From the corner of my eye, I could see Noelle's eyebrows shoot up in surprise, no doubt wondering why the hell I would suggest that when my plan had been working perfectly so far.

"I should be the one to stay," Eve protested. "I don't mind."

"It's okay with me if Aaron stays," Noelle told her, even though she still sounded confused. "Corey's probably sick of me anyway."

"Not at all," Corey assured her before turning to Eve. "Did you know Noelle knows more about our hockey team than I do?"

"She hardly ever misses a game," Eve confirmed, glancing back over at Noelle on the couch with a slightly puzzled expression. "She's a big fan of... the sport."

Noelle blushed again, avoiding her friend's gaze. "Yeah, I've always enjoyed it. It's great that we've got such a good college team, but Aaron's right, you guys can go if you want. I'll just take it easy today and by tomorrow, I'll be ready to go again."

A few more protests were made before Eve and Corey eventually agreed to go, after Eve had secured Noelle's promise to call her if she needed anything. I saw them to the door and once they'd gone, I made my way back to the living room where Noelle now wore a slightly guilty expression.

"I think Eve might suspect something," she blurted out as soon as I reappeared. "That look she gave me when she said I go to all the games, do you think she's figured out I go to watch Corey? This is getting complicated, Aaron, I don't know..."

I didn't give a fuck about any of that right now. "What do you think you were doing?"

She froze in surprise, her blue eyes looking up at me in uncertainty. "What do you mean?"

"You weren't supposed to actually hurt yourself. I never wanted you to get hurt."

Indignation flared in her eyes. "I didn't do it on purpose! Next time you can be the one to take a dive. You came up with the bright idea in the first place."

That was exactly why I felt so guilty. Rather than being angry with her, my frustration should be directed at myself, and I took a deep breath as I sat down on the sofa next to her. She still had her pant leg pulled up, and I couldn't stop myself from running my hand up her soft, smooth leg until it rested gently on her knee. "Tell me how to make it up to you. What can I do to make you feel better?"

~Noelle~

How did Aaron always manage to do what I least expected him to? He said my name the night before in the bathroom but gave me no indication that morning that anything had happened. One minute he wanted me to fake a fall so he could be with Eve, the next he sent her and Corey away together to stay with me. He practically yelled at me for hurting myself, and then suddenly, his hand caressed my leg as he told me he wanted to make me feel better.

What did he want from me? Why did I even care? And why, when I heard him mutter 'damn it, Noelle', just as he did in the bathroom, did my body flare with desire even more than it had with Corey earlier?

He confused the hell out of me, and right now, those hazel eyes were staring at me from behind his glasses, his hand still resting gently on my knee, softly enough that it wouldn't hurt me but firmly enough that I could still feel his warmth. The idea of those hands touching more of me, going higher up my leg, had me squirming in my seat as my body reacted, and this time I definitely couldn't blame it on the alcohol. I hadn't had a drop yet that day.

"I don't need anything," I tried to deflect, putting my hot chocolate down so it wouldn't spill, which seemed like a real possibility given how my hands were trembling. I folded them back in my lap to keep them steady.

"I didn't ask what you needed." Usually, his pedantic corrections would make me roll my eyes, but with the way he stared at me, intense and serious, I couldn't look away. "I asked what would make you feel better."

A few different ideas came to mind, most of them involving those hands of his, but I swallowed down those crazy thoughts before they could come out of my mouth and focused on the practical instead. "Not feeling like I'm betraying my best friend would make me feel better."

With a sigh, Aaron removed his hand and gently pulled my pant leg back down, leaving me both relieved and disappointed at the same time. He shuffled further back on the sofa to give me more space, but remained close enough to let me know I still had his full attention. "You're not exactly Judas, Noelle. What have you done? You told her some things that Corey said, actual words that came out of his mouth, and you've engineered a bit of time with Corey away from her. You haven't lied, you haven't cheated, you haven't even kissed him. You're simply dropping a seed, and if it takes root, it just means it fell on fertile ground."

He made it sound so reasonable, but my guilt refused to be assuaged. "I *have* lied. What do you call pretending to hurt myself?"

His eyebrows raised, making his glasses slip down his nose. "That bruised knee doesn't look fake to me."

"That was an accident."

"As it would have been if you'd actually fallen in the first place." His twitching lips let me know he liked debating with me, enjoyed the intellectual exercise, but did he actually mean what he said? Did he really see nothing wrong with what we were doing? I couldn't be certain.

I moved on to what I saw as the crux of the problem. "I've also lied by omission. If I'd just told Eve I liked Corey, none of this would be happening."

A scowl darkened Aaron's face. "Are you sure? Corey knew exactly how much I liked Eve and it didn't stop him."

"Really?" That didn't sound like the Corey I knew and Aaron hadn't mentioned that before. "Maybe he misunderstood. Maybe you weren't clear enough."

Aaron's eyes narrowed even further. "Give me more credit than that, Noelle. I literally told him I planned to ask her out on this trip, and he went and slept with her before I had the chance."

That sounded like a really shitty thing to do, but I still thought there had to be more to it than that. Corey could have his pick of girls, quite literally. Why would he go for the only one his best friend wanted?

As I mulled it over, my mind flashed back to the party where Eve and Corey had hooked up and how Corey had approached me in the kitchen. He asked me about Eve and commented on how we were never apart. In my naivete, I'd hoped he wanted to make a move on me, but thinking about it now, it made much more sense that he'd actually been looking for a chance to get Eve alone. I told him she'd gone to the restroom and he must have gone and found her immediately after that.

Why would he do that if he knew how Aaron felt? Had he hooked up with her *because* of Aaron? Did he care for Eve or not?

Suddenly, it felt like I didn't know Corey Davison very well at all.

"Well, Eve's not like that," I told Aaron, since I had nothing useful to contribute about Corey. "If I told her how I felt, she'd back off."

"Then why don't you?" Aaron challenged. "Why haven't you since they got together?"

Honestly, I couldn't really explain it, but since Aaron seemed genuinely interested, I tried to work it out now. "I guess because I know I don't have any right to interfere. He doesn't owe me anything. Besides, what would be the point? Everyone likes Eve better, they always have, so why should Corey be any different?"

To my horror, tears sprang to my eyes as I spoke, completely unexpectedly and I blinked them back furiously. My emotions were all over the place thanks to my guilt and confusion, not to mention the physical pain, but Aaron did not need to see me cry, not when he'd already accused me of self-pity back on the plane.

Pressing my lips together, I waited for him to call me out on it now just like he had then, but instead, he did the unexpected again.

"Maybe you're just not giving people a chance to get to know the real you." His hand went back to my leg, reaching up beneath my pajamas to rub my ankle gently. "If someone as great as Eve likes you so much, you can't be all bad."

He meant that as a joke, I knew that, but the way his touch sent tingles through my body made it hard to focus.

"Eve doesn't count," I replied shakily. "We were literally born together. She has to like me."

"What about me? I like you, and nobody's forcing me to." His hand moved higher, his fingers curling around my calf as my breath caught in my throat.

A second later, what he'd actually said sank in and I frowned in disapproval. "But you like Eve more! That's exactly my point. You don't count either."

Aaron's laugh sounded warm and genuine. "Stop making everything a competition, Noelle. Just be yourself, just like you are right now, and I think you'd be surprised how people would respond to it."

"I'm always myself," I protested, but he shook his head in disagreement, removing his hand from my leg again, leaving me just as disappointed as when he'd done it the first time.

"No, you're not. Do you know how I know?"

I shook my head back at him, not having a clue where he intended to go with this.

"Because if you were always the way you are right now, not trying too hard, not worrying about how you look or what anyone thinks, just speaking your mind and being honest, I would have done this a long time ago."

"Done what?" I started to ask, but before I could get the words all the way out, he'd got to his feet, bent down over me, and pressed his lips firmly against mine.

Chapter Seven

CLEARING THE AIR

~Aaron~

I hadn't meant to kiss Noelle. Not really. I certainly didn't plan it out in advance. With Eve, I'd imagined every possible scenario, thought of a million different ways that first kiss might happen. I couldn't help it; I liked to be prepared. Yet, with Noelle, it just kind of happened as the two of us argued and I tried to convince her that the woman I saw right now appealed to me a hell of a lot more than the woman she normally tried so hard to be.

Since I couldn't be sure my message had gotten through, I decided to deliver it in a different way.

Noelle stiffened in surprise when my lips connected with hers, cutting off whatever she'd been about to say, and for a moment, I thought she might push me away and go right back to arguing with me instead. It wouldn't have surprised me if she told me what she thought the kiss meant rather than accepting that maybe I just wanted to do it.

That didn't happen, though. After her surprise faded, she kissed me back, and it felt... really good. A whole lot better than I expected it to, actually. When I told her the day before that she had perfect lips for kissing, I hadn't exaggerated, and this time, I could feel at least a hint of desire within their movements which made the kiss even better.

Maybe she'd started to see me in a slightly different way too?

For a moment, I forgot all about the plan. I forgot this wasn't the endgame for either of us. It couldn't and shouldn't be more than a distraction, but as her hand slipped around the back of my neck, holding me closer, I let myself be distracted. I could taste the sweetness of the hot chocolate she'd just been drinking on her lips and smell her fruity perfume, sweet and playful, a lot like her. It felt less upscale than Eve's, but not in a bad way. It suited her.

My hand dropped to her stomach as she lay on the couch, resting on top of the sweater she wore, while the other stroked her cheek softly before hooking under her chin to raise her face towards me even more, letting me take the kiss deeper. My tongue brushed against her lips, teasing and testing, seeing how she'd react, and as I hoped, her lips parted just enough, inviting but not demanding, sending a flood of desire through me.

Even so, I held back a moment longer. My style involved more patience, letting her feel my interest but then holding back on it, teasing just enough by running my tongue along the inside of her lips but not going in any deeper, until she showed me she wanted more.

And she did. After a few passes of going almost in but not all the way, she came to me, her tongue pressing against mine in a way that sent shivers down my spine, yet another reaction I hadn't anticipated.

My fingers curled around her sweater, pulling it up just enough that my fingertips could brush against the bare skin of her stomach, and Noelle shivered beneath me. *Fair is fair*, I thought. If she could affect me like that, I would show her how it felt too.

I had no idea how far I intended to take this, but stopping hadn't crossed my mind when we both heard the front door open and close again, and we both froze. I didn't want her to think I had any regret about what had just happened, but on the other hand, if Corey or Eve, or both, were the ones at the door, we wouldn't want them to catch us like this.

I settled for a compromise, looking down into Noelle's blue eyes, still just a few inches away. "Do you believe now that I like you?"

She nodded up at me with that serious, startled look again, a deer in the head-lights that I found myself wanting to protect from anyone who might try to knock her down, and I couldn't help myself. I leaned over to her ear and whispered the words that, by now, I knew would work for her without question.

"Good girl."

With that, I let her go and sat back in my previous spot on the couch, settling into place just as Corey and Eve walked back into the room.

"Did you forget something?" I asked the question casually, as if we'd just been sitting here like this the whole time.

"No, but I changed my mind," Eve explained. "I'd really like to stay with Noelle. Aaron, you go ahead with the others."

What could I say to that? That I wanted to stay because I wanted to see where that kiss might have led? That I'd rather stay sitting down because the rush of blood to my dick when Noelle brushed her tongue against mine made standing up difficult? Neither of those were reasonable options, not to the girl I had come here to impress, so I simply turned to Noelle and put the ball in her court. "Is that okay with you?"

She hadn't pulled her shirt down yet, leaving a tiny bit of her stomach still exposed, and even though I'd seen a lot more of a lot of other girls, somehow, that might have been one of the sexiest sights I'd come across.

Her eyes searched mine, looking for a hint of what I wanted, but I honestly wanted her to make the call. If she told me to go, I'd go. If she wanted me to stay, I'd stay. Simple as that.

"I guess... I guess that's fine." Noelle swallowed, looking almost disappointed, but she quickly covered it up with a smile as she turned to Eve. "But Aaron said he had work to do, and I know this isn't how you wanted to spend your trip."

"I wanted to spend it with you," Eve assured her. "And it's only one afternoon. Aaron should be on vacation anyway." She gave me a teasing smile before turning to Corey who still stood in the doorway. "We'll see you guys when you get back."

"Sure." He didn't sound thrilled about the change in plan, but maybe that had to do with being hungry, as he mentioned now. "Let's go, Aaron. I'm starving, and food and beer is waiting."

I got to my feet, looking down at Noelle one more time. "Have a good afternoon. I'll see you later."

She nodded mutely, still with that almost-disappointed look in her eyes, and I gave Eve a smile as I stepped past her.

She brushed her hand across my shoulder as I went by. "Thanks, Aaron. I do really appreciate the offer to stay but it's better this way."

I couldn't agree, but I nodded anyway, only realizing once we got to the door that Eve's touch hadn't affected me nearly as much as it had the previous day.

The sun shone brightly above the snow-covered streets as Corey and I walked down to the brewery to meet the rest of the group. "How far did you get before Eve changed her mind?" I wondered, looking down at the footprints on the sidewalk. There were too many sets to guess which ones belonged to Eve and Corey.

"Not very. Eve got worried you and Noelle would end up fighting, she said you're always going at each other. Is that true?"

Did he honestly not remember? "We compete all the time. She beat me for student body president and we're in the debate club together. I've mentioned her to you dozens of times."

Corey had come to watch one of my debate competitions, though when I looked out into the crowd, I'd seen him flirting with a girl rather than paying attention to the arguments. Perhaps he really didn't remember Noelle.

He basically confirmed that now. "I guess I never put it together about it being the same girl. She's nice, though. I had a good time with her this morning."

"Yeah, she's 'nice'." The word came out more bitter than I meant it to. He had so many girls throwing themselves at him, he couldn't even recognize when he had something special.

"Why are you getting all pissy again? Fuck, you're worse than a girl." He kicked at some snow at the side of the sidewalk, his shoulders tight and his hands shoved in his pockets.

I'd just about had it with him too and I came to a dead stop, forcing him to turn back to face me. "You want to know why I'm 'pissy'? Because everything's always about you, Corey. I trusted you with the fact that I liked Eve and you went out of your way to steal her from under me. Now, Noelle's interesting all of a sudden because you decided she is. People exist outside of whether or not you notice them."

"I never said that." His brow furrowed in confusion and perhaps almost a bit of regret. "Look, I didn't mean to upset you this much with Eve." I scoffed, looking away from him, but he kept trying. "It's true. If anything, I thought maybe it would stop you from getting hurt."

Disbelief raced through me as I turned back to him. "That doesn't make any sense."

He winced at my tone. "I know what it looks like. But honestly, at the time, I just thought..." He trailed off, his lips pursing before he shook his head. "Never mind."

I had no intention of letting him off that easily. "No. You're the one who brought it up, so tell me, Corey: what were you thinking when you decided to fuck the one girl I ever told you I liked?"

My angry words echoed into the still winter air and we both glanced around to see if anyone had overheard them. Thankfully, we were still in the residential part of town and no one seemed to be around other than a few cars on the street.

When he looked back at me, a look of guilt crossed his face, a look I couldn't remember ever seeing on him before. "After you told me about Eve, I asked around about her. Everyone said she only ever dated guys who had it all: money, looks, popularity. She's got a type, Aaron, and you're not it."

"Gee, thanks?" If he thought that counted as an apology, he had even less self-awareness than I thought.

"You know what I mean. I think you're a good guy, that's why we're friends, but you don't come from money, you don't care about how you look, and people only know who you are because you hang out with me. I'm not saying that to be cruel, it's just the truth."

Objectively, he had a point, but I still didn't know what this had to do with Eve. "So... what? You thought if you fucked her first, I'd lose interest and then she couldn't break my heart?"

My words dripped with sarcasm, but Corey nodded sheepishly. "Yeah, pretty much."

He couldn't be serious. "So, by hooking up with the most popular girl in school, you were doing *me* a favour? That's a stretch, Corey, even for you."

"Maybe I didn't think it all the way through," he said defensively. "I'm not good with planning like you are, alright? But I thought once you saw that she hooked up with someone like me, you'd lose interest."

"And you honestly thought that would be a reasonable way to handle things rather than just telling me you thought she was out of my league? We're supposed to be friends."

He refused to back down. "Yeah, well, you don't always listen to me. Sometimes you just assume you know more than I do, but I figured if you saw it with your own eyes, you might actually believe it."

"All I see is someone who valued our friendship so little that he thought a 10-minute hookup at a party would be worth screwing me over for. That's what really hurts, Corey. I trusted you, and now I feel like an idiot. If you were trying to prove I'm dumber than you, mission accomplished."

His fists clenched as he grimaced. "I honestly didn't think you'd take it this hard, Aaron. I don't want to lose you as a friend and I sure as hell didn't plan to actually like Eve, but I do. I like her a lot, but I don't know if she feels anything for me."

"She spent last night with you!" Everyone thought they were dating. What more did he want?

"I know, but she's so cool and detached sometimes, and then there's the things you said she told Noelle... I don't know where we stand. With someone like Noelle, things feel comfortable and easy, but with Eve, I feel like I'm walking on a knife-edge all the time. It's exciting but it feels like one wrong move, and I'm dead."

He'd just set me up perfectly. The timing couldn't be better for me to praise Noelle and tell him how much easier it would be with her, how much happier he'd be with a girl like her.

But I couldn't bring myself to do it. I could hear the words I should say but they stuck in my throat because, although he'd called her 'nice', he hadn't seemed to realize yet that she could be so much more than that. She was a diamond in the rough, so much more valuable than we'd noticed, and I didn't want him to be the one who got to polish her up. I didn't want him to be the one to make her shine.

But where did that leave Eve? And what about the fact that Noelle still wanted Corey, not me? Would keeping silent now make me just as bad as Corey when he went after Eve instead of just being honest with me? Should I tell him the truth?

How the hell did this all get so complicated?

~Noelle~

When the door closed behind Aaron and Corey, the click of it and the sudden silence that followed sent several different emotions racing through me all at once.

Relief, disappointment, confusion, anxiety, and probably a few others I couldn't name all seemed to want to take control and I truly couldn't decide what to feel while Eve took a seat next to me, her dark eyes watching me shrewdly.

"So, are you ready to tell me the truth yet?"

My blood froze in my veins as I frantically tried to figure out what she could be talking about. The truth about my fall? The truth about how ending up with Corey for Seven Minutes in Heaven hadn't been entirely random? The truth about where Aaron spent the night? Which truth did she mean?

"Uh, I don't... I mean, I... what?"

My hopeless stuttering made her smile, the stern look falling away as her eyes twinkled mischievously. "You fooled me for a long time, Noelle, but I figured it out. I know who your mystery crush is."

Shit. I thought she might from the look she gave me earlier when Corey brought up the hockey games, but I had hoped I'd just read too much into it. Now, she would know exactly why I had been in such a bad mood the last few days and if she put the rest together about how I'd been trying to drive a wedge between them...

Wait. As my brain caught up to my racing heart, I realized something didn't add up. If she knew I liked Corey, why did she look so pleased with herself? The cat who got the cream couldn't look any happier, and that made no sense if she thought I had been lusting after the guy she was currently sleeping with.

"Who do you think it is?"

She gave me a playful nudge on my uninjured leg. "As if you don't know. I should have guessed ages ago, I can't believe I fell for all that 'I can't stand him' talk. It's so obvious!"

Her explanation made me more confused, not less. "What are you talking about?"

With her lips pursed, she shook her head at me. "It's Aaron! You like Aaron. I totally see it now."

Aaron? She thought I'd spent all these years pining after Aaron Speelman? "How did you come up with that?"

"You always get so competitive with him when you don't with anyone else," she pointed out. "You take every slight from him so personally. They say hate is just a step away from love."

"I took things personally because he meant them personally. Because he annoyed me!" I protested.

Eve shook her head again. "And all those hockey games you went to? I didn't put it together until Corey just mentioned it. Aaron must have been there! He's Corey's best friend so I bet he goes all the time too. You went to see him."

She had completely gotten the wrong end of the stick. "Eve, I..."

She hadn't finished yet. "And don't think I've missed the looks you two have been giving each other since we got here. Did something happen on the plane? Come on, Noelle, tell me!"

Her eyes were filled with such excitement that I hated to burst her bubble, but I couldn't let her go on thinking she had it right either. Aaron wanted her, not me, and if I told her that I liked him, true or not, she would never think of him that way and he'd be pissed off at me for ruining his chances.

Although he'd just kissed me, a rather astounding kiss that I still hadn't figured out how to process, and called me a good girl besides, which turned my insides to liquid in a way I really couldn't explain, he still hadn't said a word about actually wanting to pursue anything with me. He liked me, he said, but I knew he still liked Eve more. He hadn't denied that when I pointed it out. So, even if I did want more from him, which I couldn't even be sure I did, it made no difference when he didn't feel the same. We were still just helping each other out, but how could I tell Eve any of that without going into the whole story, and the longer it went on, the less possible that seemed.

High school never had this much drama, at least for me. Weren't we supposed to be adults now?

I could just tell her the truth, I supposed. Stick to the simple, honest truth, without adding any unnecessary details. That seemed the safest route.

"My crush isn't Aaron. You're wrong."

The flatness of my response seemed to convince her of the truthfulness of my words, and she deflated before my eyes, her shoulders slumping and the brightness fading from her eyes. "Really? There's nothing between you guys? The more I talk to him, the more I think you could be really good together."

As I tried to decide how to respond to *that* unexpected remark, I realized something else didn't make sense. "Wait, if you thought you had it all figured out, why would you come back here when we were alone?"

She leaned against the back of the sofa with a sigh. "Well, partly because I couldn't wait to talk to you once I figured it out... or once I thought I figured it out, I guess. It's not like anything is going to happen in the middle of the day right after you injured yourself anyway."

That showed how much she knew. What might have happened if she hadn't come back? I suspected it might not have stopped at just a kiss. I could still hear that whispered 'damn it, Noelle' from the bathroom the night before. Would I have heard it again if we...

"And also just because I needed a break," she added, her lips twitching almost unhappily as she pulled me back out of my daydreams.

"A break? From what?"

"From Corey."

My eyes went so wide, I almost saw double. "But you said things were going well."

"They are. Kind of. I know I said it would be fun to do couples things with him on this trip, but I didn't mean I wanted to spend every waking minute with him. Everyone's acting like we're a couple and we're not. They all want to make it out to be more serious than it is and it feels like Corey's starting to buy into it too."

Yet again, I felt confused, but for the first time, I started to understand Eve might too. "What do you actually want?"

She sighed again, letting me know I was on the right track. "Honestly? I just want everyone to stop reading so much into everything I do. Why can't I be the girl who hooks up with a guy at a party without it being serious? Why can't we have fun without everyone trying to find a deeper meaning? Why does everyone feel like they get to have a say in what I do with my life?"

Clearly, this went deeper than just Corey, and I put aside all the relationship drama for a minute to try to figure out what was really bothering my friend.

"Is this about the office?" Just before we went to that party back home where she hooked up with Corey, Eve's dad invited us both to visit him and my dad at Stamer Hotels' corporate office before they took us out to dinner to celebrate the end of the college term.

Nothing about that seemed out of the ordinary, but when we arrived, Eve's dad, Cole, showed Eve the office he'd chosen for her. It sat empty at the moment and he wanted to give her a chance to choose the interior decoration before she started working there in the summer. Just down the hall from his own office and her mom's, and right next door to Noah's, the whole family would soon be working together, making it a true family business.

Eve made all the right noises, but I could tell her level of excitement paled in comparison to his. I'd hardly ever seen her dad so excited. When I tried to ask her about it later, she said she didn't want to talk about it, not when we had the holidays to enjoy before we had to think about our last term and going out into the real world. With everything that had happened with Corey and getting ready for this trip, it hadn't come up again.

She didn't answer my question directly now either. "Everything feels out of control. You make one choice that doesn't seem like a big deal, something gets set in motion and before you know it, it's too late to back out. You're in too deep."

Although she had no way of knowing it, she could have easily been describing this whole arrangement between me and Aaron. When I agreed to his suggestion on the plane, I had no idea how it would take on a life of its own.

But from her perspective, did she mean her job or did she mean Corey? "It's never too late, Eve," I said, feeling like a complete hypocrite as I advised her to be honest. "If you're not into Corey, just tell him so. You've never had trouble breaking up with a guy before."

"That's just it," she moaned. "We shouldn't have to 'break up'. We were never *together*, not really. I only wanted to have some fun. I want to keep having fun with him. I just don't necessarily want it to be more than that and I don't know how to tell him that without hurting his feelings. When you told me in the car yesterday that he had been talking about being with other girls on this trip, honestly, I almost felt relieved, but that's not the vibe I'm getting from him at all."

"You want a long-term casual thing?" I still didn't fully understand.

"I don't know what I want." She hid her face behind her hands, taking a deep breath before flashing me a smile. "I'm sorry, I know I'm not making any sense. I hoped you were into Aaron so we could come up with a plan to get the two of you together. You deserve to have some fun too, and I could do with a distraction."

She had made that abundantly clear, and what were best friends for? "Well, you'll have to put your matchmaking on hold, but I have a different idea to distract us: how about we make a gingerbread house?"

As I hoped, the spark in Eve's eyes came roaring back. "Really? Right now?"

Making a gingerbread house each Christmas had always been a Stamer family tradition. As an architect, Eve's mom made the most amazing houses, while Eve and I made a mess decorating them with icing and candy. We'd never made one from scratch all on our own before, but it couldn't be that hard. We'd watched Gemma do it dozens of times.

"Sure. The kitchen's pretty well-stocked, I bet we have everything we need. I've got M&Ms in our room too."

"What about your knee?" Eve glanced down at my leg which still rested on the pillow.

"It's feeling better all the time, and I wouldn't mind a distraction from it too. You wanted a break, so let's take one. Let's forget about everyone and everything else for a while and just have some fun."

~Aaron~

"If you're looking for advice on how to win Eve's heart, you've come to the wrong guy. Even if I knew, I wouldn't tell you after what you did."

I settled on that response to Corey, and he had to concede my point, finally looking embarrassed. "I'm sorry, Aaron. I didn't mean... shit. I'm just sorry, okay?"

In his own way, I believed he *was* sorry, but I also thought he couldn't see the big picture. He might say he wanted to save me from humiliation, but I suspected he wanted to prove himself too. People never expected much from him off the ice. He said he'd asked around about Eve, and he must have realized on some level that by having a woman like Eve interested in him, he'd prove he fit her 'type', as he called it. He'd be the guy who had it all.

Behind his selfish and thoughtless actions, I saw the insecurity of a guy who had been the big man on campus for the last three years and dreaded the approaching end of college as a change he wasn't ready for just yet. Eve looked like a lifeline, a way to get people to take him seriously. Did he actually like her as a person at all? Did he even know her?

Did I, for that matter? I thought I did, based on everything I knew *about* her, but she had taken me by surprise a few times on this trip already, just like Noelle had. Maybe I didn't know either of them as well as I'd imagined.

Had Noelle had the same thoughts about Corey as she got to know him better? Would she still want to be with him if she knew him like I did? Maybe some more time together would help all of us to get a lot clearer about what and who we actually wanted.

With that in mind, after Corey and I had a long lunch with the others and walked around town for a while, I told him that I wanted to head back to the house where the two girls were still on their own. He took that as an invitation to join me and the two of us made our way back together. Things still weren't completely comfortable between us but our little blowout and Corey's apology helped to smooth things over a bit. It felt less tense than it had.

The smell of gingerbread and the sound of Christmas carols and laughter greeted us as soon as we walked in the door. "Sounds like they're having fun," Corey said, smiling in anticipation as we took off our outdoor gear.

It did. I'd rather foolishly imagined them still sitting in the living room where we'd left them, waiting for us to come back, but they had clearly moved on.

Even though we could smell the gingerbread, the scene in the kitchen still took me by surprise. Wearing matching aprons they'd found somewhere, Eve and Noelle were perched on stools at the kitchen island, covered in flour and multi-coloured icing, with various pieces of decorated and undecorated gingerbread laid out on the counter in front of them. Noelle added some more icing from the bag in her hands to the piece of gingerbread in front of her and they both laughed again, without a hint of self-consciousness, not having noticed us in the doorway yet.

Corey soon spoiled that. "What's so funny?" he asked, walking into the room with his usual swagger.

Both girls looked up in surprise, but while Eve grinned, Noelle turned beet red, glancing down at the piece of gingerbread she'd just been decorating, and before anyone could say anything else, she broke it in half and shoved one piece into her mouth while covering the other with her hand, which made Eve laugh louder than ever.

Corey and I exchanged bemused looks. Obviously, we'd missed something.

"Hi," Noelle mumbled around the cookie. "We're, uh, just making a ginger-bread house."

"Do you want to help put it together?" Eve asked us, still grinning, but with a note of challenge in her voice.

The carols were coming from a digital radio on the kitchen counter, and Eve directed us to the pantry where we could find more aprons to wear. When Corey protested at the idea of putting one on, Eve gave him a wink.

"It's better to be prepared. Things might get dirty."

I liked the sound of that. With our aprons on, Corey and I joined the girls at the island and looked over the pieces they'd made so far.

"These are the main walls and the roof," Noelle explained, pointing to the largest pieces. "The roof is always the tricky bit."

"Sounds like you know what you're talking about." Corey gave her a warm smile and she beamed back at him, setting off an uncomfortable constriction in my chest.

"Always."

Whatever had happened while we were away was working for her. She looked happy and confident, and Eve looked a lot more relaxed too. Noelle still hadn't done anything further with her hair or makeup since the morning, it made me glad to see. Her lips were redder than usual thanks to the icing she'd just eaten, and I couldn't help imagining if they'd taste even sweeter than before.

Had she been thinking about that kiss like I had? From the way her eyes were glued to Corey now, I had to guess that answer would be no.

"Neither of us are engineers, though," Eve pointed out with a laugh. "I think we better get some cans to help prop things up or the whole thing will collapse."

I took the hint, grabbing some soup cans from the pantry, and the four of us worked together to assemble the basic structure, laughing and teasing each other the whole time. Hands brushed against hands, icing got squirted around accidentally and not-so-accidentally, bodies got pressed against each other as we changed positions to hold onto different pieces, and by the time we had the house entirely together, I honestly didn't know who was flirting with who anymore.

Eve took a step back to admire the finished product and to laugh at the state of us all. "Noelle, you've got icing in your hair. Aaron, there's some on your glasses too."

"You're one to talk," I pointed out. "You've got some on your nose."

"Do I?" She rubbed her nose with her hand furiously. "Did I get it?"

"Nope. It's right... here." I reached over with a glob of icing and placed it right on the tip of her nose while Corey and Noelle laughed.

"You don't want to start that with me," Eve warned.

I raised my eyebrows back at her. "Don't I?"

From the corner of my eye, I saw Noelle whisper something to Corey who grinned in response, and the next thing we knew, they both had a handful of icing sugar.

"Don't even think about..." I started to say, but it was too late. They both blew into their hands, sending the powder flying all over me and Eve.

Food began flying as the kitchen devolved into chaos and soon, the four of us and the entire room were a complete mess.

"We didn't think this through," Noelle moaned as she looked around when we'd run out of things to throw at each other. "It's going to take hours to clean this up."

Corey just shrugged. "The house comes with a housekeeper. I'll throw in a tip."

Money solved most problems, at least in Corey's world.

"Well, we'll have to clean up ourselves," Eve pointed out. "I need a shower."

"I think we all do," Noelle agreed. "I guess you can go first and I'll wait."

"That's not necessary. We can pair up," Corey offered. He obviously meant Eve could go with him, but I saw Noelle's cheeks begin to flush anyway.

"That's a great idea," Eve said breezily. "Noelle and I will go together and you two can use yours."

I had to laugh at Corey's look of disappointment, but he had given me an idea. "Sharing *would* save water. How about we let the gingerbread decide?"

Both girls looked at me curiously but Eve asked the question first: "What do you mean?"

I picked up one of the extra gingerbread pieces that hadn't made it onto the house. "Like spin the bottle, but with gingerbread. We put an icing arrow on it and Corey can give it a spin. Whoever it lands on has to share with him."

I specifically phrased it to sound like the person he chose would be the loser, though I knew neither woman felt that way.

"Sounds interesting," Eve said, glancing over at Noelle. "So, if Corey gets Noelle, then I shower with you?"

I nodded in confirmation as they all thought it over. The night before, I manipulated the game to get the result I wanted, but now, maybe we should let fate play its part. Maybe Noelle and I would end up with the people we'd come here to be with, or maybe we'd end up with each other. Either way, it would give us an opportunity to take things further than we had before, in a relatively low-risk way. After all, we all knew it would just be a game, and we were all willing players.

Maybe it would be worth the gamble.

Chapter Eight

THE GAMBLE

~Noelle~

What the hell was Aaron doing now? Did he have a way of fixing the game he just suggested? I didn't see how, not when he said Corey would be making the spin. He hadn't been involved in making the gingerbread, so he couldn't have weighed the piece down on one side or anything, if something like that would even be possible. My heart raced and my mind whirled as I tried to figure it out.

Could he really just be leaving this to chance?

"What do you think?" Eve whispered in my ear as the two men in front of us waited for our approval.

I honestly had no idea. On the one hand, the idea of showering with Corey made me incredibly nervous. I'd imagined getting naked with him so many times but never in this context. Could I really strip down in front of him? How far would things go? Would this be another letdown like Seven Minutes in Heaven, where it sounded like we were all being edgy and up for anything, but in reality, nothing would happen when we got alone?

And what if I ended up with Aaron? Just the thought of it sent a pulse of energy through my body because, while I couldn't really imagine anything happening with Corey, no matter how much I might want it to, with Aaron, it seemed possible. The way he fantasized over me the night before and the way he kissed me earlier made it seem very likely that if he couldn't have Eve, he would accept me as a substitute, at least temporarily.

Did I want that? Could we keep it casual, finding pleasure in each other as an alternative to the people we really wanted to be with? My body screamed at me to go for it while my mind wavered indecisively. I'd never really done casual sex before, and falling for *another* guy who preferred my best friend to me was the very last thing I needed. At some point, I needed someone to put me first.

"What do *you* think?" I whispered back to Eve. After all, she and Corey had already been intimate together, but how would Corey feel if Eve ended up with Aaron? Would she actually do anything with him? Why did the idea that she might leave such a bitter taste in my mouth?

She shrugged. "Everyone's already deciding things for me. Why not let a piece of gingerbread make my choices too?"

I couldn't tell how seriously she meant that, but it didn't sound like a good reason to agree to something like this. "If you don't want to, I'll say I'm uncomfortable with it. They don't need to think it has anything to do with you."

Her eyebrows raised in surprise. "But if it were up to you, you would go ahead?"

That confirmed my suspicion that she might be hoping I'd provide her an out, but I did my best to copy her shrug. "Why not? Like you said, we're here to have some fun, and if you and Corey aren't serious and we all agree it wouldn't mean anything, what's the harm?"

I hoped that sounded a lot cooler than I felt, because inside, panic had started to rise as the thought began to solidify inside my head. Could I really be about to have sex in a matter of minutes? It suddenly felt entirely realistic, even though my partner remained undetermined. It felt crazy, but also kind of like the most exciting thing I'd ever done.

Eve pursed her lips thoughtfully before turning back to the boys with a nod. "Alright. We're in."

"Really?" Corey sounded shocked. "You know you might end up with Aaron, right?"

Aaron shot him a withering look as indignation bubbled up inside me on his behalf. Eve would never put me down like that, and she stood up for Aaron now, in a roundabout way. "And I might end up with Noelle if you pick Aaron. Looks like I win no matter what."

She gave Aaron a wink that I both appreciated, since it helped smooth over Corey's putdown, and disliked for reasons I couldn't entirely explain.

"I'll make the arrow," I offered, picking up one of the icing bags in an effort to distract myself from my contradictory thoughts. My hands shook as I tried to pipe in straight lines onto the square gingerbread piece Aaron had pointed out. The air around us seemed to have grown heavier, the laughter of our earlier food fight forgotten as tension and anticipation built up around us.

Corey's shoulders had tightened when I looked up, but he gave me a smile anyway, trying to maintain some control over the situation. "You think you can handle me, Noelle?"

I'd been waiting so long to hear words like that from him, but knowing that they were mostly for Eve's benefit, trying to make her jealous like she had obviously made him, took the shine off them for me. Rather than melting beneath that steely gaze and mumbling something submissive, I simply raised my eyebrows back at him.

"I think the question is whether you can handle me."

Eve laughed in delight while Aaron's lips curled in approval, sending a shot of warmth through me far stronger than Corey's words had.

"Alright, so we all know the rules?" Eve confirmed. "Corey spins and whoever it lands on goes with him, no complaining and no do-overs. Got it?"

We all nodded our agreement and I took a step back into line with the other two, Eve in the middle, as Corey took hold of the gingerbread square.

"Let's see just how good those hands of yours are," Eve teased, sounding far more blasé about the whole thing than I felt. Which outcome would please her most? I had no idea, no more than I knew which one I wanted for myself.

Corey's lips pressed firmly together as he took hold of the edges of the square and gave it a firm twist, sending the cookie spinning across the counter.

We all leaned forward for a better look as it skittered and slowed, until coming to a rest pointing straight at...

Eve.

~**Aaron**~

I waited for disappointment to hit me as Corey managed to land on the one person he wanted to. Things always seemed to go that way; give us both a 33% chance of success and luck would be on Corey's side rather than mine, every fucking time.

And yet, this particular time, any disappointment I might have felt paled in comparison to the reaction in my body caused by the flush that immediately spread up Noelle's cheeks. She didn't look over at me, didn't make eye contact at all, but that red colour creeping into her face told me all I needed to know: the thought of us showering together made her just as hot as it made me.

Maybe we were both just overstimulated already. Maybe we were only channelling the attraction we felt to Eve and Corey onto each other instead. Maybe we had found ourselves more compatible than we expected. I couldn't say for sure what lay behind it, but I recognized the feeling well enough and I had no plans to hide it. Now that the opportunity had presented itself, I would freely admit that I wanted her, and I felt damn sure she wanted me too. If Eve and Corey were going to have fun together, I couldn't think of any reason Noelle and I shouldn't do the same.

"That settles it, then," Eve announced, walking over to Corey and slipping her arm around his waist as if it had been her plan all along. "Have fun, you two."

She gave us another wink as the two of them headed downstairs, leaving Noelle and me standing alone in the messy kitchen, the silence descending over us like a blanket as we both waited for the other to make the first move and set the tone.

Noelle broke the silence with her now-familiar self-deprecating apology. "I know you wanted to go with Eve, so if you want to just shower separately, we could just lie and tell them..."

I didn't want that at all, and I took a step closer to her, cutting her off. "What happened to the girl who just told Corey he might not be able to handle her?"

She blinked up at me with that utterly irresistible desire for approval. "You want me to say things like that?"

"I want you to think that you're the grand prize, Noelle, not the consolation. I want you to show me why you are. Can you do that for me?"

She swallowed before nodding hesitantly. "That's what you think Corey would like?"

Who gave a fuck about what Corey wanted? Those words were on the tip of my tongue until I remembered that *she* did; she wanted him and not me, but right now, we only had each other. Right now, we could forget about the scheming and the backstabbing and the misguided intentions and just enjoy ourselves.

Right now, I knew I could show her a damn good time and I intended to do it.

"It's what I would like," I answered her. "Forget about everything else and just focus on me, alright?"

She nodded again, more firmly this time, and I gave her an approving nod.

"That's my girl."

I could literally see the shiver that ran through her, sending a spike of adrenaline through me too. Fuck, this was going to be fun.

~Noelle~

Aaron actually wanted to do this. Those hazel eyes stared at me intensely from behind his glasses, sending tingles through my whole body, and when he called me 'his' girl, saying it with pride and approval, the tingles erupted into a full-blown explosion of electricity, travelling through my body like a shockwave.

Why did I like that so much? How did he know just what to say?

He told me to forget everything else, and right now, I honestly couldn't remember what he wanted me to forget. My thoughts had all been swallowed up by that firm voice, that unexpectedly commanding and affirming tone, and what he might say to me when we were naked together. I would have a hard time saying no to anything he asked me to do when he said it that way, and I didn't even really want to attempt to resist. Nothing existed right now outside of this moment and the possibilities it held.

"Do you need help getting upstairs?" Aaron stepped closer to me, reaching out to run his thumb down the line of my jaw, his touch light and warm and distracting, so distracting that it took me a second to figure out why he asked.

My knee. Right.

"N-no. I think I'm okay." My mouth had gone dry all of a sudden, the words struggling to come out, and Aaron's lips pursed.

"Don't lie to me, Noelle. Is it going to hurt on the stairs?"

It did hurt when I put my full weight on it, but what alternative did I have? "I can manage."

The look of reproach in his eyes left me almost as bereft as his earlier words had warmed me. Why did his approval mean so much to me? It truly confused me. "I'll let you try that one more time: is it going to hurt?"

Beneath the firm look and demanding tone, I felt myself nodding even though I hadn't meant to. For some reason, I really didn't want to disappoint him. "A little."

His brow immediately cleared, the critical look giving way to approbation. "Was that so hard to admit? Let's go, then."

Before I had a chance to prepare myself, he leaned down, his arms grabbing hold of me as he lifted me up against his chest, one arm behind my back and the other on the back of my thighs, avoiding the sore area of my knee. To my surprise, it felt almost as secure and solid as when Corey picked me up earlier. Aaron's sudden proximity and the heat of his body against mine sent waves of warmth through me, my heart beating fast and a steady pulsing rhythm kicking off between my legs.

Fuck, this was really happening.

He fixed his gaze forward with determination as he walked out of the kitchen and carried me up the wide staircase. Over his shoulder, I could see the trail left behind by the icing sugar from the kitchen floor, one set of snowy footprints leading straight to my bedroom door.

Inside the room, he didn't put me down until we reached the bathroom. Once he'd steadied me on my feet, he reached into the shower and turned the water on, getting the temperature warm and ready for us before turning back to me, his gaze just as heated as my body felt.

"I want you to be honest with me, always, Noelle. It's very important. If you don't want me to do something, say so. If you *want* me to do something, say so. If you want to stop, just say the word. I can't know what's in your head unless you tell me, and when I know what you want, we'll both be much happier. Can you promise me that?"

I'd never had such a set-up for sex before. Usually, I just kind of fumbled towards it, never entirely sure what my partner expected of me or even if it would really happen until we were naked. But now, while we were still fully clothed, he set out his ground rules, rules that were all about making sure I enjoyed myself.

Who *was* this guy?

'I'll try,' would have been my default response, but I knew even before I said the words that they weren't going to be enough. He wanted me to be confident, he'd told me that downstairs. He wanted me to think of myself as the prize. And the way he looked at me now, the anticipation and the desire, made me feel that way too. Neither of us were thinking about what might have been if the cookie had spun in a different direction. We were both completely in the moment, and in this moment, I wanted to please him.

Fuck, I wanted to please him.

So, I nodded firmly, my answer surprising me in its firmness. "I'll tell you what I want."

The satisfied smile that spread across his face somehow made me feel weak and strong at the same time. "Good girl."

My thighs clenched as Aaron stepped towards me and kissed me again.

Unlike our kiss earlier, this one had nothing slow or exploratory about it. His lips staked his claim, letting me know that for as long as I allowed it, he would take what he wanted and make me feel good while he did it. No kiss had ever sent me such a clear message before, but I heard it loud and clear and felt it in every inch of my body.

He took hold of the bottom of my sweater, tugging it up just a little before pausing, giving me the chance to tell him to stop if I wanted him to, but nothing could be further from what I wanted. My heart pounded as I waited for him to pull it the rest of the way up, and a moment later, he did, lifting it gently but firmly over my head.

His lips returned to mine immediately afterwards, distracting me from any nerves I might have felt about my clothes coming off. His warm hands splayed across my back, pulling me closer to him, my chest pressing against his and my nipples hardening at the sensation. Deftly, his fingers undid the clasp of my bra, and again, he paused before going any further, his hands running up and down my back, giving me a chance to change my mind.

This time, I did pull back from him, breaking our kiss as I took a step away to put some distance between us. Confusion and a strong disappointment flared in Aaron's eyes, but I knew without a doubt that he wouldn't stop me. If I said that I wanted to end it right here, he wouldn't try to convince me otherwise.

Luckily for both of us, I had no such intention. Instead, I pulled my bra off my shoulders myself, letting him watch as it slid down my arms away from my chest, leaving me fully exposed to him.

The disappointed look melted away in an instant, and desire and appreciation quickly took its place. "You look incredible."

His voice sounded heavier and throatier than usual, letting me know those weren't just idle words. He truly meant them.

His eyes on my chest, he reached out and ran his hands across my breasts, slowly, taking his time as he explored them. His thumbs flicked over the nipples, making me bite my lip to keep from moaning, and he cupped and squeezed and tweaked them, all without shame or self-consciousness, which made me feel more confident too. "These are beautiful," he confirmed when he'd finished his examination. "The perfect size."

"For what?" I blurted out, flushing beneath his praise but also not entirely sure what he meant. Most men preferred them slightly bigger, like Eve's.

My question made Aaron grin unexpectedly. "For this," he replied just before he leaned down and took one of the stiff nipples into his mouth, sucking on it firmly.

"Oh, fuck!" I didn't mean to say that out loud but the words came out anyway and Aaron laughed, his lips vibrating against the tender skin of my breast.

"Soon," he teased me, glancing up at me with his mouth still pressed against my chest. "I still need to see the rest of you first."

He returned to his task, his tongue flicking across my nipple as the pulsing between my legs grew even stronger. My thighs pressed together again in a desperate attempt to soothe the growing ache, and Aaron noticed me squirming, his eyes twinkling as he looked back up at me from behind his glasses.

"Are you getting impatient, Noelle?"

Maybe I should say no, but he asked me to be honest, so I pointed out the obvious. "The water's going to get cold."

Although he laughed, he couldn't deny it either. His glasses were already starting to steam up, along with the bathroom mirror. The humid air around us only made me hotter. I couldn't wait to get out of the rest of my clothes and to get him out of his. As good as all of this felt, I wanted more.

He stood back up, our faces nearly level to each other. "Normally, I like to take my time, but you're right. Let's get clean first."

He pulled his glasses off, placing them on the bathroom vanity before pulling off his own shirt, and my jaw nearly dropped as I got my first look at him.

He didn't have Corey's width and bulk, obviously, his body narrower and slimmer, but his muscles were surprisingly well defined, the lines of his abs clearly visible and a rather inviting V-line that disappeared beneath the waist of his jeans. I had no idea his ill-fitting clothes hid all of that.

His hands went to the buttons of his jeans as he looked up at me with a challenge in his eyes. "Are you sure you're ready?"

~Aaron~

Noelle's confidence growing with each passing second had my whole body buzzing. Seeing her take control of her desires turned me on, and the more she realized she had my complete attention, the more positive energy I gave her, the more she absorbed and returned to me.

When I asked her if she still wanted me to take my pants off, she raised her eyebrows at me just as I hoped. "Is the view going to shock me?"

Fuck, I couldn't ask for more than this version of Noelle, the one sure of herself and willing to play dirty at times to get what she wanted. So long as she wanted me, she could get as dirty as she wanted.

"Shock is a strong word, but I think you'll be satisfied."

I'd seen enough naked men in my life to know that while my dick may not be the biggest out there, it fell into the above average range. I'd certainly never had any complaints. I just didn't feel the need to go around, like some guys did, acting like my dick made me better than anyone else. The only time it really mattered was times like these when I could use it to bring pleasure to someone I wanted to please.

The pressure of the zipper against my dick as I pulled it down made me wince. I'd been ridiculously hard ever since I picked Noelle up downstairs, seeing the way her body reacted to me and anticipating all the pleasures that lay ahead of us. Getting her beautiful tits in my mouth hadn't helped the situation at all, so by the time I pulled my pants down, kicked them off and removed my socks too, I was fully erect and ready to go.

Noelle's lips parted as she took in the whole picture as I stood completely naked before her. "You... uh... I didn't... um, oh."

No complete sentence seemed to be forthcoming as her cheeks flushed, and that made me just as happy as if she'd teased me again. I had actually begun to grow fond of these swings of hers, going from confident to stumbling in a matter of seconds. I found both sides of her appealing. I found every damn part of her appealing.

Only one part of her remained that I hadn't seen yet, but I had no doubts I would like it just as much as the rest.

"Your turn," I reminded her as she stood there motionless, still staring at my dick. "Unless you plan on showering in your pants?"

That seemed to wake her up and her hands went to her remaining clothes, fumbling as she grabbed hold of the elastic waist and slowly pulled them down.

She winced as she bent over, her knee still bothering her, and I quickly got to my knees in front of her.

"Stand back up. I got it. Put your hands on my shoulders."

Gently, I helped her out of her pants, making sure not to bump her knee. I couldn't help noticing the dampness of her panties as they hit the ground, not that it really surprised me. From the way her body reacted to me, the flush in her cheeks and the dilation of her pupils, I knew she wanted this just as much as I did.

And when she stood there, just as naked as me, I couldn't stop myself from running my hands up her legs, just like I had on the sofa earlier but not stopping this time, travelling her thighs until I reached that irresistible junction between her legs. My fingers slid naturally into the small gap there and when the proof of her desire coated my fingers, I groaned out loud.

"Damn it, Noelle." Her whole body shuddered as she gripped my shoulders tighter. "Such a good, wet girl. Do you know what this does to me?"

My fingers slipped through her wetness again, brushing against her clit as she let out a soft moan.

Standing back up, I held up my fingers for her, letting her see how they glistened. Even without my glasses, I could see them shining. "Do you think it tastes as good as it looks?"

Her eyes widened as she blinked at me. "I don't know?"

The fact that she phrased it as a question made me smile. "Maybe we should find out then."

Keeping my eyes locked on her, I took the fingers into my mouth, sucking on them hard as her taste danced on my tongue.

"Fucking delicious. You taste amazing."

A small whimper slipped through her tightly pressed lips, and I made note of every reaction. She loved the praise, I knew that already, but possibly even more than anyone else I'd ever been with. She didn't just love it; she *needed* it. It turned her on and she craved it almost as much as she wanted my touch right now. Luckily for her, I could give her both.

"Let's get in," I said, gesturing towards the shower. The rest of the room had gone blurry for me, but as long as I kept Noelle close, I could see her reactions, and I only needed that for now.

The warm water poured over us both as we got in, the drops that hit me bouncing off onto her body and vice versa.

"You do have icing in your hair," I reminded her. We had all decided to shower in the first place for that reason. "Let me wash you."

She nodded in agreement and I picked up a bottle, squinting to read the words. "Is this shampoo?"

With a smile, she took it from me and placed it back down, picking up a different bottle instead and teasing me as she handed it over. "Is it true that when you're blind, your other senses are heightened?"

The quip made me laugh, as did her confidence in delivering it. She could be such a contradiction, such an enticing, intriguing mix of personalities. "You tell me. Close your eyes." When she instantly obeyed, I praised her for her compliance. "Good girl. Now, see how this feels."

Squirting the shampoo into my hand, I massaged it into her head slowly. My fingers pressed firmly against her scalp, rubbing in slow circles as she moaned in appreciation.

"God, that's amazing," she breathed.

If she liked that, the rest of what I had planned would really blow her mind.

"You've got such pretty hair," I told her honestly as I continued washing it. "You should leave it natural more often. The way it curls around your face is beautiful."

"Really?" Those words seemed to shock her almost more than anything else I'd said so far.

"Really," I confirmed. "I like it curvy, just like the rest of you."

My soaped-up hands left her head and travelled downwards, tracing the lines of her collarbone, the swell of her breasts, the curve of her hips, and back to that sweet spot between her legs. Her hands grabbed hold of my arms as I brushed against her clit again, and this time, I went deeper too, letting my fingertips find her entrance and pausing there, as always, to give her a moment to recognize what I meant to do and tell me to stop if she wanted me to.

She said nothing, her eyes still closed and her lips parted, so I pressed my fingers further inside.

"Yes," Noelle moaned, the word whispered and breathless.

Yes was right. She felt incredible, and I told her so. "You feel amazing on my fingers, Noelle. Your pussy feels so good, nice and wet just for me."

She whimpered again as I pumped into her, reaching further until I found her g-spot and her grip on me tightened.

"There you are. Your body knows just what to do. You want to be a good girl and come for me, don't you?" My thumb circled her clit as I said the words and she nodded, biting her lip as she tried to hold back. "Show me then, Noelle. Let me see how good you look when you come. Give it to me like the fucking good girl you are."

I hit all her spots at once, her sensitive clit, the one deep inside her warm pussy, and the one in her brain that responded to my words. Overloaded with pleasure, she jolted and shuddered on my hand, her nipples gathering to a stiff peak as her orgasm hit, letting me know she definitely hadn't faked a thing.

That was the real deal, and we were only getting started.

Chapter Nine

IF ONLY

~Noelle~

Holy shit. As I clung onto Aaron's surprisingly firm arms, water running down my body as my legs trembled with the release of my orgasm, those words formed the only coherent thought in my head.

Gradually, a few other things filtered too, like the memory of the things the other girls had said about Aaron on the way here to Leavenworth, about how his confidence might indicate that he knew his way around the bedroom. I could now confirm that on that point, they had been entirely correct. No one had ever made me feel anything close to this before, and the fact that Aaron Speelman should be the one to do it only made it more surprising.

But the most surprising thing of all had to be the words he spoke, the absolutely filthy yet encouraging words that made me want to do anything he said, anything to please him, yet made me feel powerful at the same time. How did he *do* that? Did he know what it would do to me? How could he, when I hadn't even known myself?

Would it do the same thing to Eve? Based on her reaction to what he said during the game of Spin the Bottle, I suspected it wouldn't. She already had the praise and admiration of everyone she met, so why would it matter to get it from one more person?

And why did he do it anyway? Did saying those things make him feel as good as it made me? That seemed impossible, but he must have gotten *something* out of it or he wouldn't have done it.

I'd rarely been so confused in my whole life, or so completely satisfied.

"That was perfect," Aaron whispered to me now, his breath hot against my ear as his fingers stroked me gently a few more times and then, disappointingly, withdrew. "You looked just as good as I imagined."

He had imagined it? Did he mean the night before when he jerked off right there in that very bathroom while saying my name? Had he thought about me other times too? Or was it simply a turn of phrase, something that sounded good in the moment but ultimately meant nothing?

Could I be overthinking this? It felt like I might be.

Maybe I needed to just slow down and enjoy the moment, especially since his rather prominent erection still required some attention.

I'd been surprised by his unexpectedly toned physique when he took off his shirt, but when his pants came off, I honestly thought my eyes might be playing tricks on me. Who would have guessed that Aaron, of all people, possessed such an impressive piece of equipment?

I'd been itching to get my hands on his dick since he revealed it and now that he seemed satisfied with how he'd just made me come, I seized the opportunity, quite literally.

My hand moved from his arm down the firm planes of his chest and stomach, following the trail of hair that led even lower until I reached the base of his thick, hard shaft, and I wrapped my hand around it, giving a firm squeeze.

Aaron inhaled, the air hissing between his teeth in perfect harmony to the splashing of the water still raining down on us from the shower. He placed his hands on the wall of the shower behind me, steadying himself as I continued to touch him. "Your hand feels so good," he groaned, his eyes closing in pleasure as I moved slowly up towards his head. "Touch me just like that."

No one had ever given me this kind of direction and encouragement before, but I loved it. My confidence grew as he continued to praise me, commenting on the firmness of my grip and the pace I set. He told me he loved when I stroked his balls too, but when I rolled them around in my hand, he stopped me.

"I liked what you were doing before better," he explained between grunts as I continued to stroke his dick. "It felt amazing."

Honestly, I appreciated the direction, especially phrased that way. And when I went back to my previous action, his approval warmed me through and through.

"That's it, fuck, Noelle. Good girl."

Those particular words sent a jolt of electricity straight to my core, every single time.

He hardened even further beneath my touch until I knew he must be close. If I made him come now, that would be the end of things, but I wanted him to anyway. I wanted to see his cum painted across the shower stall and know that I'd been responsible for it.

"Shit." Aaron's breath grew shorter as I pumped him faster. "You're doing such a good job."

A whimper of pure delight came out of me. Even though the physical pleasure belonged to him right now, his words turned me on almost as much as his touch did.

"That's it... ugh... yes..."

He kept encouraging me as he reached his climax, his words coming out hot and heavy in short bursts. When he finally let go, exhaling heavily as he came, spurting out onto the shower and my stomach too, a sense of achievement and pride raced through me, heightening my own pleasure in return.

Fuck, I felt really close again myself and his next words didn't help.

"Damn it, Noelle." The heel of his hand tapped lightly against the shower wall as he came down from his high, but those words, the same words he'd said the night before, the words that suggested I turned him on almost against his will, really got to me. I whimpered once more and his eyes immediately opened, looking down on me with their hazel intensity. "Again?"

He only said the one word, but I got the message. He wanted to know if I could go again, and when I nodded truthfully, he immediately took charge. One hand returned to my clit, rubbing it firmly as his other hand played with my breast. Adding to that near overload of sensation, he kissed me, that hard, demanding kiss that took my breath away.

"You earned this," he murmured into my mouth, his hands working their magic as his words made my brain short-circuit again. "You deserve this reward."

My body seemed to agree as it surrendered to his onslaught of pleasure, and I came again, crying out his name into the steamy air. "Aaron!"

He pulled me close to him, my head against his chest as my body shivered through the aftershocks of my orgasm, his hands gently caressing my back. I could hear his heart pounding just as loudly as mine as reality settled back in between the water and the steam and the shower walls.

That really just happened. Aaron and I just made each other come, but what it meant, and where we went from here, I had no idea.

Aaron spoke first, pulling himself back from me gently. "Are you clean now?"

I had to laugh. He'd just made me dirtier than I'd been in a long time. "My hair's clean, at least."

"Here." He turned us around so I stood directly beneath the shower's stream, and while I rinsed my hair one more time, his hands rubbed the rest of my body clean, moving firmly over my arms and legs but more gently over my more sensitive areas, like my knee, my breasts, and between my legs. When he seemed satisfied with the state of me, he gave himself a quick wash too. I watched as his hand quickly scrubbed his now-soft dick, wondering how long it would take to get it hard again if I really tried.

I wouldn't get a chance to find out. The spell seemed to have broken, and though Aaron remained considerate as he stepped out of the shower first and handed me a clean towel to dry off, he seemed ready to move on.

That had all been part of the game, I had to remind myself. As incredible as it had been, it only happened because Corey's gingerbread spin landed on Eve. Aaron would have gone with Eve instead if the arrow pointed that way. He still wanted Eve, not me. He told me not to think of myself as a consolation prize, but how could I really think otherwise? All of this had only been a distraction, a way to pass the time while he continued laying the foundation towards his ultimate goal of getting together with Eve.

That shouldn't bother me. After all, I still had Corey.

Except I didn't. I'd never really *had* Corey, and the more I learned about him, the less certain I felt that we were meant to be together the way I'd always hoped. The things Aaron told me earlier about Corey going after Eve despite knowing how Aaron felt made me see him in a whole new light. We all had fun with the gingerbread house earlier, but even though Corey had been friendly enough, Aaron was more solicitous of me, always seeming to be aware of me and making sure I had a good time.

If I'd known everything I knew now back before any of this began, if I knew that Aaron's single-mindedness could be a good thing as well as a frustrating one and if I knew just how good he could make me feel, maybe I would have felt differently about him and about Corey too. Even those thick-framed glasses, which he stuck back on his face now, seemed less off-putting than they had before. They transformed him from Superman to Clark Kent, but the guy underneath remained the same.

If only I'd known that earlier.

But would it have made any difference anyway? The guy who let me lean on him to get dressed since it still hurt to stand on my knee wanted my best friend. That hadn't changed, no matter what else had, and the thought of him whispering things to her like he just had to me made my stomach twist even more than it had when I saw Eve and Corey coming out of that bedroom at the party.

Of all the things I'd ever been jealous of Eve for, this one might just surpass them all.

~Aaron~

I carried Noelle back downstairs. She tried to protest that she could manage on her own, which had nothing to do with it. She shouldn't have to *manage*. She should expect more from the world, expect more for herself, and in this case, more from me, since she wouldn't have hurt herself at all if she hadn't been following my instructions in the first place.

Although she gave in to having me carry her, as soon as we reached the bottom of the stairs, she insisted that I put her down, and since her firm tone suggested she truly meant it, I did as she asked. I had a pretty good idea why: she didn't want the others to see me carrying her. In particular, she would prefer that Corey not see it. If he did, he might think something more existed between us than a quick, dirty game in the shower.

She might not have said those words, but I understood the situation well enough.

For the time we were in the shower together, naked and focused on each other, we were completely compatible. *Completely.* Giving praise and pleasure was my own kink, it brought me more satisfaction than anything else I'd ever found, and Noelle was a natural sponge for it. She soaked it up until it filled her, until just a little pressure would give her a release of pleasure that would give me mine in return.

I loved how well she took my compliments, exactly the way they were intended. I loved how well she took my direction, and I loved how she got so turned on by pleasing me that she came a second time with only the minimum of help from me.

When she called out my name, it felt practically as good as a second orgasm for me too. Fuck, it felt amazing.

But as soon as our mutual high faded, as soon as that moment of connection passed, I forced myself to take a step back and remember our situation.

She only agreed to do this with me because of the game. She would have gone with Corey if he'd chosen her, and probably been happier about it too, though I suspected she wouldn't have had nearly the same reaction to him if they actually got physical. I had to guess, based on everything I knew about him, that Corey would be just as focused on his own pleasure during sex as in every other aspect of his life. Noelle might think she would be satisfied by simply being with him, but she wouldn't. Deep down, she needed something else.

All these years we'd argued and faced off against each other, and I'd had no idea what a perfect treasure hid behind the belligerent, defensive, overcompensating facade. She and Eve were different but that didn't have to be a bad thing. It could even be a very good one.

If only I'd known that sooner.

As I helped her back into her clothes, I waited for her to say something, anything, to indicate that what just happened between us had rocked her foundations as much as it had for me, but she remained silent and finally, I had to accept that my hopes were probably misplaced.

"I need to redo my makeup," she said as she looked at herself in the mirror, the first words to come out of her mouth since we got out of the shower. "And my hair."

Who did she want to impress? Not me, clearly. "Just brush your hair and do what you did this morning with your makeup. It looked perfect."

That adorable blush spread up her cheeks. "I had no time this morning. I can do better than that."

My eyebrows raised at her disagreement. "Are you insulting my taste?"

Her eyes went wide, exactly as I would have predicted. "What?"

"I said you looked perfect. If you put yourself down, you're suggesting I'm wrong."

"No, I... I just..." She stared at me through the mirror in confusion. "You really liked it?"

"Do I ever lie, Noelle?"

This time, she raised her eyebrows, always ready to argue a point of order. "What do you call fixing the game last night?"

"Cheating. It's different."

I held her gaze, refusing to back down, until her lips twitched and we both laughed. "Alright," she conceded. "Just give me a minute, then."

I left her in the bathroom, returning to her bedroom to wait, looking again at Noelle's clean, tidy side of the room versus Eve's haphazard one. The bed had been made, but I could picture Noelle in it, just as enticing as she'd looked the night before. If Eve spent the night with Corey again, would Noelle invite me back here? Now that we'd crossed the intimacy line in the shower, what might happen if we shared a bed again?

And why did that possibility seem far more appealing to me than any other possible scenario that might play out?

"I'm ready." It hadn't taken her long at all, and when I turned around, she had followed my instructions precisely. Her hair hung down over her shoulders, brushed but still damp, and she had just a hint of makeup on, not hiding any of her own natural features.

"Perfect," I confirmed, repeating my earlier word, and she flushed with pleasure even as she tried not to show it.

After I set her down at the foot of the stairs, we walked together to the living room, where we found not only Corey and Eve but some of the rest of the group too.

"We're just about to order pizza," James told me as Noelle went to sit next to Eve and I found a place with the guys. "Since you all destroyed the kitchen."

"Worth it," I told him unapologetically. It turned out to be a far better afternoon than I could have imagined.

Corey also sat over with the guys, away from Eve, but I couldn't guess if that had any significance. No further chances to speak to either Eve or Noelle appeared for the rest of that night. People came and went while we ate supper, watched Christmas movies on TV, and shot the breeze as a group. Some people went out for a walk to see all the lights in town, but since Noelle's knee needed a bit more recovery time, Eve stayed with her, and Corey and I remained behind too.

Eventually, Eve stood up and announced that she and Noelle were going to bed, and deep disappointment flooded my body. It sounded like nobody would be having any more fun that night.

After they left, Corey and I stayed up a while longer, but as soon as he excused himself, I followed after him, curious to know what had happened. He and Eve had hardly said two words to each other all evening.

"Is everything okay between you and Eve?" I asked the question as we both got ready for bed, and Corey scowled over at me.

"Why? So you can swoop in if there's trouble?"

"You're the one who did the swooping," I reminded him. "Don't act all offended with me. I asked because you seem upset and that's what a friend does. It shouldn't be any surprise you misunderstood, since you don't know how to be one yourself."

Corey exhaled, his big shoulders drooping in defeat. "Fuck. I'm making such a mess of everything."

"We can agree on that, at least." My sarcasm was only half-serious, and he knew it. "What happened?"

Corey sighed again as he collapsed down into the bed. "We got back here and I asked Eve if she really would have showered with you if I'd landed on Noelle instead. She said of course because we're all just here to have fun."

She really would have? That surprised me, but when I tried to feel some regret about the way it had turned out instead, the feeling refused to surface.

"I told her I wouldn't have liked that and she got upset, telling me I had no right to make decisions for her. I wasn't trying to force her to do anything, I just don't want the girl I like getting naked with another guy. That seems reasonable to me. Am I crazy?"

It would be reasonable if they had committed to each other in any way, but they hadn't and, apparently, Eve didn't want to.

I should be thrilled. Things were working out exactly as I hoped, but the best I could do was give Corey a shrug as I grabbed my pajama pants out of the dresser. "Maybe you need to back off and give her some space. And before you go accusing me of anything again, I'm not just saying that so I can get with her instead. I mean it."

"You're right," Corey agreed. "That's why we agreed to spend tonight apart. And tomorrow too. In fact, I thought I might ask Noelle if she wants to go out and do something tomorrow."

My head shot up in surprise. "What?" How did Noelle get involved in this?

"Eve wants to keep things casual, so we'll be casual. She can hang out with whoever she wants, even you, and I'll get to know her friend."

'Even' me. He managed to be insulting even when he didn't intend to be.

"And absence will make the heart grow fonder?" I guessed. "You think that after a day away, she'll see what she's missing?"

"It's possible," Corey replied defensively. "And if she's really not interested in more, then fine. I don't have to beg a girl to be with me. I'm not that hard up."

His reasoning jumped all over the place, but I thought I understood the base feeling behind it: afraid of being rejected, just like we all were deep down, he would push her away first. If she came back, he'd feel justified. If she didn't, he could claim the whole thing had been his idea.

My plan had taken on a life of its own, working out far better than I could have anticipated, but as I went to sleep haunted by the idea of Corey and Noelle spending the next day together, I couldn't help feeling I'd had the wrong plan all along.

~**Noelle**~

Eve asked if I needed help up the stairs, but honestly, my knee felt fine. If I accidentally touched it, it still hurt, but otherwise, I could forget all about it.

The orgasms earlier certainly helped take my mind off it.

"So, you didn't want to spend the night with Corey again?" I asked her once we were alone in our room and getting ready for bed.

Though I would never admit it to her, or to anyone, I'd been kind of hoping she would sleep downstairs again so that Aaron would need a place to stay. I'd seen what he could do in the shower, but what extra skills might he have in bed? I could only imagine, and the more I imagined it, the stronger the aching inside me grew.

It would only be while we waited for our plan to pan out, I reminded myself, but we could still have some fun in the meantime. I had been almost certain he would agree, but now, with Eve sleeping in our room, the question became moot.

Eve shook her head in response to my question about Corey. "No, we're going to take some time apart. He started getting all possessive and I don't need that."

We really did have different turn-ons, it seemed. She hadn't liked Aaron's compliment during the game, and now this. "I think it's kind of sexy when guys get like that," I admitted.

"In the right circumstance," Eve amended. "Not when we've only hooked up a couple of times and are on vacation. I just want to have some fun."

"Is there someone else on the trip you're thinking about having fun with, then?" My mouth felt dry as I asked the question, hoping she wouldn't say Aaron and trying not to think about how happy he'd be if she did.

"I really haven't put that much thought into it," she demurred. "Not every waking second has to be about men. Just making the gingerbread house with you today was by far the best part of the trip so far."

Guilt ran through me as Eve gave me a warm smile. I had really enjoyed it too, but I couldn't agree about it being the highlight of my trip. The shower that followed had definitely topped it.

She seemed to read something in my expression, or maybe she just realized she hadn't asked me about it yet, and she brought up the shower now. "You and Aaron didn't actually shower together, I assume?"

"Why do you assume that?" I hadn't decided yet how much I wanted to tell her about what happened, if anything, but I didn't understand why she had jumped to the conclusion that nothing happened at all.

"Well, Corey and I showered separately and we were still ready way before you guys. You took a really long time."

It hadn't seemed like very long to me. I would have happily stayed longer.

But what should I tell Eve? Aaron and I hadn't talked about it, but since he still hoped to get together with Eve, would it put her off if I said we'd fooled around a bit? Or would it make him seem like the kind of guy worth fooling around with? What did he want her to think, and what did I want her to think? I went back and forth in my head so many times that Eve gave me a concerned look.

"Noelle? Did something happen? You know you can tell me if he tried something, right?"

Oh, shit. Now, she thought he'd done something I didn't want. Aside from being very much *not* the case, I didn't want her thinking of Aaron as some kind of creep.

"We actually did shower together," I admitted, and her eyes widened in genuine surprise. "And some... touching took place. All completely, one hundred percent consensual. Actually, I really enjoyed it."

"Oh. Well, good for you." She looked a bit stunned, and also confused. "Why wouldn't you just tell me?"

Thankfully, I had a plausible excuse for that. "You already thought I had a crush on him and I thought you might read too much into this. It only happened because of the game. It didn't mean anything."

She laughed as she crawled into her side of the bed. "Alright, message received. You and Aaron, not a thing. We're all here to have fun. I got it."

Exactly. Not a thing. I had to remember that too. "Good night, Eve."

The next morning, I woke up to the smell of coffee, and looked over to find Eve in her pajamas, standing next to the window holding onto a mug as she looked outside.

"Did I sleep in again?" I had no excuse this time, I'd slept well the whole night with no late-night noises coming from the bathroom.

"No, I'm just up early," she admitted apologetically. "But I brought you some coffee too. And look, it's snowing!"

I scrambled out of bed to join her at the window, the two of us looking out eagerly at the lightly falling snow just like we used to when we were little girls.

"Do you have more secret plans today?" I asked as I picked up the cup of coffee she'd left for me on the bedside table.

"Of course," she teased me. "Just don't go falling over again, okay?"

I wouldn't do it on purpose again. "What are we doing?"

"You'll see." Her eyes sparkled with excitement. "Dress warm, though. No jeans."

We both got dressed in our fleece-lined leggings and sweaters, and I did my hair and makeup the same as I had the day before, the way Aaron said he liked it, before we headed downstairs for breakfast. The housekeeper exited the kitchen just as we got there, and both Eve and I avoided her eye as we thanked her before she left, both of us dissolving into giggles as soon as she'd gone. "I hope Corey really did provide a tip," I groaned. "We made such a mess."

My dad would kill me if he knew I let someone else clean up after me like that. My parents hadn't raised me that way at all.

"If he forgets, I'll do it," Eve assured me. "Now, what should we make for breakfast?"

By the time the rest of the group joined us, we had bacon, eggs, pancakes and fruit prepared, a full breakfast buffet that quickly disappeared into the mouths of twenty hungry college students. Aaron and Corey sat together at the other end of the table from me and Eve, as if Corey wanted to demonstrate that he and Eve were taking some time off from each other.

At the end of the meal, Eve announced her plan for the day: we were all going horseback riding. A bus would soon be arriving to pick us up, and there would be a two-hour ride with views over the Cascade Mountains, followed by lunch and some games at the lodge. Everyone split up to finish getting ready while a few stayed behind to clean up breakfast.

"I didn't really expect this kind of wholesome entertainment on this trip. I thought we were going to be drunk the whole time and naked for half of it." Corey's deep voice surprised me as he reached past me to pick up some empty plates from the table. I quickly glanced around to see who he might be talking to, but I couldn't see anyone else, leaving me to assume it must be me, as unlikely as that seemed.

"I'm sure we've got enough time to be both wholesome and drunk," I replied with a shrug. "Besides, you wanted to ride the reindeer yesterday, so this is pretty close."

He gave a surprised laugh. "You remember that, huh? Do you remember what else I said?"

Of course I did. He mentioned how he preferred to be ridden, but he said it to Eve, not to me. I didn't want him thinking I'd been paying that much attention. "No," I lied, even though I could feel my cheeks growing warmer.

Corey laughed again, deeper this time. "I think you do. I think you might be a bit of a dark horse yourself, Noelle."

Was he... flirting with me? It certainly felt like it, but I couldn't understand why. It felt completely out of the blue.

And to my surprise, his choice of words, implying I had a naughty side, affected me far less than when Aaron accused me of being a good girl. Maybe because deep down, I knew I wouldn't fit anyone's definition of bad, especially compared to the girls Corey would have been with. I'd rather be praised for being good.

"Well, for now, you're only riding the actual horses," I blurted out, almost in a panic, and Corey's eyes gleamed with amusement.

"For now," he agreed, smirking as he walked away.

What the hell was that?

"Come on, Noelle, let's go!" Eve called from the front door, and I quickly swallowed down all my confusion as we set off to get our next adventure started.

Chapter Ten

TWISTED

~Aaron~

Corey wasted no time. As soon as we arrived, he offered to help Noelle up onto her horse, because of her knee, he said, and when we were told to buddy up for the trail ride, they were already side-by-side. He effectively froze Eve out, making me wonder if he wanted to make Eve jealous or simply wanted to leave her without a partner of her own? Maybe he thought he could kill two birds with one stone. Did that explain why he'd chosen Noelle out of all the girls there?

Noelle, meanwhile, shot me a look that I couldn't interpret as she and Corey set off together. Excitement? Gratitude? Fear? Indigestion? I honestly didn't know.

"Have you got a partner, Aaron?" I'd been so distracted by Noelle that I hadn't noticed Eve behind me.

"No, not yet." I tried to swallow down the uncomfortable feeling in my chest at the sight of Noelle and Corey together. "But I understand if you want to choose someone else. I've never been on a horse in my life. I'm going to be focused on just staying on."

Maybe the rich kids on this trip grew up with horses of their own and huge open spaces to go riding, but my childhood hadn't been anything like that.

"I'll take care of you," Eve promised. "It's really not that hard. The horse does most of the work, especially seasoned ones like these."

She gave me a few tips once we were in the saddle, and when we got underway, I had to admit, she hadn't lied. The horse knew where to go, I simply had to hold on, which gave us plenty of time to talk. With two hours ahead of us, it would be the perfect time to get to know her better.

"Did you ride a lot growing up?" I had to assume she had, she looked so comfortable and natural on the horse.

"My aunt has a farm upstate," she explained. "We'd go up to visit a few times a year, so she made sure we knew how to ride. In the winter, we'd go on sleigh rides. Christmases there are the best."

"That sounds pretty idyllic," I couldn't help pointing out, and Eve laughed.

"Pretty much. I wouldn't want to live there all the time, I would miss the city too much, but my aunt loves it. Things were different when she grew up. No one expected her to go into the family business with my dad, so she could do what she wanted."

The wistful tone that crept into her voice reminded me of the things she'd said the other night when we talked about her family's company. "And you can't do what you want?"

The question seemed to startle her, and she quickly changed the subject, getting back to the topic of the farm instead. "Noelle and I spent a whole month at the farm when we were teenagers. My brother had gone to college and Noelle's sister went to a volleyball camp, and I think our parents just wanted to get rid of us but somehow made us think we came up with the idea."

She looked ahead to where Corey and Noelle were chatting to each other, and my chest tightened again as I followed her gaze. I wanted to know what they were talking about, but since I couldn't, I asked Eve a follow-up question instead. "What did two teenage girls get up to on the farm all summer?"

Eve happily launched into stories of their exploits, and over the next two hours, along with enjoying the views, we ended up talking far more about Noelle than anything else. Every story seemed to lead back to her, and I honestly couldn't say if I kept bringing her up or if Eve did. Either way, by the time we returned to the lodge, I felt I knew Noelle better than ever, but Eve still remained a bit of a mystery. Every time we got close to talking about her future plans or her family, she clammed right up and diverted the conversation down a different path instead.

When I thanked her for her help and praised her riding ability and the way she looked on the horse, she shrugged it off, the words not affecting her at all. Noelle would have responded differently, I couldn't help thinking.

We all had lunch together in the lodge after the ride. Corey seemed to be in a better mood and he and Eve seemed more at ease with each other than they had the day before or even first thing that morning. Perhaps the time away from each other had been helpful after all.

The lodge had a number of board games for us to use after we'd eaten, and Corey's eyes lit up when they landed on the Twister box.

"No way." Eve laughed as he held the box up to her, me and Noelle. "Noelle's hurt, remember?"

"I'm not," Noelle protested, clearly not wanting to disappoint Corey. "As long as no one lands on my knee, I'll be fine."

"I say we go into the room next door and make it a little more interesting," Corey suggested with a grin. "A strip version, maybe?"

A few smaller rooms sat off the main dining area, perfect for breakout gatherings. Another group had already taken one of the Clue boxes into one of them and shut the door behind them.

It seemed harmless enough to me; nothing too crazy would happen while we were still essentially out in public. It would just be a bit of fun. And if Noelle got thinking about me without my clothes on, it couldn't hurt.

I meant Eve. If *Eve* got thinking about me. I shook my head at my internal slip of the tongue.

MELODY TYDEN

With the rest of us on board, Eve gave up her protest and the four of us went into the empty room next door. The room contained two sofas and a coffee table, all of which Corey and I pushed back to give us more space. As I laid out the mat on the floor, Corey set out the ground rules.

"Because there's four of us, we'll each take turns spinning and only that person has to move. Anyone who spins a yellow has to remove a piece of clothing. If anyone spins red, we *all* remove a piece of clothing. And if you fall, that's obviously another piece."

Noelle looked down at herself, mentally calculating how many pieces of clothing she had on. "That's not going to take very long."

"Only if you're clumsy," Eve teased her.

When we'd all agreed, Corey went first, landing on green. Eve got blue, and so did I, and Noelle got yellow.

"Of course," she muttered under her breath, but she gamely removed one of her socks and took her place.

Corey spun red, meaning we all had to remove something. Eve and I also went for a sock while Noelle removed her other one, but Corey took off his shirt instead, keen to be the centre of attention as usual. It seemed to work as Eve cast an appraising glance over him and Noelle did her best *not* to look, which only made it more obvious that she wanted to.

Eve landed on blue again while I got yellow. Following Corey's lead, I took my own sweater off, replacing my glasses afterwards so I could still see the rest of the players. Eve's eyebrows raised as she looked me over and she gave Noelle a pointed look, which Noelle did her best to ignore. What did *that* mean?

Noelle got green, to her relief. With all of us fully on the board, Corey spun red again.

"You're doing that on purpose," Noelle accused, which only made him smile. Corey went for a sock this time while Eve and I removed our other ones. After a moment of indecision, Noelle tugged down her leggings.

146

Her knee still looked bruised, but my attention didn't linger on it for long, not when I got a glimpse of the pretty pink panties she wore. Unfortunately, her sweater hung low enough that we *only* got a glimpse.

Eve spun green, and I hit red. Noelle had been right; this really wouldn't take very long at all to get us out of most of our clothes. While Corey removed his second sock, I took off my belt. With a sigh, Noelle pulled her sweater over her head.

I hadn't really taken a chance to look at her in her underwear the day before. She'd admonished me for letting the water go cold, so I'd removed everything as quickly as possible, but now, I could enjoy the view. Although I'd seen what lay underneath, she still looked incredibly sexy in the pink satin bra that matched her panties and the colour on her cheeks.

Eve, meanwhile, removed one of her earrings, leaving Noelle gaping at her in disbelief. "Wait, our earrings count?"

Eve shrugged. "If Aaron's belt does, then I don't see why not."

Noelle looked so put out as she glanced down at her own exposed body that I had to laugh. "Look at the bright side. You've got your next two turns sorted and you look fantastic."

"You do," Corey quickly added, sounding a little *too* surprised.

We made it through a round of everyone hitting blue or green, and as we began to bend and twist over each other to find a spot for our hands, some skin-to-skin contact soon proved inevitable. Corey stuck his hand on the spot right between Noelle's legs. Eve remained pretty much fully clothed, but her hand brushed my arm as she reached past me. When my turn came again, I turned my back to Eve, only because it made sense as the easiest move to make.

Noelle was the next to hit red, and she triumphantly removed an earring while Eve took her other one off, and Corey and I, with little other choice, both removed our pants.

"Where's my camera?" Eve teased us all from her comfortable, clothed position as the rest of us stood there in our underwear.

147

Things got more tense as the amount of skin on display grew. Noelle got yellow again so she removed her second earring, and then Corey spun yellow too. He had nothing left but his underwear, so I looked over curiously to see what he had planned.

"I have no problem getting naked," he told us all, and from experience, I could confirm the truthfulness of that statement. "But we could do this another way if you like."

"What way?" Noelle asked.

"Well, rather than taking my underwear off, I could let someone touch me. A quick grope, and obviously the same goes for you all once you get to this point." He gave Noelle a wink, his gaze drifting down to her chest, which looked even more appealing now that she'd bent over.

"Do we get to choose who does the groping?" Eve asked. "Because I nominate Aaron."

"Only if I get to choose the kind of contact," I amended. "A kick should do it."

We all laughed, but it didn't fully disperse the growing tension at the idea of getting our hands on each other. "I guess it's that or game over," Noelle spoke up, and none of us were ready to quit just yet.

"I'll spin again to choose who gets to cop a feel," Corey suggested. "Blue or green is Eve, yellow or red is Noelle."

Both girls gave their agreement and I held my breath as he made the spin.

~Noelle~

It amazed me how much things could change in such a short amount of time.

I'd dreamed of being in an intimate situation with Corey for years. *Years*. And now, only three days into our vacation, the opportunity to touch him, to actually lay my hand on his dick, even if only over his underwear, dangled in front of me - no pun intended - and I couldn't muster any real enthusiasm for the prospect.

It had to be the situation, I told myself. If we were on our own, that would be one thing, but with Eve right there, and Aaron too, it simply felt awkward. So, when Corey spun the spinner to see which of us would get the privilege of touching him, I actually hoped it would land on Eve.

As always, the fates were against me.

The spinner came to a rest clearly on the red, one of my assigned colours, and Corey looked over at me with a smirk. "Guess it's your lucky day."

I tried to smile back while avoiding eye contact with either Eve or Aaron. Neither of them made any protest, so it seemed like they expected me to go ahead.

"Do I have to stay where I am?" I asked. We were already rather twisted up with one of Corey's hands between my legs and me bent over his arm.

"That's the game," he reminded me. "And if you fall, then you have to spin."

Right. Then either he or Aaron would get to touch *me*.

Doing my best to keep my balance, I raised one of my hands and reached out. I could barely see what I was doing, but hopefully that meant nobody else could see very much either. My palm hit his firm stomach and I slid it lower until I hit the top of his underwear. From there, I easily found his semi-erect dick, and I ran my hand across it as confidently as possible, not lingering too long. It all felt rather impersonal and not at all as sexy as I had always imagined this moment would be.

Corey chuckled as I took my hand away. "You enjoyed that, am I right?"

I honestly didn't know how to answer that. "Whose turn is it next?" I asked instead, my voice squeaking as the words came out, which made everyone laugh.

Eve spun next, landing on green, of course, and Aaron spun yellow. Since he had also already stripped down to his underwear, that meant someone would touch him too, and once again, the spinner landed on me. This would have to be the time I suddenly became popular.

He stood further away from me than Corey, so I had to reach further, making my balance even more precarious as I stretched.

Aaron leaned closer to me, whispering into my ear. "You didn't have any trouble finding it yesterday."

The shiver that ran down my spine at the reminder nearly made me fall over. "I'm not having trouble. I just need to..."

With the last stretch, I lost my balance and fell directly onto Aaron. Eve cackled with laughter as the two of us ended up tangled together on the ground.

"Sorry," I quickly apologized, trying to get off him, but Aaron pulled me closer.

"At least you found what you were looking for," he teased me, which drew my attention to the fact that my hand did indeed cup his groin right now. "And since you fell, I guess I get to touch you back?"

His hand slid up the back of my thigh onto my ass, his fingers flirting with the edge of my panties as he gave the cheek a gentle squeeze. My fingers tightened too, almost subconsciously in response, and he whispered in my ear again.

"Fuck, that feels too good."

I knew exactly what he meant.

"Alright, let's keep it PG," Eve teased us both, making me jump. I'd almost forgotten we weren't alone. "I think we should probably wrap up anyway, the bus will be ready to take us back to the house soon."

Quickly, I scrambled to my feet and redressed, my mind whirling as I compared the difference between Corey and Aaron in the game. Not the physical differences; a more thorough inspection would be needed before I felt confident in making a comparison there, but what I found curious was the way they responded to me touching them. Corey told me that I must have enjoyed it, while Aaron told me how good it felt. One assumed I got more out of it than he did, while the other praised the effect I had on him.

My body's reaction made it pretty clear which response I preferred.

Corey had been kind of the same way on the whole trail ride too. Everything we talked about seemed to come back to him and his perfect life. I honestly didn't know who he was trying to impress, or maybe he simply wanted to make himself feel better after Eve's rebuff the day before. But where I once thought I'd be perfectly happy just to bask in his presence, I found myself glancing back at Eve and Aaron more than once. They seemed to be having a more interesting conversation, their attention entirely focused on each other. I never saw either of them looking at me.

On the way back into town, we found out that the game of Clue in the next room to us had also turned into a stripping game, though how Strip Clue worked, I couldn't guess. Everyone seemed primed for more risqué pursuits after the chilled-out pizza and movie night the previous evening, and as soon as we got back to the house, the alcohol came back out, as did the Seven Minutes in Heaven concept.

"I say we make some amendments though," James suggested. "First, seven minutes is too short. It should be twenty, minimum. And so that none of us are wasting time, we each submit a list of people we want to end up with."

"How does that work?" Sabrina wondered, but Corey had an answer.

"Aaron can do it."

All heads in the room turned to him and his eyes met mine for just a second before he pushed his glasses up his nose. "Sure. It's just setting some different parameters on the program I used on my phone the other day. We give the program a list of all possibilities, and it'll spit out random pairings. It means you'd all have to share your lists with me though."

Nobody seemed to have a problem with that, except for me. What was I supposed to say? Would he only want me to choose Corey, and he would only choose Eve? Or would we give it the option of choosing each other? Or anyone? I had no idea.

But when my turn came to go talk to him to input my selections, he just gave me a knowing smile. "I've got yours already, Noelle."

He did? What did that mean? What names did he put down?

He moved on to the next person before I could find out, so when he began to read through the list, my stomach fluttered with uncertainty.

"Eve goes with... me."

His brow furrowed as he read the words, and the disappointment sank in my stomach like a lead weight. If I'd needed any further confirmation that he still wanted Eve rather than me, I had it now. He must have manipulated the program just like he did the other night, and he chose Eve.

"Noelle and Corey."

The words should have made me happy. I *should* have been thrilled, but as the disappointment hit, I couldn't really lie to myself any longer.

I would rather be with Aaron.

Unfortunately, it made no difference, not when he still wanted Eve instead, as he clearly did. And maybe I was being too hard on Corey anyway. I'd had such huge expectations of how amazing it would be with him, maybe nothing could live up to that. I owed it to him, and myself, to give him a proper chance, so when Aaron said our names, I smiled over at Corey, and he winked back at me.

When all the couples had been assigned, Corey came to take my hand. "Let's do this properly this time," he suggested, pulling me towards the basement door. I couldn't help glancing back one last time before we headed downstairs, to see Aaron watching us with a completely unreadable expression on his face.

~**Aaron**~

What the fuck just happened?

As soon as Corey suggested I run the draw, I knew immediately how I could work it to my advantage. All I had to do, while entering everyone's lists of suitable partners, would be to put that Noelle only wanted me and I only wanted her. The program would match us, and the rest of the group would take care of itself. What happened to them made no difference to me, but after seeing and touching Noelle during the game of Twister earlier, I desperately wanted an excuse to be alone with her again. If she complained, I could blame it on luck, but I had a feeling she wouldn't complain.

I had been so confident of my plan, that when I got to Eve and my name popped up, my mind went completely blank. It took me by surprise so much that rather than simply lying, as I should have, I read it out loud instead, and once the word had come out, I couldn't take it back. I glanced over at Noelle to try to gauge her reaction, but she looked down, her face hidden from me, giving me no idea what she might be thinking.

My confusion grew even stronger when I got to Noelle's name and found her paired with Corey. How did that happen?

They were the last names on the list, so as soon as I read them out, everyone began breaking off into their pairs, secure in the knowledge that the people they had chosen had also chosen them.

For me, that was no great compliment. Eve had literally told me she would take anyone, and Corey told me the same. So how did this happen? It didn't make any sense.

My throat tightened as I watched Noelle head down the stairs with Corey. He'd been hitting on her all day, with absolutely zero subtlety, and I had no doubt he would get physical with her when they were alone. Fuck, after seeing her in her underwear, even a man who'd sworn off sex would be tempted, and Corey could hardly be called a saint.

She turned back to look at me just before they went downstairs, but I couldn't tell what the look on her face meant. Her excitement seemed muted, but maybe her nerves were getting the better of her. She did have a habit of getting adorably flustered when things got out of her control. I would know just how to calm her down, just how to take control and make her feel good.

Except this time, I wouldn't be there to do it. *Fuck.*

"Are we staying here?" Eve's question alerted me to the fact that the room had emptied. A quick glance around confirmed we were the only two people left. "You know, I'm starting to think you might be rigging these games. You got me in Spin the Bottle, and now both times we've done Seven Minutes."

Her light tone suggested she meant it as a joke, not actually accusing me of anything, but she had come closer to the truth than I liked. Except I *didn't* rig this draw this way and I still had no idea how it could have happened.

"I guess I'm just extra lucky these days." I gave her as confident a smile as I could muster, but my thoughts were still with Noelle. "I just need to check something really quick."

Tapping on my phone screen, I exited the results list and returned to the input. Under my name, where it should have said Noelle, Eve's name had taken its place, and under Noelle's entry, it only said Corey when it should have been me.

What the actual fuck?

"Noelle chose Corey?" I'd been so taken aback by what I saw that I hadn't noticed Eve leaning over to see my screen. "*Only* Corey?"

The confusion painted across her face mirrored my own. "I'm not sure what happened," I admitted. "I must have mistyped. She told me something else."

I didn't elaborate any further than that, mostly because I had no idea what to say. The explanation might fool her, but I knew I hadn't mistyped anything. I'd been very clear about what I wanted and what I entered.

Suddenly, it hit me. *Corey* suggested we use this program. Corey, who had seen me use the app multiple times, and who I'd shared my login with so he could use it with his teammates when they were arguing over who had to sit where on the team bus or whatever other nonsense they couldn't decide like adults.

Did he log in and change the entries for me and Noelle while I entered the choices for the others? I had to admit it could be possible. I hadn't been watching him since I had been busy with my own task instead. But why would he do that? Not satisfied with taking Eve from me, now he wanted Noelle too?

I couldn't answer those questions right now and neither could Eve, so I shoved my phone back in my pocket and pushed down all my conflicting feelings. Though a part of me wanted to storm downstairs and break the door down to 'save' Noelle, I had to admit she hadn't asked to be saved. She'd signed up for the game along with everyone else, trusting me to enter her choices for her when I'd previously schemed to set her up with Corey, and she'd gone downstairs with Corey willingly. She'd given me no indication that she had wanted anything else.

She'd stood up to me enough times in the classroom, during the campaign for student body president, and in our debating club that I knew she could stand her ground when she wanted to. If she changed her mind about being with Corey, I had to trust that she would tell him so. If I stuck my nose in now, she might resent it.

My best option was simply to proceed as if nothing had gone wrong.

"I guess we're heading to your room," I said to Eve, offering her my arm. "Shall we?"

She smiled at the old-fashioned gesture, but she took my arm anyway, and we walked side-by-side, hip-by-hip, up the stairs.

"You impressed me when you took your shirt off during Twister today," Eve told me once we reached her room. As confident as ever, she came right up to me and placed her palm on top of my shirt, against my chest. "You should show it off more."

"You've got a good eye." Noelle would have flushed at the compliment, but Eve simply laughed, so I took a more teasing tone instead. "Did you miss when I took my pants off, though? That's the star of the show."

She laughed again, taking a step back. "Well, you don't need me to tell you how good you look, apparently."

"I could tell you how good you look instead." There was no point denying it; everything about her looked as stunning as ever. Only a blind man wouldn't appreciate that.

"You're a charmer." She gave me a curious smile. "Do you ever take those glasses off?"

"I can, but then you'll look worse, at least to me. It'll be all blurry."

"Good." With a nod of determination, Eve stepped towards me again and gently pulled my glasses off herself. I offered no resistance. "Now, I could be anybody, huh?"

"Pretty much." Her edges had all gone soft, all her features blurred. If I squinted enough, I could even pretend to see Noelle. As soon as that thought crossed my mind, the realization hit me with complete clarity, making me wonder how I'd missed it before.

I wanted Noelle.

Here I was, alone in a room with the girl of my dreams, the girl I'd been fantasizing about for far too long, and I couldn't get her best friend off my mind. The burning desire I'd felt for Eve had faded. Somewhere during the last three days, the slightly awkward, unsure girl who kept surprising me had snuck in and taken over the spot in my heart I'd reserved for Eve.

But even after the amazing shower we had together, and all the little moments ever since the plane, she still wanted Corey instead. She went with him without a peep of protest, knowing as well as we all did what would happen if she did. They might have even been fucking at that very moment, for all I knew.

The thought made me groan out loud, and though I couldn't see Eve's face very well anymore, I could hear the concern in her voice. "Are you alright?"

Rather than trying to explain myself, I simply kissed her instead.

Chapter Eleven

REALIZATION

~**Noelle**~

Corey hadn't held my hand the other night when we went down to his room for our Seven Minutes in Heaven, but things had changed since then. We'd gotten to know each other a bit better, and he seemed a lot less concerned about me being Eve's friend now that their relationship had turned rocky.

He held the door to his room open for me this time, letting go of my hand so I could go in first, and when he followed me inside, he locked the door behind him. He hadn't done that last time either.

Shit, this might actually be happening. Ever since I first laid eyes on Corey Davison, I'd wanted to be alone in a locked bedroom with him, and now that I had finally got there, I could only think about his best friend.

What was wrong with me? Did I only want guys I couldn't have? I'd pined after Corey for so long, but now that I had him looking straight at me with lust in his eyes, I'd developed cold feet. Now, I wanted Aaron, who had made it clear his interest lay elsewhere. Maybe I *wanted* to sabotage myself?

"We keep ending up together." Corey's blue eyes glinted as he stepped closer to me. "Must be destiny."

Sure, if destiny had a helping hand known as Aaron Speelman. "Do you believe in fate?"

I always found people's ideas on the subject interesting. My dad firmly did, trusting that everything in our lives happened for a reason. Even the painful things taught us important lessons, which meant that mistakes were just a learning opportunity. He liked to point out that my mom and Eve's mom could have chosen any hotel in London to hold their Christmas party on the night that Eve's parents met, and if they hadn't met, my mom and dad wouldn't have met either. He thought nothing else could explain it other than fate.

"Fate and a discount on the room rental for the party," my mom would always add, giving me and my sister a wink. She always took a more practical approach, but even she would agree that sometimes, luck and coincidence played a part.

Corey smirked at the question, coming down closer to my mom's point of view. "I believe we make our own luck."

He stepped towards me again and I took a step back, my mind racing. Did that apply to how he went after Eve, despite knowing how Aaron felt? Maybe Aaron's accusation explained why my feelings towards Corey seemed to have cooled. Maybe if I got Corey's side of it, I'd feel differently. Since I could hardly ask for a better set-up than the one he just gave me, I put on my debating hat and went for it.

"The way you made your own luck when you approached Eve at that party?"

Corey stopped moving, his eyebrows drawing together warily. "What do you mean?"

"You know what I mean." My voice sounded surprisingly strong considering the nerves playing havoc with my stomach. "You came up to me in the kitchen and asked where to find her, and you went to hit on her, all while knowing that Aaron liked her. You made it happen."

His eyes widened in genuine surprise. "He told you that?"

I hadn't fully thought this through. If Corey ever found out *why* I knew Aaron liked Eve, because I told Aaron how much I liked Corey, our whole cover would be blown, but I still wanted to know why he'd done it. "We'd been drinking at the time. Alcohol's got a funny way of turning off your filter."

Corey snorted in agreement. "That's the truth." He took a step back from me, and another, sitting down on the edge of the bed before looking up at me almost nervously. "Can I ask you something?"

The complete change in him caught me off guard. A few seconds ago, he looked like a man who always got his way and intended on having it; now, he resembled a little boy who'd been caught with his hand in the cookie jar. Or as much as a six-foot-three solid man could look like a boy, anyway.

I sat down too, keeping a bit of distance between us. "Sure. What is it?"

"Do you think people take me seriously?"

The earnest look in his eyes almost made me wince as I remembered Eve's words after their first night together: *I still don't think he's anyone I could be serious with. The guy's all style and no substance.*

I turned the question back on him instead of answering. "Why do you think they don't?"

He tapped against his temple lightly with his knuckles. "People joke about me taking one too many blows to the head on the ice. Everyone expects me to be the life of the party, the player, but never the guy you go to when you need help figuring something out. That's always Aaron."

Really? Corey compared himself to Aaron like I did with Eve? I never, ever would have guessed.

"Aaron takes you seriously," I pointed out. "He's a smart guy, and he obviously thinks you're worth being friends with."

Corey grimaced. "I know. Which makes what I did even worse."

"What you did?" I had lost him somewhere.

"With Eve," he explained. "I told him I went after Eve so he wouldn't get hurt when she shot him down, but that's not exactly true. I did it out of jealousy. Because Aaron *is* smart, and he's confident and he's going to be a success and have this great life, and when he told me about how she would be the perfect girl for the life he imagined, I just... I don't know. I guess I wanted that life for myself, so I took the one part of it I thought I could get."

I exhaled slowly, taking that all in. "Shit, Corey. That's really low."

"I know." He groaned as he put his head down in his hands. "I swear, I'm not usually that guy. It's just all the pressure of school ending, and the pro scouts aren't as interested in me as I hoped they'd be, and when I look at my future, I see a washed-up former athlete who peaked in college. Eve's got it all together. With her, I could still be somebody."

So, he'd not only set out to steal Eve from his best friend, he only wanted to use her too? "She's just a meal ticket to you?"

He looked up at me in panic, his eyes wide. "No! I mean, she might have been, at first, but when I started to get to know her, I found I really liked her. Too much, apparently. More than she likes me, and now everything's a mess. Aaron's pissed off at me, Eve thinks I'm coming on too strong, and I can't even score with a girl like you. I'm losing whatever touch I used to have."

"A girl like me?" I repeated. What the fuck was that supposed to mean?

His eyes closed in regret as he realized what he'd just said. "Fuck, maybe I really am an idiot. I didn't mean to say it like that, Noelle. You're really nice, and pretty, and all the rest, but I know you've got a thing for me. One thing I usually am smart about is when girls are interested. I could have taken you up to the bedroom at that party too, couldn't I? I saw it in your eyes when we talked in the kitchen."

He knew I liked him? For how long?

I had no idea what to say, but he didn't make me answer. He carried on with his explanation. "I've got a fan club. I'm not trying to brag but it's true: the puck bunnies, the girls who just want a piece of me because of who I am. I figured you were another one of them. After all, you barely even know me."

"And you were planning to sleep with me just now to make yourself feel better since Eve doesn't want you?" The longer this conversation went on, the less attracted to him I became.

"Well, when you say it like that, it sounds creepy." He smiled when I raised my eyebrows in disapproval. "And I thought you wanted it too. You've been hanging around me ever since we got here. Isn't this what you were hoping for?"

He had me there; this *was* exactly what I'd been hoping for. Except now that I had it, I didn't want it anymore.

And I had to admit that, although I certainly didn't agree with the way he'd gone about things, Aaron and I had done some questionable things too. None of us were saints here, except perhaps for Eve. As far as I knew, she hadn't manipulated anyone.

"So, that's why you chose me for the game?" He must have had me on his list, the same as Aaron had put Corey on mine.

"Actually, I chose you so that Aaron could go with Eve."

Just when I thought I couldn't get any more lost, he managed to confuse me once more. "What?"

"Eve wants a break from me and Aaron always wanted a shot with her. I put them together so they could see if there's something there. Maybe he'll stop being so angry with me now once he figures it out."

"*You* put them together?" What did that mean? I thought Aaron had rigged the game.

Corey, however, disagreed. "Yeah. I went into his app and fixed it so he ended up with Eve. If we had a good time too, that would just be a bonus."

A 'bonus'. A consolation prize. I would never be anything more than that to him; I saw it completely clearly now.

"Well, we're not having sex, Corey."

He chuckled. "Yeah, I kind of gathered that, but thanks for listening. I needed to get a lot of that stuff off my chest, apparently." That much, I understood. Sometimes, it really did help to have someone to talk to, and it helped things make sense too. A moment later, his expression turned wary as he considered one more thing: "Are you going to tell Eve?"

She deserved to know about it, but it probably shouldn't come from me. "If you're serious about having any kind of relationship with her, you should get it all out into the open. A relationship needs to start with trust."

My dad always told me that, too.

Corey exhaled deeply. "You're right. I guess I'll have to wait and see what happened with her and Aaron. If they hooked up, it might not matter anyway."

My stomach twisted as I realized that this whole time Corey and I had been talking, Eve and Aaron had been alone together. The odds didn't seem very likely that they'd have only talked like we had, and as I imagined him holding her and whispering those hot, sweet words of praise in her ear like he did to me, I almost felt like I might be sick.

"I guess we'll have to wait and see," I managed to choke out, and held my hand out to Corey. He might have made some terrible choices, but I thought there might still be a decent guy in there somewhere. He just needed to have a bit more confidence in himself and take other people's feelings into consideration more. A little like me, maybe. "Friends?"

He gave me a genuine smile as he took my hand and shook it. "I'd really like that, Noelle. Thanks."

That handshake officially marked the end of my three-year-long crush. Now, I had to figure out what the hell I should do next.

~Aaron~

Eve didn't resist my kiss at all. If anything, she met it more eagerly than I anticipated, her arms wrapping around my neck as she pulled me closer.

Fuck, this could actually happen. I was alone in a bedroom with Eve Stamer, kissing her while she kissed me back. This had happened in my head so many times, it seemed almost impossible that it had now become reality, especially after all the craziness of the last week.

She really must not have been serious about Corey after all, just like Noelle said.

As soon as Noelle appeared in my head, I pushed her back out, trying to focus on the kiss instead. I told Eve the other day that she kissed well, and I meant it. I never gave false praise; that would diminish its worth. She obviously had a lot of experience, and she liked to take the lead, I quickly realized.

Her tongue pressed against my lips, and as soon as I opened them, before I could do anything, she slid her tongue inside my mouth, teasing but determined. My body responded, as anybody's would to such a blatant come-on from a beautiful woman, and when I tried to shift my hips away from her so my reaction wouldn't be immediately obvious, she refused to let me, tilting her hips against me instead.

"You're very good at taking control," I praised her truthfully. "You know what you want, and that's very sexy."

Eve raised her eyebrows at me, a smirk on her lips. "What I want right now is less talking."

With her hands on my arms, she turned me around and pushed me down onto the edge of the bed, so forcefully that I bounced up and down with the impact. With a confident smile, Eve pulled her sweater up over her head. Though I couldn't see her all that clearly without my glasses, I could definitely make out the shape of the pretty, black bra, covering a pair of breasts that were everything I'd always imagined they'd be.

The image of Noelle in her sweet pink bra flashed back into my head, but once again, I pushed it away. Corey probably had her out of that bra by now, I reminded myself. We were both getting exactly what we wanted. I needed to focus on that.

"Take your shirt off too," she commanded, and I obeyed, getting undressed in front of her for the second time that day. Once my shirt had gone, she climbed up onto my lap, straddling me on the edge of the bed as her lips pressed against mine again.

My hands ran along her smooth back as her hands traced the muscles of mine. Her classy, understated perfume made an interesting contrast to the way her hips were grinding into mine, working my dick into a frenzy. Not messing around, every action of hers seemed calculated for maximum arousal. She knew exactly what she was doing.

Although I had wanted this for almost as long as I could remember, I'd never imagined it being this way. I always pictured being the one to seduce her, my words winning her over and driving her crazy before my body finished the job.

Just like it had gone with Noelle in the shower, to be honest. As beautiful as I found Noelle, the way she responded to my words had been the biggest turn-on of all.

I tried to elicit that same kind of response from Eve now. "Your skin is so soft," I murmured against her lips as my fingertips trailed over her back, brushing against the strap of her bra. "It feels incredible against mine."

Eve pushed against my chest, pushing me down onto my back. "What did I say about the talking?"

She hovered over me, her red hair framing her beautiful face, her breasts swelling over the top of her black bra, and a determined look in her eyes. To some people, it would have been irresistible.

To some people, it would have been their fantasy come true.

Unfortunately, I wasn't one of those people.

"Wait." When she leaned down to kiss me again, I placed my hands on her arms gently to hold her back. "What's the rush?"

Her eyebrows raised in impatience. "We've only got twenty minutes, remember? No time to waste."

"You think I'd have trouble making you come in twenty minutes?" I matched her blunt tone precisely, which made her smile.

"That's more like it." She leaned closer again. "Stop telling me how perfect I am. Tell me what you'd do to me instead."

My stomach sank as her words seeped into my brain. This was worse than I thought. Not only did Eve not respond to my praise, she actually wanted the opposite. There was absolutely nothing wrong with that; I made no judgements about what got other people off, but the problem lay in the fact that our turn-ons were completely incompatible. While a little dirty talk could do wonders, I wanted to build her up, not dominate her.

Maybe a couple of days ago, I would have tried anyway, but after being with Noelle and knowing just how good it could be when I did what came naturally, when someone matched me so completely in their own inclination, I didn't want to pretend. In just a few short days, my perspective had shifted. Eve was no longer the be all and end all for me. I still found her incredible, but in a way meant for someone else. I could see clearly that we'd never work, not in the way I had always hoped.

Gently, I pushed her back up as I sat up too, reaching for my glasses. I wanted to be able to see her face properly while we talked this out. "Eve, I don't think this is going to work."

Her expression reflected a perfect blend of confusion and disbelief. "You're turning me down?"

I knew she hadn't meant that to come out as condescending as it did. I'd simply caught her off guard. "Trust me, I'm as surprised as you are. You're perfect, Eve. Absolutely perfect, but maybe not perfect for me, and I don't want to have sex with you just for the sake of it. Believe it or not, I'm not that hard up."

A brief smile flashed across her face. "So I've heard. Noelle seemed to have a good time with you yesterday, and I've heard a few other things too. I thought I'd see what the fuss was about."

Noelle had said good things about me to Eve? My body reacted to that idea even more than it had with Eve half-naked on top of me.

"Well, I guess it'll just have to stay a mystery." I gave her a smile to let her know I meant it in good humour. "I've got particular turn-ons and they don't seem to match with yours. Ultimately, I don't think it would be satisfying for either of us."

Eve looked me over shrewdly. "That's very mature of you, Aaron."

"Compared to Corey, you mean?" The words slipped out before I could stop them, and Eve arched an eyebrow at me again.

"You're just full of surprises. I guess Corey's talked to you about us."

"He and I have talked about you, yes." I couldn't put it much more mildly.

The next question out of her mouth made my stomach sink all over again. "Do you think he and Noelle are having sex?"

Fuck, I would rather not think about that, but I couldn't ignore her question either. "Maybe. Would it bother you if they did?"

Eve took a moment to truly think it over as she picked up her shirt and pulled it back over her head. "I don't think so, not if Noelle really wanted to. She's seemed happier these past couple of days, more confident. If having some extra attention from Corey built that up, I wouldn't complain. He doesn't belong to me, so she might as well have some fun."

It seemed like Corey's plan to make Eve jealous had turned out to be a bust then, if that had indeed been his intention in switching the names in the first place.

"I don't think we should tell anyone we didn't have sex," Eve added. "Keep them guessing. I'd like to see how Corey reacts. If he handles it maturely, maybe we can pick up where we left off. If he loses his shit, then we're done."

I promised not to say anything to Corey and we spent the rest of the twenty minutes just talking. Now that any lingering sexual tension had vanished, I could see how we might be friends. I could even see myself asking her for advice about Noelle, once we'd put a little distance between ourselves and what just happened.

Because when it came to Noelle, I wanted a whole lot more than friendship. The whole day had made that much clear, and now, I just had to hope I hadn't left it too late.

~Noelle~

As we headed back upstairs at the end of the twenty minutes, Corey took my hand again. "Will you do me a favour, Noelle? Don't tell anyone that we only talked, okay?"

"You want me to lie to Eve?" I had done enough of that over the past few days. Now that I knew Corey and I were never getting together, I wanted to put all of that nonsense behind us. We could start this whole trip over with a clean slate.

"Not lie to her," he corrected. "But keep it vague. If she asks what we did, just say we got to know each other better. That's true, isn't it?"

Technically, but lying by omission still counted as lying and he knew it.

"Only until I have a chance to talk to her," he pleaded, sensing my resistance. "And it's not so much for her, it's for everyone else. I have a reputation to uphold."

"A reputation as a manwhore?" I raised my eyebrows at him in challenge and he grinned, not in the least offended.

"It's not such a bad thing. And besides, if everyone thinks I slept with you, it looks good on you too."

I could have pointed out how arrogant that sounded, but unfortunately, I couldn't actually argue with him. Corey's taste in women skewed towards the sexy and desirable and everyone knew it. Putting myself in that category could raise my standing among the group and, by extension, everyone else at home too, even though, at the moment, I only wanted to impress one particular guy. I supposed

I could tell Aaron the truth in confidence if he asked me, and if he didn't ask, if he'd actually slept with Eve, at least I wouldn't feel like a complete loser.

So, in the end, I gave Corey my agreement, on the provision that if Eve out-and-out asked me if we had sex, I wouldn't lie.

He kept hold of my hand as we made our way back into the kitchen where some of the others had already gathered. My eyes immediately scanned the room for Eve and Aaron, but they weren't back yet. What did that mean?

Corey stayed close to me, his arm draped casually around me, and just as he'd predicted, several of the other guys gave me a more thorough look than ever before. With Corey's seal of approval, I had suddenly become someone worth noticing.

A full two minutes after we arrived, Eve and Aaron showed up, her arm linked through his, and my spirits immediately sank. They looked cozy and comfortable together, and when they came over to the island where the rest of us had gathered, Aaron leaned over to whisper something to Eve, his hand resting on her hip. What sweet, hot thing might he be telling her?

I watched wistfully until he glanced over and caught my eye, and I immediately froze. Shit, he would have noticed me staring. I couldn't pretend otherwise, so I simply smiled as brightly as possible, trying to give nothing away, not about what happened between me and Corey or how I felt about him with Eve either.

"Twenty minutes worked much better," James announced to the group, giving Sabrina a playful smack on the ass, which had her grinning too.

A general chorus of agreement swept the room, everyone nodding and exchanging smiles with the person they'd gone off with. Did *everyone* get laid except for me? It certainly looked that way.

It certainly looked like Eve had.

My throat grew tighter and tighter as everyone laughed and teased each other, until Eve made her way over to me and Corey while the others started discussing what we should do for supper. Eve had booked us all on an evening sleigh ride, so we couldn't get too drunk before then. It looked like we were actually going to cook.

Eve's thoughts had already moved on to the later part of the night. "Are you guys excited for the sleigh ride?" she asked me, Corey, and Aaron. "It's supposed to be really clear out, we should have a great view of the stars."

"I've never been on a sleigh," Aaron admitted. "Isn't it going to be cold?"

"They have blankets we can all snuggle up under." She grinned up at him, making my stomach sink further. "And they'll have hot chocolate for us afterwards."

"Did you know hot chocolate used to be considered medicinal?" I blurted out, trying to keep the conversation neutral. "They thought it helped the liver."

"Where exactly is the liver?" Corey wondered, his hand snaking around my waist. "Here?"

He started to poke and tickle my side, making me squirm and shriek. I had always been ticklish there.

"Corey!" Charlie called out. "We're going to fire up the grill in the back, can you help?"

"Sure thing." He let me go, giving me a wink. "Excuse me."

Eve and Aaron both watched him walk away before turning back to me, Eve's eyebrows raised curiously while Aaron's expression remained unreadable. "Looks like you guys had fun," she commented, leaving it for me to confirm or deny it.

I stuck to the words Corey had given me, especially since they weren't giving anything away either. "We got to know each other a bit better."

"Good." Eve looked genuinely pleased about that. "I found out there's more to Aaron than meets the eye too."

Those words and the smile they shared seemed to confirm my worst-case scenario, and my stomach churned in jealousy. Could I have possibly screwed this up any worse? After my devastation over Eve and Corey, I had done everything in my power to push her into Aaron's arms, and now that it had worked, I regretted it more than I'd ever regretted anything.

"Let me make sure they aren't *only* cooking meat," Eve said with a laugh as she looked over at the guys gathering around the grill on the snowy back deck beneath the winter sky. "I'll be back."

She walked away, leaving me and Aaron alone at last. He didn't seem to know what to say and neither did I. I should be happy for him, but I couldn't bring myself to pretend, or even to look him in the eye.

He broke the silence first, after several excruciating seconds. "So, things went well with you and Corey?"

I nodded, keeping my gaze focused on the countertop. In their own way, things *had* gone well. At least I wouldn't waste any more time hoping for a relationship with him that would never happen. "He told me he fixed the game so that you and Eve ended up together."

I glanced up just enough to catch the look of surprise that crossed his face. "He told you that?"

I gave another nod. "He said he felt bad about going behind your back before and wanted to give you a proper chance with her."

"Huh." That seemed to take him off guard as much as it had for me. "I didn't expect that."

"I guess it all worked out for the best, then," I suggested, putting the ball in his court just as Eve had done for me, leaving things open-ended so he could tell me as much or as little as he wanted to. Meanwhile, I knew what I wanted him to say. I wanted him to say he'd reached the same conclusion I had, that what he thought he'd wanted wasn't actually what he wanted at all.

I'd given him the opening. All he had to do was take it, but those weren't the words that came out of his mouth.

"I think it did," he agreed instead. "I think I really needed this."

Well, that settled it. I'd missed my chance, with my usual rotten luck and terrible timing, and I had never felt quite so foolish in all my life.

With a heavy heart, I forced a smile onto my face. "Me too. Well, I had my doubts, but you pulled it off, Aaron. Your plan worked."

"Yeah. It looks like it did." He didn't sound as happy about it as I expected him to, but maybe he would rather not be overheard. We were, after all, still in the middle of the kitchen where anyone could walk up to us at any time.

Exactly like Eve did just a few seconds later. "Come on, Noelle, let's make a salad while the guys take care of the main course. I'm starving."

She looped her arm through mine and, with one last glance at Aaron, I went to join her and the others to get ready for dinner.

Chapter Twelve

BETTER

~Aaron~

Frustration ran through me as Noelle walked away; frustration and jealousy and regret. My worst fears were coming true: I waited too long. It took me too damn long to come to my senses and realize that the perfect girl for me had been right there the whole time. Now, I'd been left out in the cold, and fuck it all if I actually kind of deserved it.

I'd been blind and selfish, and though a huge part of me wanted to chase after her right then and tell her how I felt and what I wanted, would it really have been for her sake or for my own? She'd told me all along that she wanted Corey and now, she had him, or at least a piece of him. If I went after her the way I wanted to, would it be any better than what he did to me by making a move on Eve?

Fuck, how did this all get so complicated?

Somehow, I made it through dinner. Corey sat next to me while Eve and Noelle sat at the other end of the table with the other girls. There were too many people around to ask him the kinds of things I really wanted to know, like how he felt about Noelle or what had happened with him and Eve. That conversation would have to wait until we could get some privacy, and that didn't seem to be happening anytime soon as everyone bundled up after dinner to head out into the snowy darkness of the evening.

The sleigh ride left from yet another farm just outside town, this one close enough to walk to, and our breath formed puffs of mist that drifted up into the air as we made our way there. Despite the cold, our movement helped to keep us warm on the journey to get there. Once we sat down on the sleigh, it would be another matter.

Three sleighs awaited our arrival, and we split into smaller groups to fit. Corey immediately offered his hand to Noelle to help her up into one, so I did the same with Eve. The benches were wide enough that we could sit four across and Corey took his seat on one end with Noelle next to him. Eve looked set to sit down next to her, but at the last second, I snuck in instead, grabbing the spot on the bench before either of them could react. Eve looked surprised, and Noelle had that sexy, startled look in her eyes that I found so damned appealing, and I honestly didn't know what I would say if either of them asked me to move.

Thankfully, no one did. With a shrug, Eve took the end seat on the bench on my other side, and when the farm staff handed out the blankets Eve had promised, we spread them out over the four of us to try to trap our combined body heat within them. It went without saying that we also pressed ourselves together as much as possible to conserve heat, Eve on one side of me and Noelle on the other.

Also as Eve had promised, the moon and stars were bright overhead, and as we left the farm to begin our journey through the snowy valley, I asked Noelle to tell us about them. "What do you know about the constellations?"

Based on the way she kept spouting random facts about things whenever she got nervous, I had surmised that she had a wealth of general knowledge stored up and that being able to share it made her feel more comfortable than simply making small talk in the way other people did.

Sure enough, as soon as I asked, she smiled with pride and pleasure. "Well, Orion, the hunter, is the most obvious one." She pointed above us with her fuzzy mitten, and we all dutifully looked up. "The band of three stars there is his belt.

Next to him are his dogs, and if you look at the bright stars on the head of each dog plus the one on Orion's shoulder, that's the Winter Triangle."

She pointed out a few more things until Corey began to lose interest, wondering how cold it would have to be for the river next to us to freeze over and if you could skate on it when it froze, and Noelle tucked her hands back beneath the blanket.

I leaned over to whisper in her ear. "I really enjoyed that, and I like the way the stars reflect in your eyes when you look up at them."

As praise went, it ranked pretty low on the scale: a statement of fact, followed by a compliment specific to her and our situation. Eve would have simply brushed it off, I knew that by now, but Noelle's cheeks flushed as she looked down, and I could almost feel the way her heart must have sped up.

The same way mine had at her reaction.

And that simple reaction on both our parts, simple yet profound, finally, *finally*, made me see exactly what an idiot I would have to be to keep my distance.

Something had happened between us whether we admitted it to each other or not. She might have slept with Corey, but that didn't mean game over. If I wanted her to choose me over him, she needed to know she had me as an option. I needed to show her exactly what she'd be missing if she chose him instead.

"Where are your hands?" I whispered, my lips still right next to her ear. Groping around blindly could have been risky if Corey was already touching her. That could make things very awkward, very fast, but with the blankets covering us, I honestly couldn't tell whose hands were where.

"Between my legs, to keep them warm," she responded innocently, obviously not grasping the reason for my question, and I almost groaned out loud. Fuck, she turned me on, and now that I'd made up my mind to do something about it, my body thrummed in anticipation.

"Put one between my legs instead," I instructed at the next natural opportunity, when Eve and Corey were both distracted, and as I would have predicted, Noelle's eyes went wide with surprise. "Just to keep it warm," I added. She wouldn't be touching me, not just yet.

She didn't even ask me why. With complete trust, and only a tiny bit of hesitation, she moved her left hand, the one closest to me, onto my thigh, following the curve of it down and pressing it between my two legs, where I gave it a slight squeeze, confirming she'd done a good job.

I said it out loud too, just in case she doubted it. "Good girl." The words were heavy in my throat as I muttered them into her ear. "Tell me if you want to stop, okay?"

With a slight look of confusion, she nodded in agreement. Her confusion stemmed from the fact that my intentions were still a mystery to her, but it would become a lot clearer very soon. Beneath the blanket, I pulled the glove off my right hand and slid my hand between her legs, just as she'd done with mine, but a lot closer to her hips. As my fingertips brushed against the sensitive skin directly between her legs, she shivered, and Corey gave her a knowing smile.

"Not used to the cold, huh? Here." Without giving her a chance to protest, he put an arm around her, pulling her towards him. My hand froze in place, waiting to see what would happen next.

"I guess you must be used to it with all the time you spend on the ice," Noelle said, not pulling back from him, but not telling me to stop either. They got talking about hockey, again, Corey's favourite subject, with his arm still around her and my hand still between her legs, unknown to anyone but the two of us.

When she made no move to push me away, I kept going. Chatting with Eve about Christmas traditions, my fingers trailed up and down over Noelle's leggings, pressing down just enough to get her craving the friction. Her legs widened ever-so-slightly; none of us had a lot of room to maneuver, but even that slight movement told me everything I needed to know: she wanted more.

Our separate conversations merged, Noelle telling us how her dad always watched the world junior hockey championships in the week after Christmas, making hockey and Christmas go hand-in-hand in her house. As Corey told us all about how he almost made the junior team, I withdrew my hand, watching Noelle's reaction carefully. The frustrated crease of her forehead gave me all the permission I needed to go a step further.

Reaching up beneath her coat, I found the waist of her leggings and, moving slowly to make sure no one noticed anything, my hand slipped beneath it, beneath her panties too, feeling along the soft skin and the trim hair that led to my goal. That wonderful heat between her legs that I'd felt in the shower beckoned me, and when she shifted in her seat to give me a better angle, satisfaction joined the anticipation I felt.

Things definitely weren't over between us yet.

My fingers slipped between the folds of her skin, finding her just as warm and wet as I could have hoped. Coating my fingertips in her wetness, I curled them back up until I found her clit, making her whole body jolt as a whimper left her mouth.

"Are you okay?" Corey looked down at her in concern, his arm still around her back, and my hand froze again. If anyone pulled the blanket back now, this could be very tricky to explain. There would be no quick way to remove my hand from her pants.

Thankfully, Noelle had an excuse. "Just a cramp in my foot. Sorry. It's okay."

Accepting that answer, he went back to talking, while I returned to the conversation between my fingers and Noelle's body. Over and over, I traced circles around her clit, brushing the top of it before bringing my fingers back down to her hole and prodding at the entrance but never going more than an inch or two in. I was being a tease, but right now, I wanted it exactly that way.

I wanted to drive her crazy. I wanted her weak with need and knowing that no one could meet it as well as I could. I brought her as close to the edge as I dared and then backed off, every single time.

When the farmhouse came back into view, I pulled my hand back out completely, slipping it back into my glove beneath the blanket as Noelle exhaled in pent-up frustration. I felt the same frustration too, because I knew just how good she looked when I let her go all the way. I wanted to see it again, desperately. She definitely wasn't suffering alone.

The whole group walked back to the house together, me walking next to Corey but fully aware of Noelle and Eve ahead of us. Excited chatter filled the air as we all removed our winter clothes at the door, leaving piles of coats and boots and hats and gloves at the door as everyone returned to the kitchen, the guys pulling out the booze and everyone settling in for another drinking game.

I'd had enough of games though. I announced to the room that I would be taking an early night and going down to my room. I caught Noelle's eye as I said it, making myself perfectly clear: if she wanted me, if she wanted to finish what we started under the blanket, she knew exactly where to find me.

My heart had never beat so fast as it did when I got to my room, leaving the door open just enough to make the invitation clear. I went to the ensuite bathroom and washed my hand that had been teasing her earlier, and I even ran a comb through my hair for good measure.

I wanted to impress her. I wanted her to remember this night *if* she decided to turn up.

Each second contained an agonizing mix of anticipation and anxiety, the hope that she'd appear and the fear that she wouldn't, until, at last, the door pushed gently open.

"Aaron?" Noelle said my name first before stepping inside, catching sight of me in the bathroom door. Her eyes flashed as they met mine, full of desire, fear, hope, and a touch of indignation. "You kind of left me hanging!"

Her accusation made me laugh, that fire in her exactly what I wanted to see right now.

"I know. I wanted you to come find me so I could finish the job." She quickly closed the door behind her, and I smiled even wider. "Lock it."

She did as I said, her hand fumbling with the lock. When she turned back to me, I could see the tiniest bit of hesitation in her blue eyes. "About this afternoon..." she began, but I shook my head.

"I don't care about this afternoon."

There would be time to talk afterwards. Right then, I only wanted to give her another option. I only wanted to show her how good it could be before she made any kind of decision.

"But Corey and I..."

Again, I didn't let her finish. "I don't care what happened," I told her bluntly, as firmly as I could, my eyes fixed on her as I stepped towards her. "I don't care if he fucked you, Noelle, because I'm about to fuck you better."

~Noelle~

The whole walk back from the sleigh ride, my body alternated between arousal and annoyance. What Aaron did on the sleigh had been incredibly hot, at least to me. Having his fingers playing with me with Corey's arm around me went beyond anything I could have dreamed of. Somehow, despite being the very opposite of what a 'good girl' would do, he made it feel incredibly right. Corey and Eve were both completely clueless about our activities beneath the blanket, but every time my eyes met Aaron's and I saw the approval and the satisfaction in them, pleasure rushed through me just as strongly as the pleasure he brought with his fingers.

Although it frustrated me that he didn't help me finish, it secretly relieved me too. I might not have been able to keep *that* a secret.

All of those feelings were joined by my confusion over the whole situation. If he slept with Eve, which it certainly seemed he had, why would he be messing around with me? Unless he had done the same thing with her on his other side? Did that explain why he wanted to sit between us?

I didn't think so, though. He never whispered anything to her. Although he had been discreet about watching my reactions, he faced my direction far more than he did hers. It definitely seemed like he had been focused on me.

But *why*? My lack of understanding frustrated me, and feeling confused and uncertain all the time was getting very old. I spent the walk back to the house trying to think of a way to get him alone and find out what the hell kind of game he was playing at now, but it all proved pointless when we arrived and he suddenly announced his intention to go to bed. He shot me a look as he left the room, as if I should have any idea what *that* meant.

I waited a couple of minutes to see if Eve would follow him, thinking perhaps that had been some sort of prearranged signal between the two of them, but she stayed put. Grabbing a drink with the others, she settled in to discuss the plans for the rest of the evening.

That seemed to give me an opening, then, and I intended to take it. "I'm actually going to call it a night too," I announced to the room. With Aaron already gone, we had an odd number of men and women, so I expected that no one would be too upset with me leaving too.

The only exception, as usual, was Eve, who gave me a concerned look. "Is everything alright?"

I smiled back at her brightly. "Yeah, of course. We'll catch up in the morning, okay?"

She agreed somewhat reluctantly, and everyone else said goodnight, forgetting me the minute I walked out the door, I had no doubt. I headed towards the stairs, but rather than going up to my room, I took a quick glance behind me to make sure no one could see me, and headed downstairs to the basement instead, my heart racing with nervous energy. I had no idea what might happen when I got there, but for now, I really just wanted some answers.

Aaron's room had started to be almost as familiar to me as my own since I'd been in there twice already, but I'd only been inside with Corey before now. This would be the first time Aaron and I were alone down there, and I took the open door as an invitation, pushing it open without knocking.

"Aaron?" He stood in the bathroom doorway, and the sight of him there combined with the memories from my bathroom upstairs, of walking in on him in the middle of the night and the shower we took together, started my body pulsing again, reminding me of just how unsatisfied he'd left me earlier. I blurted those words out as soon as the thought crossed my mind. "You kind of left me hanging!"

He laughed, as if it were a joke. "I know. I wanted you to come find me so I could finish the job."

Seriously? I hadn't expected that response, and I quickly closed the door, just in case anyone else followed me down and might overhear. The drumming in my body grew stronger as his words sank in.

"Lock it."

His firm tone of voice made it even clearer that he actually wanted to pick up where we left off, so I followed his instructions. The click of a lock had never sounded quite so significant before.

I still wanted to clear things up, though. I wanted to know what his intentions were, and I wanted him to know how I felt. All this beating around the bush had gotten exhausting. "About this afternoon..."

He shook his head, not letting me finish. "I don't care about this afternoon."

He might think that, but I wanted to tell him anyway so I tried again. "But Corey and I..."

"I don't care what happened." He stepped towards me, his hazel eyes blazing behind his glasses. "I don't care if he fucked you, because I'm about to fuck you better."

My knees nearly buckled right there and then. *Holy fucking hell*, he sounded serious. There wasn't a hint that this might be a joke, and the idea that he would try extra hard, thinking that I'd compare him to Corey, excited me far more than it should have. However, I still didn't understand. "But... Eve..."

"Noelle." With another step, he stood right in front of me, taking my face in his hands. "I'm not thinking about Eve right now. I don't want you to think about Corey. All I want to do is focus on us and see what happens if we just let go and enjoy each other properly. I want to give it a chance, right now. Can you do that with me?"

Corey who? Even if I *had* slept with him earlier, I would have had a hard time remembering. All other thoughts, every intention I had of telling Aaron what happened earlier, all of it flew out of my head at the touch of his hands, the sound of his voice and the look in his eyes. When I nodded, not even able to form the words but my body willing me on anyway, a satisfied smile slowly spread across his face.

"Good girl."

And just like that, I would have done anything he asked of me.

"I've been thinking about that pink underwear of yours all day," he murmured, kissing my forehead. "It looked so good against your skin. Show it to me again."

Having told me what he expected, he took a step back, his eyes still heated behind his glasses as he watched me, while my heart pounded in anticipation. I'd never really had the confidence to do a proper striptease before. When I took my clothes off during Twister earlier, I did it as quickly as possible. But with the words Aaron had just spoken and the look of anticipation on his face, I knew that he hoped for more than that and would appreciate any effort I made. And I *wanted* to make the effort. I wanted to please him and to hear those words of approval from his mouth.

So, I stepped back, going to the centre of the room with as much confidence as I could and, with his eyes on me the whole time, I pulled my sweater up slowly, giving him a flash of stomach, just a bit of skin, then a little more, teasing him and making him wait. The way his hands clenched at his sides gave me a pretty good indication I was on the right track.

Finally, I pulled the sweater all the way up, over my head, and let it drop to the floor beside me. My hands ran over my breasts, over the bra, as he followed their movement with his eyes. "Is that what you wanted?"

"Fuck, yes." His voice sounded thick and heavy, mimicking the way the air around me felt too. "Keep touching yourself. Squeeze those fucking perfect tits for me."

Perfect. No one ever used that word for me before.

I did as he said, moaning as my hands pressed against my hard nipples, and I had to squeeze my thighs together too, the need between my legs growing stronger by the second.

Aaron immediately noticed, his gaze dipping lower. "Take the leggings off too."

I obeyed, quicker this time. As fun as it could be to tease him, I wanted him to touch me too. I was getting desperate for it. My body remembered the feel of his hand on the sleigh earlier, very well, and it wanted more.

When I got down to my bra and panties, Aaron circled me, keeping his distance and taking his time, looking at me from all angles. Everywhere he looked seemed to heat up beneath his gaze, leaving me flushed all over.

"How is it even possible you look this good?" He sounded genuinely confused as he stepped closer to me from behind, and his words confused me too until he clarified them further. "How have I spent three years around you and never guessed you had skin this soft?"

His fingers brushed against my shoulder, sending a shiver down my spine.

"Why didn't I see the way your ass is begging to be touched?"

His palm ran down it as he spoke, giving the cheek a gentle squeeze, making me whimper in need and anticipation.

"You're beautiful, Noelle. Just looking at you has me rock hard. There's not a man alive who wouldn't want you right now, but they're out of luck, because right now, you're all mine and I'm not the kind of guy who shares."

Shit. I'd never been so turned on by anyone's words before. "Then maybe you should do something about it," I suggested shakily. I wanted him to touch me properly. I needed it so badly.

He chuckled into my ear. "Don't worry. I absolutely will."

With a practiced snap, my bra came undone and he pushed the straps down over my shoulders, still standing behind me as he pulled it off and tossed it to the floor. A second later, his hands were on my bare breasts, grabbing hold of them and using them to pull my body back against his as he ground his firm erection directly into my ass.

"Aaron." I moaned his name as his fingers kneaded my breasts, tugging gently on the nipples, his hips rotating against mine. My panties were growing damper by the second as my body pulsed with need.

"I love the way you say my name." His hands left me, but only to pull my panties down in one firm movement. "I'll like it even more when you're screaming it in a minute."

He sounded pretty damn sure of that, and right then, I couldn't disagree. As soon as I stepped out of my panties, he picked me up, those solid, unexpected muscles of his barely straining, and carried me the few steps over to the bed. My back had barely hit the mattress before he parted my legs, his head between them.

"Fuck, I've been dying to taste you properly. I only got a teaser yesterday. I need to know if you taste as good as you smell."

I could only manage a moan as he dove in. Only when he kissed my lower lips, his tongue exploring me eagerly, did I realize he hadn't even kissed my mouth yet. This was no slow seduction but an explosion of built-up tension, confirmed by the writhing of my body. Aaron hadn't taken any of his clothes off, even still wearing his glasses, although he pulled those off a second later so he could get his face even further between my legs as he kissed and sucked and licked me, praising me all the while.

"So sensitive," he murmured as his tongue swirled around my clit. "So responsive. Such a good fucking girl."

"Aaron, please!" I had been close on the sleigh, but now, I could practically taste the summit. His words and his tongue were driving me crazy and I craved the release like I never had before.

"You've got it," he encouraged me. "You're there, Noelle. Come on my tongue, let me taste it."

That did it. The dam inside me broke, releasing a wave of pleasure through my whole body more intense than any orgasm I'd ever had before. My body trembled, my thighs squeezing around Aaron's head still between my legs.

How the hell did he know how to do that to me? And, just as importantly to me as my thoughts began to clear, could I do the same thing to him?

~Aaron~

I couldn't have imagined this going any better. The confident, assured way Noelle stripped for me, the feel of her on my tongue and the taste of her surpassing my highest expectations, and most of all, the way that my words drove her over the edge, all of it filled me with satisfaction. When I praised her for being responsive, I meant it, but not only for the way she responded to the things I did to her body. The way she reacted to my words topped it all.

The contrast between her and Eve couldn't be clearer, and the contrast definitely worked in Noelle's favour as far as I was concerned.

I withdrew from between her legs after she came only because I had to, only because my jeans had begun cutting off my circulation as all the blood in my body continued to divert straight to my dick. I needed to get myself some breathing room, but as I stood up to do so, Noelle sat up too.

"Let me," she offered, reaching for my belt. "Please?"

I had no intention of saying no. Although I couldn't see her face clearly without my glasses, I could make out the way she bit her lip as she shuffled towards the edge of the bed, her attention focused entirely on my jeans which were just below her eye level.

The heel of her hand brushed against my stiff cock as she undid my belt. Intentionally or not, it made me groan in growing desperation. I had never felt so confined before.

"That's it," I encouraged her, reaching down to thread my fingers through her hair. "Don't tease me, Noelle. I'm choking here."

Her giggle suggested she thought that might be an exaggeration, when it most definitely wasn't. When she pulled my zipper down, I exhaled in relief, my dick immediately swelling even more into the small amount of extra space it now had.

She tugged my pants down to mid-thigh before running her hand over my dick more firmly, still over my underwear. "You're so hard," she commented, sounding almost baffled by it as her fingertips followed the length of my shaft, brushing over the ridge of my head which made it jump in excitement.

"Of course I am. It's all because of you, Noelle. You turn me on so fucking much."

Those startled blue eyes looked up at me, sending yet another rush of blood to my groin. "Really?"

I let out a choked laugh. "Do you think I'm faking this? Take a look for yourself if you don't believe me."

Thankfully, she took my invitation willingly. Her fingers slipped beneath the waist of my underwear, lifting it gently up and over the head of my dick, letting me breathe fully as it sprung loose. I helped to kick off my pants and pulled my shirt over my head too, leaving me completely naked, and when her eyes went back to my dick, it jumped again in anticipation.

I would never tell a woman she *had* to suck me but fuck, I wanted her mouth on me right now. So, when she lowered her lips to the tip of my dick, I groaned in approval. "That's it. Show me what you can do, Noelle."

She took that as exactly the challenge I meant it to be, and, as always when she went for something, she didn't hold back. Her tongue flicked across the bottom of my head as she took me into her warm, wet mouth, her hands stroking my shaft and balls, and my grip on her hair tightened.

"Fuck, just like that. It feels so good, Noelle, fucking hell." The encouragement spurred her on as she moved faster, taking me in even further. "Good girl, you've got it, you can take it."

With each bit of praise, she went deeper, until she took me all the way, her nose hitting my abs as her throat squeezed around the head of my dick.

"Oh, fuck!" That felt far too good. I pulled back from her before I came right there and then. As good as it would have felt, I still had other plans first. "Do you want me to use a condom?"

Her eyes widened, even though she couldn't have any doubt about my intentions. I'd told her flat out that I wanted to fuck her. Didn't she believe me?

"Not if you don't need to," she replied breathily. "I'm taken care of."

I would have bet any money she had birth control meticulously taken care of, just like everything else in her life, and the idea of being inside her without that barrier had my dick twitching yet again. I wondered briefly if she used a condom with Corey before pushing the thought out of my mind. In the end, I didn't care. By the time I had finished, she wouldn't remember him anyway. I was about to give her an orgasm she'd never forget.

Lifting her under her arms, I shifted her back further onto the bed, lying her head down on the pillows as I climbed up on top of her. My fingers went between her legs again, priming her for me, making sure she was ready to go again after her previous orgasm.

"I love the feel of your pussy," I whispered to her, staring down into her eyes as I fingered her, daring her to hold my gaze. "My dick is going to feel so good in there. Are you ready for me?"

She nodded, her lips parted in arousal as my fingers continued to tease her. "I want to feel it, Aaron. I want to feel you."

Those words were music to my ears. Hearing her take ownership over her own needs was incredibly sexy. "Good girl, Noelle. Tell me what you want. I love when you ask for what you need. You deserve it."

Emboldened by my encouragement, she went a step further. "I want you to fuck me, Aaron. I want that big dick of yours filling me up."

Fuck, yes. That confidence sent a wave of pleasure through me, knowing she felt secure enough and strong enough to be honest with me. I knew she wanted it, but to hear her saying it took everything to another level. "You're sure you can take me?" I teased, reaching down to grab my dick and bring it up to where my fingers had just been, running it through the dampness of her folds, getting the head nice and wet and rubbing it against her clit as I drove her need higher. "Are you a good enough girl to take me all the way in, filling every inch of you as I fuck you harder than you've ever been fucked before?"

She whimpered as her hips bucked against me, trying to draw me in. "Yes," she moaned, her eyelids heavy with lust. "Please."

"Yes what?" I rubbed my dick over her clit again, watching her body jolt in response. "Say it, Noelle. Let me hear the words from your perfect lips."

Her blue eyes looked up into mine, sweet and wanting and submissive. "I'm your good girl."

"Yes, you fucking are." My own body filled with pleasure as I thrust fully into her, hard and deep.

"Aaron!"

Her legs wrapped around me as I did exactly as I promised, fucking her as hard as I dared. Resting on my elbows, I held her head in my hands, keeping eye contact with her as much as I could, whenever her eyes weren't closed in pleasure, or mine weren't. I whispered more praise to her as our mutual pleasure grew, telling her exactly what she did to me.

"You take me so well, I knew you would. It feels so good inside you. You have no idea what you do to me. It's going to feel incredible when I come inside you."

That last one made her whimper my name, letting me know just how close she was, and I reached down to her clit to help her over the finish line.

"Come on my dick, let me feel you squeeze it, my fucking perfect girl."

With one more cry, she came around me and I couldn't have held back even if I wanted to. And I *didn't* want to. My orgasm hit me so intensely, I nearly lost my balance, my arms trembling as I emptied myself deep inside her.

When I finally regained control of my body, I leaned down and kissed her on the lips, the first kiss we'd shared since we got to my room, which made it feel even more significant. It put a seal on everything we'd just done and how good it had been.

Hopefully, I'd made my point. Hopefully, she knew now exactly what I could offer to her.

And hopefully, when I told her I wanted more of this, more of her, more of us, she wouldn't be able to disagree.

Chapter Thirteen

No More Games

~Noelle~

That. Was. Incredible.

I couldn't have played it down even if I wanted to. I'd had sex before, but I'd never had sex like *that* before.

On the girls' nights when we kicked my dad out of the room and my mom, my sister, and I would sit around and drink cosmos and talk frankly about sex and love and anything else that we felt like talking about, the two of them would always tell me that things were different when you found the right person.

"It's about respect and trust and the freedom to be completely yourself," my mom tried to explain. "And respect doesn't have to mean it's boring or that he won't do absolutely filthy things to you. It just means he respects the fact that you know what you want, and he'll find a way to give it to you."

"Exactly," Olivia agreed. "I feel comfortable telling Noah anything. He would never judge me."

I did have to wonder exactly what kinds of things the two of them were into that would make that a concern, but now, I thought I could understand.

I never knew how much it would turn me on to have someone praising me like Aaron did, to have him telling me what to do, not in a dominant way, but with encouragement, and the rush I would get when he told me I'd done a good job. I couldn't imagine asking someone else to do that, but it came so naturally to Aaron. He knew I wanted it even before I did.

And the best part had to be that he liked it too. I could tell he did by the way his body reacted and the heat in his eyes when I told him I was his good girl. He craved it too.

Was that what people meant when they talked about finding your other half? Did we each have someone out there who completed us so perfectly?

Or had I let myself get carried away again? The excellent sex could have clouded my judgement. After all, he hadn't said a word to me about wanting anything more than this moment. As far as I knew, he still wanted Eve. He'd slept with her too, I still felt pretty certain. Did he call her his good girl too? That thought left a bitter taste in my mouth and a sting in my chest as he softly kissed me.

Gently, I pushed Aaron back. "What are we doing here?"

He grinned down at me, his hazel eyes still full of warmth and his hair tousled from the exertion of what we'd just done. I couldn't deny that he looked incredibly sexy, and I would never think of his messy hair the same way again.

"I don't know about you, but I'm catching my breath after a pretty amazing orgasm." His hips rotated against mine once more, sending a shiver down my spine as he rubbed up against my sensitive clit before pulling out of me and rolling over onto his side next to me. "I'm pretty sure you had a good one too."

He sounded awfully sure of himself, but on the other hand, I couldn't argue. Me calling out his name the way I had must have been a bit of a giveaway.

"That's not what I'm talking about." I rolled over to face him, which I immediately regretted. Those hazel eyes close up were far too distracting.

But to his credit, he kept the conversation on track. "You want to talk about Corey and Eve."

Now, we were on the same page, so I nodded. "I want to tell you about this afternoon. Corey and I..."

A thud at the door cut me off as someone tried and failed to open it, followed quickly by a firm knock. Seriously? What now?

"Aaron?" Corey's voice called out from the other side. "Let me in."

"No," Aaron called back, not taking his eyes off me. "I'm busy. You can find yourself somewhere else to sleep tonight."

Corey's silence suggested he hadn't been expecting that answer at all, and it took him a few seconds to respond. "Look, Eve's looking for Noelle. She's not upstairs, have you seen her?"

My eyes went wide as I gave Aaron a helpless look. If he told Aaron I was here, after just claiming to be 'busy', Corey would guess pretty darn quickly what we'd just done. He'd tell Eve, and that would ruin Aaron's chances with Eve. But if he said he hadn't seen me, Eve would panic. I couldn't see how he could get out of this.

Aaron, however, seemed completely unbothered by the whole scenario. "Yeah, she's here with me. She'll be spending the night."

My mouth fell open in disbelief at the absolute certainty in his voice. What the hell did he mean? I hadn't agreed to that.

"Oh." Corey sounded even more surprised. "Alright, I guess. I'll let Eve know. See you in the morning, then."

We both waited a moment more to be sure he had really gone, and when it seemed the coast was clear, I asked for an explanation. "Why did you tell him that?"

"Because it's true," he replied with a shrug. "I don't want to play any more games, Noelle. No more schemes, no more half-truths. You're here and I want you to stay here, and I told him so. If you really didn't want him to know something happened between us, you wouldn't have had sex with me in the first place."

None of what he said was false. He'd always had a way of laying out his logic and making it sound reasonable. It made debating against him very frustrating.

"What about Eve, though?" I challenged. "He's going to tell her that too."

"I know." He held my gaze calmly. "It won't bother her and it doesn't bother me either. There's nothing between us."

Just when I thought I couldn't get any more surprised, he dropped that on me. "What do you mean? Having sex with her is 'nothing'? What does that make this, then?"

I gestured down at our naked bodies, making Aaron's lips twitch. "This," he repeated, mimicking my gesture, "is a hell of a good time. And there's nothing between me and Eve because we didn't do 'this'. I didn't sleep with her, Noelle."

I couldn't see how that could be true, but he'd just said we weren't lying anymore, so I gave him the benefit of the doubt and simply asked for more information. "Why not? I thought she wanted to have some fun."

Aaron's eyebrows raised. "What makes you think she's the one who said no?"

"You turned her down?" Each word out of his mouth shocked me more than the last.

"Yes."

He left it at that, his lips twitching again as he knew it wouldn't satisfy me. "Why?" I demanded.

"Because I realized over the past few days that she isn't the girl I want after all. I still think she's wonderful, but we're not wonderful *together*. She's not right for me."

My heart began to pound as I read between the lines, trying to hear the words he hadn't said. Something had changed for him in the last few days, the same as it had for me. I knew what had shifted on my end, but he hadn't said what changed for him. Were we both feeling the same way?

One of us would have to say it, and it might help if he knew the full story.

"I didn't sleep with Corey either," I blurted out. "I know you think I did, because of what you said before, but I... I changed my mind too."

"You turned him down?" Aaron's lips twitched again, but this time, rather than showing his amusement, his expression almost looked hopeful.

"Yes. Kind of. I mean, he would have had sex with me, but I don't think he ever would have been interested in anything long-term, and I see that now. We're not as compatible as I hoped we were. And..."

The words stuck in my throat, my heart racing wildly. I could do this, I encouraged myself. Aaron told me to think of myself as the grand prize. He made me *feel* that way, so if I told him now that I wanted to be with him, he should be excited about it.

He respected me and I trusted him. If we were meant to be, then just like my mom and sister had told me, I shouldn't have to be afraid to share what I wanted.

"The truth is, Aaron, the more time we spend together, the more I think that you're more right for me than Corey ever could have been. I... I really like you. I like the way I feel when I'm with you. If you don't want to be with Eve after all, then maybe we can..."

Before I could finish, his lips were on mine, his hand sliding around the back of my neck to pull me closer. A moment later, as the kiss deepened and my desire began to grow again, he rolled over onto his back, pulling me on top of him.

"Damn it, Noelle," he whispered, smiling against my lips. "I think we can."

~Aaron~

Noelle's giggle when I told her I thought we could be together wasn't exactly the reaction I'd been going for.

I could hardly believe it when she said she hadn't slept with Corey. She'd had him, ready and willing, and she turned him down because she'd rather be with me instead, exactly as I had with Eve. And yet, she hadn't said anything to me until now because she thought I still wanted to be with Eve, the same as I'd held my tongue about my own feelings earlier in the day because I thought she wanted Corey.

We really were a rather perfect match. I understood her perfectly, most of the time, but what had her laughing right now, I had no idea.

"What's so funny?" I asked, pushing her up just enough that I could see her face. Her expressive face told me so much, even without my glasses on, and I looked for hints there about what made the idea of us being together laughable.

She bit her lip hesitantly, not sure whether she should tell me, but in the end, she gave in. "You said that the other night: 'Damn it, Noelle.'" She lowered her voice to repeat my words, mimicking me in an affectionate way. "I heard you."

"What other night?" I had no idea what she meant.

"The night you spent in my room. I got up in the night to go to the bathroom and you were in there. I heard you."

It took a second before it all came back to me: the frustration and desire I'd been feeling, the frenzied release in the bathroom, and finding the door open on my way out. So *that* explained it. I must have really been lost in the moment if I missed her opening the door.

I could have been embarrassed about it, but why bother? By now, she knew just how sexy I found her, and I felt no shame over that fact.

"Why didn't you say something?" I asked her instead.

"What was I supposed to say?" she scoffed. "Oh, hey, Aaron, I know you're in love with my best friend but you said my name while you were jacking off, what's that about?"

Those kinds of absurd questions were one of her favourite debate tactics, but where I would normally formulate a logical argument back to her, I simply reached up and poked her in the sides instead. I'd noticed her ticklish response when Corey did it earlier and I'd been dying to try it for myself. She didn't disappoint, shrieking as she wriggled on top of me, trying to get away. The movement of her naked body against mine, and especially the friction against my dick, stirred it back to life in record speed.

My hands went to her hips, pulling her down even tighter against me, and as she felt me hardening, her movement slowed to a gentle rocking, stroking my dick with her pussy, letting it slide across her opening and rub against her clit as her laughter quickly shifted to sighs.

"This is exactly what I imagined that night," I told her honestly. "I imagined your hand touching me, your body against mine. It got me so hard."

Blood pumped to my dick again, making it throb, and from the way Noelle whimpered, I knew she felt it too.

"If we're going to do this for real, I have a few ground rules." I raised my hips as she slid across me again, pressing against her clit as she gasped.

"What we did before doesn't count as real?" she asked breathlessly, her eyes closed as she focused on the sensations between her legs. "Besides, I don't think you're in a position to be making demands. You kind of need me right now."

Fuck, I loved the way that confidence looked on her, even when she was only half right. "You need me just as bad, Noelle, but I'm not talking about sex right now, I'm talking about a relationship. If we're going to do all of it for real, I have some rules."

That opened her eyes, and she looked down at me curiously. "Like what?"

"Like when you're mine, you're fully mine. No messing around with other guys. No flirting. No trying to make me jealous. If you've got a problem with me or if you start to feel something for another guy, you talk to me about it before anything happens. I don't want any games."

"That's kind of rich coming from you," she pointed out. "It's been nothing but games since we got here, and interfering in other people's relationships. Eve and Corey were together and you still went after her."

"Only because I thought they weren't for real," I argued back. The distinction might be small, but it existed. "They never made any kind of commitment to each other but that's what I'm asking for now, Noelle. I'm asking you to be mine, and I'm telling you what that means to me. If it doesn't mean the same thing to you, this isn't going to work, so I want us to be clear about it up front. Do you understand?"

She must have had more arguments she could use, more of my own actions she could hold up against me, but she let them go and nodded instead. "I understand."

"Good girl." Using those words might have been playing a bit dirty, since I knew how hard she found it to resist, but I appreciated her agreement and I wanted her to know it. "There's one other big rule for me."

"What is it?" Her gaze had turned hesitant even as she continued to rub herself against my dick, which was nearly rock-hard again.

"No putting yourself down. Not in front of other people and not in private either. If you're ever feeling inadequate, you come to me and I'll tell you why you're wrong. I don't date runners-up, Noelle. I'm choosing you because you're fucking amazing, and if you say otherwise, it's an insult to me. Got it?"

Those blue eyes looked down on me with something close to wonder in them. "I got it."

"Good." I pushed my hips up again, increasing the pressure between us. "What are your rules for me?"

"You're making it kind of hard to think right now," she complained, making me smile.

"I know you, Noelle. You already know what you want. Even if you've never said it out loud to someone before, you've thought about it. What's important to you in a relationship?"

She bit her lip again, that telltale sign that she had something she wanted to say but doubted whether she should say it. I didn't want her to ever be afraid to tell me what was on her mind, so I softened my tone to encourage her.

"I'm not going to judge you," I promised. "If it's important to you, it's important to me."

"Well, the first I guess is pretty close to yours," she admitted. "No cheating, and I don't want you checking out other girls when we're out together or telling me I should be more like them."

What kind of fucking guys had she dated before? "That won't be a problem. What else?"

I grabbed hold of her ass as she continued rubbing herself against me, momentarily distracting her. I could see the effort as she tried to remain focused.

"I... I want to tell Eve and Corey the truth about what's been going on. I think this could really be something special, Aaron, and I don't want to feel guilty every time I think about how it started."

That one genuinely took me by surprise. "Are you sure?"

She nodded firmly. "You said no games and that should apply to our friends too. Agreed?"

As she pressed down against my dick, I could hardly argue. It wouldn't be a fun conversation, but if she wanted me to tell Corey the truth, I would. "Agreed. Now, will you fucking ride me properly already?"

She grinned at my impatience, lifting her hips as I reached down to line up my aching dick with her slick entrance, and as she sank down onto me, we both exhaled in satisfaction. *Fucking perfect.*

"Sit up," I instructed, pushing her back gently so she sat astride me. "You look incredible with my dick inside you."

Although she blushed at the compliment, she couldn't resist the chance to tease me too. "How do you know? You can't see anything without your glasses."

A surprised laugh slipped out of my mouth. She constantly surprised me, in the best way. "I'll just have to use my sense of touch then."

My hands went to her hips, helping her to find a rhythm to start us off with, and as she continued to raise and lower herself onto me, my hands travelled up further, over her soft stomach to her perfect breasts, squeezing and stroking them as she kept up her pace. She looked incredible, she sounded wonderful and she felt fucking amazing.

One hand drifted back down to her clit, circling and rubbing it as her breath grew shorter. "You ride me so well, Noelle. Just look at you. I can't wait to show you off to everyone when we make this public, but the way you look right now is just for me to enjoy."

She whimpered again, moaning my name as her legs began to tremble.

"That's it. It's going to feel so good when you let go. It's going to feel so good when you come all over my dick. Fuck!"

I groaned the last word as her orgasm started and my hands went to her hips, holding her steady while I thrust up into her, fast and hard, drawing out her orgasm as mine drew closer, and when she whispered my name once more, I came again too.

She drove me absolutely wild, and as we drifted off to sleep together, warm and content, I couldn't imagine ever getting enough.

When my eyes opened in the morning, I could see even less than usual thanks to the darkness of the basement room. I could, however, feel the bed shift beneath me as Noelle shuffled away.

"Where are you going?" I mumbled. "What time is it?"

"It's almost eight," she whispered back. "I wanted to brush my teeth and hair before you woke up."

There she went, worrying too much about her appearance again. I didn't expect to wake up to a perfectly put together woman next to me. In fact, I would have considered it a failure if a woman spent the night in bed with me and looked untouched. I would have to have done something wrong.

"This isn't your room," I pointed out. "You don't have your toothbrush or hairbrush."

"And you're telling me I won't find an extra, unopened toothbrush in your toiletry bag?" Although I couldn't see her, from her tone of voice I could imagine how her eyebrows raised as she asked the question.

She knew me way too well already. "Fine, brush your teeth but don't worry about your hair. We're going to have a shower anyway."

She had no protest to make about *that*.

I followed her into the bathroom when she had finished and we had a long, steamy shower together. Naturally, it reminded me of that first amazing shower we shared, but this time, it got even hotter. As I drove into her against the shower wall, I thanked my lucky stars that I hadn't backed out of this trip after Corey hooked up with Eve. Though I never could have anticipated this outcome, I also couldn't be happier about it.

We got dressed next to each other back in the room and I put my glasses back on, bringing the world back into focus. Noelle had no extra clothes with her so she put her clothes from the day before back on, hoping to sneak upstairs before anyone saw her.

The pretense seemed pointless to me. "You know they'll already be aware we spent the night together, right? Corey already knows and there's a good chance that he announced it to everyone else as soon as he found out."

"That doesn't mean they need to see me like this," she argued. "You're going to talk to him this morning, right?"

She meant talking to him to tell him the truth about what we'd been doing on this trip. It wouldn't be easy, but, with a grimace, I gave her my word. "I'll talk to him when he comes in to get ready. We'll get it all out in the open."

"Thank you." She flashed me a grateful smile that sent a wave of desire through me and firmed up my resolve too. If talking to Corey would make her happy, I'd do it. I couldn't think of much I wouldn't do to see that smile; it had such power over me. How had I never noticed it that way before?

In the end, her scheming proved as useless as I expected. Noelle's attempted stealthy getaway was thwarted almost immediately as she opened the door to find three of the guys sitting in the living room, including Corey. They all wolf-whistled after her as she gave them an embarrassed wave and ran up the stairs. I rolled my eyes at all of them, leaving the door open so Corey could come in to get ready.

"You didn't spend the night with Eve?" I kind of expected he would have once they knew that Noelle would be staying with me.

He shook his head as he pulled his clothes off and threw them on the floor. "No. We had a long talk last night and we've decided to just be friends."

Honestly, I thought they'd made the right decision, but after all the backstabbing and the angst and the fighting, it surprised me that he seemed to be taking it so well. "Are you okay with that?"

Corey shrugged as he took some new clothes from his suitcase. "Yeah, I think so. She's going through some stuff and I am too, and I think we were both looking for a way to feel in control again. We might have let it influence the way we felt."

I had a feeling those were Eve's words. Corey wasn't usually quite so philosophical.

"I would say that opens the door for you, then, but it seems you've already moved on." He gave a meaningful glance to the unmade bed with its rumpled sheets.

"I have," I confirmed. "Noelle and I are together now."

His shirt went over his head. "Like, for real together? Not just a one-night thing?"

I nodded firmly. "Yeah, for real. But aside from that, there's something else I need to tell you. I owe you an apology."

That got his full attention as he stopped getting ready and turned to face me fully. "For what?"

I told him the whole story, just as Noelle asked me to, starting with the plane ride and the deal we'd struck, rigging the game and Noelle's fake injury that turned out to be not entirely fake, all the way up to the point where I realized Eve and I wouldn't be right together after all.

He listened silently, not giving anything away until I reached the end. His eyebrows raised as he studied me, looking at me like he'd never fully seen me before. "You're a bit of an asshole."

"I'm not denying that." Put all together like that, it really didn't cast me in the best light. "And if my interference actually led to you and Eve not working out, then I'm sorry. Honestly. In spite of how this looks, I don't want you to be unhappy."

With a sigh, Corey sat down on the end of the bed. "I don't think it had anything to do with you. I don't think it would have worked no matter what, and let's be honest, I did deserve a bit of payback after what I did to you. I've been an asshole too. That's actually why I put you and Eve together yesterday. Part of it was about making her jealous, but I also thought if you had a shot with her, you wouldn't be so angry at me anymore. I didn't realize you actually wanted to be with Noelle and I screwed that up."

"Actually, with hindsight, I'm glad you messed with the game." I took a seat next to him, both of us making an effort to really listen to each other. "It helped me see for sure that Eve wouldn't be right for me. I think I still would have reached that conclusion eventually, but you made it come around quicker. What you did by going after Eve in the first place was pretty shitty, but trying to sabotage you wasn't any better. I guess we're equally as shitty as each other."

"Maybe that's why we get along." Corey gave me a nudge to let me know he meant it as a joke. For the first time in over a week, I could actually see the guy I became friends with in the first place.

"So, you're not upset with me?" He seemed to be taking this way better than I imagined he would.

"Nah, I'm good. We're on vacation and it's just been one drama after another. You and Noelle look good together. I've still got a half-dozen other girls I can have some fun with before we head home. Not everything needs to be life-changing."

He had that right, but in my case, my life definitely had changed for the better since we arrived. As we called a truce and finished getting ready for the day, I could only hope that Noelle's conversation with Eve went half as well.

Chapter Fourteen

OUT IN THE OPEN

~Noelle~

An empty room greeted me as I opened the door to my own bedroom but I could hear the shower running in the bathroom. I quickly changed out of the previous day's clothes into some fresh ones as I tried to decide how to broach the conversation with Eve about everything that had transpired since we left for our vacation.

I knew how happy she would be for me once she found out Aaron and I were together. She had just told me the other day that she thought we'd make a good couple, and how she thought our years of arguing had actually been sexual tension in disguise. Maybe she had a point. Maybe we rubbed each other the wrong way because we simply hadn't realized yet how good rubbing each other the right way would feel.

However, starting with announcing our relationship felt like a cheat. I wanted her to go through the whole thought process with me, to be there every step of the way as I came to realize why Aaron would be the right guy for me. I wanted her to be a part of it, like she always had been before, and like she would have been if I'd simply been truthful with her in the first place. My deception would hurt and confuse her, and I hated that idea, but I had to own up to it too. I had done all those things, I couldn't deny it, and I had to make it right, no matter how hard it would be.

I had just finished putting my new clothes on and doing my hair and makeup in the vanity mirror when Eve appeared from the bathroom, still wrapped in her towel. Her eyes widened in surprise as she saw me and she tried to turn away, but not fast enough. I noticed her red eyes before she could hide them and I immediately got to my feet.

"Eve? What's wrong?"

She waved her hand as she gave a small laugh, pushing the question away. "It's nothing. I'm fine, just feeling emotional for no good reason."

That didn't sound like the Eve I knew. "If something's upsetting you, it's not nothing. Please, tell me. Is it Corey?"

I had no idea what happened between them, but when I left Aaron's room that morning, it looked like Corey had slept downstairs with the other guys. Did they fight? Was it because of what Aaron and I had done? My guilt grew even stronger at the idea that I'd caused her any kind of distress.

Thankfully, Eve dispelled that notion. "It's not him. We talked last night and we've come to an understanding. We had our fun together but we're ending it now."

Her announcement made me feel even worse. She had been looking forward to spending time with him on this trip, and I'd done everything I could to disrupt that. Now, it seemed I'd been successful, but I didn't even want the prize anymore. How selfish could I have been?

Eve still hadn't answered the question either. "So, what's wrong, then?"

She sighed as she sat down on the edge of the bed, pulling her clothes for the day out of her suitcase. "It's just this whole job situation. Again. I told you: it's stupid."

I sat down on the other side of her suitcase, my brow furrowed in concern. "It's not stupid. It's your life, Eve. Your future. It's kind of a big deal. Did something else happen?"

She reached over to the bedside table for her phone, pulled up an email and handed it to me. The email came from both her mom and mine with architectural sketches and plans for Eve's new office at Stamer Hotels. It looked wonderful, but I knew she hadn't shown me for that reason.

"Everyone wants this," she pointed out as I handed the phone back to her. "Everyone's excited and things are moving ahead and it feels like I'm stuck on a runaway train with no way off. I think that's why being with Corey appealed to me so much because I made the decision, even if it might not have been the smartest one. Honestly, I just kind of used him to make myself feel better, and that's a pretty terrible thing to do, especially since he liked me more than I realized. I feel awful about it."

Every word out of her mouth made *me* feel worse. Here she was, blaming herself, when out of the four of us in the equation, she'd been by far the least selfish.

Her unhappiness stemmed from her concern over her future, though, not the situation with Corey, and I tried to focus on that. "It's not too late to change anything, Eve. I know it'll be hard but you need to tell your dad the truth. He loves you, and even if he's disappointed, he wouldn't want you to be unhappy. He'll want to know how you feel."

I couldn't sound like a bigger hypocrite, talking about being honest when I'd been keeping so much from her for so long. And even though I wanted to tell her the truth now, the timing felt off. We were dealing with her problem and I didn't want to make it about me.

"I know you're right. The longer I let it go, the harder it will be. I guess I could try to talk to him at Christmas," she said, not looking at all happy with that prospect. "Would you come with me when I do?"

"Of course, if you want me to." Hopefully, we would still be friends then, after I'd told her what I had to say.

We talked about our upcoming Christmas plans as Eve got ready, and her spirits lifted to the point where I started to think I could bring up the conversation I wanted to have in the first place, but before I got the chance, someone knocked at the door.

"You both decent in there?" Corey called out before opening the door without waiting for an answer. "Damn, too bad. You are."

Eve and I both rolled our eyes, but it made me happy to see Corey not acting any differently after the talk they had. Eve seemed comfortable enough around him too.

"What's up?" she asked.

"A bunch of us are going to go ice skating this morning. I figured it'd be right up your alley."

Eve's eyes lit up. "Absolutely. We'll just have a quick breakfast and we can be ready."

He headed back downstairs as Eve grabbed a couple of last things.

"Actually, there's something I want to talk to you about," I tried to tell her. "It's about Corey."

Eve shook her head. "I'm not worried about Corey right now. I want to just have some Christmas fun, like we came here for. We can gossip about the men later."

She headed out the door before I could say anything else, and I reluctantly followed her down the stairs, kicking myself for letting the opportunity pass me by.

Aaron smiled at me as soon as we walked into the kitchen. I flashed him a quick smile back before heading to the fridge to find something to eat, and a moment later, he came up behind me. "Is something wrong?"

He could read me so well, it almost scared me. "I haven't had a chance to talk to Eve yet," I admitted, glancing over to where she sat chatting to some of the other girls. "She doesn't know about us or about any of it."

His lips pressed together unhappily. "So, you're going to pretend like we're not together?"

He made it sound like I *wanted* it to be that way. "Only until I have a chance to tell her everything. I'll do it as soon as I can."

It sounded weak, and Aaron obviously agreed. "Well, I wish I'd known you were going to wait. I already told Corey."

Shit. It both pleased me that Aaron had kept his word and dismayed me that he'd beaten me to it. "Do you think he'll say something to her?"

We both looked over at Corey, standing with some of the other guys. At the moment, he and Eve weren't paying any attention to each other, but we couldn't keep them apart if he chose to talk to her.

Eve's metaphor of the runaway train began to feel eerily prescient as the group finished up breakfast and started to get ready to go to the rink. I could have held Eve back, but I didn't want her to miss out on this. She looked so excited and it made such a nice change from how unhappy she'd been that morning.

I would talk to her as soon as we got off the ice, I decided. I could stick next to her the whole time and make sure Corey kept quiet. One more hour and we could go for a walk together and get it all out in the open.

It would be just fine.

When we arrived at the rink, kids, families and a big group of teenage girls already filled the ice. There wouldn't be room for Corey to show off his moves as we'd talked about earlier this week, but he had probably forgotten that conversation anyway. He and Aaron went off to the men's changing room while Eve and I went with the other girls, even though we only had to swap our shoes for skates. The separate dressing rooms felt like a bit of overkill.

Eve and I had taken skating lessons together when we were younger, so we both knew our way around the ice and of course, Corey blew us both away with his skating skills. Aaron surprised me by holding his own too. He never told me which sports he used to play, but he kept up with the other guys who circled the rink as a pack, drawing quite a bit of attention from the teenage girls. Watching the way they couldn't keep their eyes off Corey, I had to smile. I had been just like them not very long ago at all, barely even noticing the guy next to him, but now, Aaron had my full attention. In my view, he stood front and centre while Corey had faded completely into the background.

After Eve and I went around several times with the other girls, the opening strains of All I Want for Christmas rang out through the rink's tinny sound system, and Eve excitedly linked her arm through mine. "Listen! Do you remember our program?"

Just the thought of it made me groan. "We're not doing it here," I protested. "There's no room."

During our last year of skating lessons, we took part in a Christmas carnival where the older skaters were expected to do solo performances. I'd been so afraid of having everyone's attention on me, judging me against the other girls, that I wanted to back out entirely, but Eve convinced me to do a routine with her instead. We choreographed it ourselves and thought we were incredibly edgy and fresh. I suspected the passing of time wouldn't be too kind to that assessment, not to mention the fact that we hadn't done it in years.

"We can do it in the middle," she told me, pulling me into the centre of the ice. "Come on, I want to see what we remember. It'll be fun!"

Her growing enthusiasm proved infectious, and as soon as we started, it all came back to me as clearly as if we'd done it just the other day rather than eight years ago. I could remember not only the performance but all the time we'd spent putting it together too, laughing together and practicing in Eve's room while we stressed about school assignments and boys we liked. We'd always shared everything; I'd never shut Eve out of any part of my life before. As the rest of our group gathered around to see what we were doing and I caught sight of Aaron watching us with an amused smile and a degree of pride in his eyes, I felt even worse about everything I'd kept from her in the last few days. I really couldn't wait to come clean.

Maybe those thoughts distracted me, or maybe I simply wasn't as coordinated as I used to be, but when we went to do our final spin, my edge caught in the ice and I tumbled over, landing directly on my bruised knee as a collective gasp rippled through the crowd of onlookers.

"Shit," I groaned before remembering all the children around us. "I mean: shoot. That really hurts."

Tears sprang to my eyes as I tried to get back up. Putting weight on it only made the pain worse, and in a moment, Aaron had his arm around my waist. "It's okay, Noelle, I've got you."

He took most of my weight as he helped me glide over to the door and, stepping off the ice first, he picked me up and carried me to a nearby bench. Eve and Corey followed behind us, Eve's face drawn in concern as Aaron gently placed me down.

"I'm so sorry, Noelle, I forgot about your knee." She wrung her hands guiltily. "Is it bad?"

"It's okay," I assured her even as I winced. "I forgot too, and we both know I can be clumsy."

"Maybe it's a bit of karma for faking the fall in the first place," Corey suggested with a laugh.

Oh, fuck. My blood seemed to freeze in my veins as his words sank in. Aaron must have told him that, but of course, Eve had no idea what he meant, and as her brow furrowed in confusion, my eyes darted to Aaron. What did we do now? He grimaced sympathetically, but before either of us could say anything, Eve asked Corey for clarification. "What are you talking about?"

He looked confused by her confusion. "You know, how she only pretended to fall the other day so I'd look after her."

That didn't clear anything up for Eve, naturally, but it did manage to distract me from the pain in my knee as my whole body went numb. I hadn't wanted the conversation to go this way at all, but I seemed to have lost the power of speech.

My brain refused to cooperate as I tried and failed to find any way to stop this train wreck.

Eve's eyebrows drew further together as she looked over at me and then back to Corey. "Why would she want you to look after her?"

Corey's expression grew more uncertain but he answered her anyway. "Their whole plan to break us up? Rigging the games, talking us down to each other, how Noelle's had a thing for me for years? She told you, right?"

My mouth had gone completely dry and when Eve looked back at me again, her eyes now full of suspicion and hurt, I tried to say something, *anything*, to diffuse this before it got any worse, but the words simply refused to come. I'd debated in front of hundreds of people before, but right now, I couldn't find a single word in my defense.

"No," Eve said softly, her eyes fixed on me, reading in my silence the confirmation that Corey's words must be true. "She didn't tell me."

"Eve..." Finally, one word came out, but it made no difference. In fact, as soon as I said it, she turned on her heel and walked away, her skate guards squeaking on the concrete floor as she walked briskly back to the dressing room.

I tried to stand up to go after her but pain shot through my knee again and Aaron pushed me back down. "You can't even walk, Noelle. You're not going to catch her."

"I have to." Sure, *now* I could speak. Typical. "I have to explain. I have to make sure she's okay."

When she already felt conflicted and overwhelmed, I'd just made it a thousand times worse.

"I'll go and talk to her," he promised. "I'll get her to come back and talk to you. Corey, will you stay with Noelle?"

"Sure," he agreed before giving me a sheepish shrug. "I'm sorry, I didn't know you hadn't told her. I thought because Aaron told me..."

"It's not your fault." I did this and no one else. He might have been a little insensitive, which seemed to just be part of his personality, but he hadn't outed me on purpose. This screw-up belonged to me and I needed to take responsibility for it. "Please, hurry, Aaron."

With my agreement, he took off to try to catch Eve while I pulled out my phone and sent her a text.

I'm sorry, Eve. Please, let me explain. I love you.

Although it went to read almost immediately, no reply came through.

~Aaron~

Eve had a minute or two head start on me so I would have to be quick. Confronting her in the women's change room seemed risky for a variety of reasons, so I quickly changed out of my skates and back into my boots before heading to the door. When I couldn't see her in the lobby of the rink, I went outside and caught just a glimpse of her red hair already a block away. Shit, she moved fast.

On the way to the rink, I had decided not to say anything to Corey about Eve not knowing the whole story since it seemed unlikely to come up while we were on the ice. Planting the idea in his head might actually have made him blurt something out unintentionally. I did my best to keep him away from Eve, but when Noelle hurt herself, that became my priority and I lost sight of Corey. What were the odds he would say the one thing that we didn't want him to?

Pretty good, apparently.

The snow crunched beneath my feet as I ran down the sidewalk after Eve, my breath puffing out behind me. I saw her turn the corner and lost sight of her behind a building, but although she walked quickly, I ran, so I caught up to her on the next block.

"Eve! Stop, please," I called out as soon as she seemed to be within earshot and she did stop, mostly out of surprise. As soon as she saw me, however, she turned back around and began walking again.

"Leave me alone, Aaron. Why can't everyone just leave me alone?"

I didn't know what she meant by that, but I'd made a promise to Noelle and I wouldn't go back on it. "I can't do that, Eve. You have to talk to Noelle."

"Don't tell me what I have to do." Her dark eyes flashed in anger or frustration, or maybe both, as I fell into step beside her. "I don't want to talk to her and I don't want to talk to you either. I don't even know you, apparently."

I could see why she'd feel that way. The guy Corey had described in his brief rundown of events barely sounded like someone I recognized either.

"Well, let me introduce myself, then. I'm Aaron Speelman, and I had a crush on you for the longest time."

She hadn't expected me to say that, I could tell by the way her eyebrows raised and the surprise that flashed across her face before she turned away from me again.

"You don't know anything about me," she pointed out, sounding disillusioned and perhaps even a little bitter. "Everyone thinks they know me but they don't. They all just have this idea in their heads about what I'm like."

I knew how that felt. People judged me on the way I came across too, thinking me awkward and geeky and uncoordinated. "Well, the Eve the rest of the world sees is pretty damn impressive. I thought I'd fallen in love with her. I convinced myself she was the right girl for me, I even enlisted her best friend to try to help me prove it."

At the mention of Noelle, Eve glanced over at me again. "Why would Noelle help you?"

I would rather not steal too much of Noelle's thunder, but with the truth already out there, I could fill in a few of the broad strokes and Noelle could add the fine detail later. "Because, as Corey so eloquently put it, she 'had a thing' for him for years. She fell for the idea of him just like I did with you. We thought we could help each other out since you and Corey told us you weren't serious about each other."

As I would have expected, that didn't make Eve any happier. "So, you decided to mess around in my personal life because you thought, based on some public image of me, that we were meant to be together? Do you even hear how creepy that sounds?"

She definitely had a point, and hearing it in those terms made me wince. "We were drinking and it sounded like a good idea at the time. I have no other excuse."

"And that's the other thing." Eve's voice went up a notch in volume, her fists pounding the air as she continued to stride angrily down the street. "You're one thing; you might just be a creepy guy for all I know, but Noelle is supposed to have my back. She's the one person I thought I could count on."

"She never wanted to hurt you, Eve." She might not give my words much weight after what I just admitted, but I had to try. "She honestly thought you weren't that interested in Corey and we know each other well enough that she knows I'm not a total creep. All we wanted to do was create some opportunities for you to spend time with me and her to spend time with Corey to see how things developed. No one would have ever forced you into anything."

"And if by some miracle I did actually fall for you, you thought this would be a charming meet-cute story? How you manipulated your way into my company?"

Fuck, she really wasn't taking this well. I tried a joke to lighten the mood. "I thought it might show my inventiveness and creativity."

She shot me a look of disapproval that told me the time hadn't come to joke about it just yet. As we rounded another corner, the town's main park came into view and I pointed over at it.

"Come on, let's go sit down and talk properly. I'm not arguing with you that we behaved badly. Looking back on it, I can see we made the wrong choice, and I'm sorry, Eve. I truly am. I'm sorry for presuming to know what you would want, and I'm sorry for involving Noelle in anything that would hurt you. The whole thing was my idea. Hate me if you want to, but please, talk to her about it. You mean the world to her, and she wanted to come clean about it. I only told Corey because she asked me to. She planned to tell you this morning, she just didn't have a chance."

As I'd been talking, we reached one of the park benches and took a seat in the snowy park beneath the bright blue winter sky. Eve's lips pursed as she thought over what I'd said.

"She did tell me she wanted to talk to me about something. Something to do with Corey."

I grabbed onto that. "You see? Even though she knew you'd be upset with her, she respects you enough to tell you the truth. If it were up to me, I would have just kept my mouth shut."

Eve raised her eyebrows at me again. "You're not painting yourself in the best light here."

I could only shrug. "I'm just being honest. And to be frank, it doesn't matter that much what you think of me. As I already told you yesterday, I think you're amazing, but now that we have spent a bit of time together, it's clear to me that we don't work in the way I hoped we would. There's someone else who suits me much better, and there will be someone else out there for you who will be a perfect match. Not me, and not Corey either."

For the first time, she almost smiled.

"But this isn't about me," I continued, pressing the advantage while I had it. "This is about you and Noelle. You know her. You know the kind of person she is. Give her a chance to explain everything and talk it out. You guys have been friends for way too long to let an idiot like me mess things up for you."

She stayed silent, her lips pressed together, so I pulled out my phone and held it up to her.

"I can let her know where we are so she can come over here and you can talk right now. Would that be okay?"

After a moment, Eve nodded, and I breathed a sigh of relief as I sent our location to Noelle. It still wouldn't be an easy conversation, but if anyone could win Eve over, Noelle could. I had complete faith in her.

~Noelle~

Corey helped me limp back to the changing room, and once I'd taken my skates off and put my boots back on, my knee already felt better. The fall hadn't been as bad as the other day, it just hurt because I had already bruised and battered my knee the first time. I would just have to spend the next few days staying away from any hard surfaces.

But first, I needed to talk to Eve. She still hadn't responded to my text, and though I wanted to go after her, I had no idea where to start. It made no sense to start walking and hope I'd run into her. I could wind up going in the complete opposite direction.

"Do you want me to take you back to the house? I could call a cab." Corey obviously felt guilty enough to make the offer, but I waved him away. Only a week ago, I would have thought it a dream come true for him to want to spend time with me alone, and now, he had become just another guy. Funny how a little thing like finding my perfect man could completely change my perspective.

"I'm fine, thanks, Corey. Go back on the ice with the others. We'll catch up with you all later."

Gratefully, he took the out I provided, and I pulled my phone from my pocket to check my messages yet again. Nothing new had come in, but before I could put it away in frustration, a text popped up; not from Eve, but from Aaron.

We're in Front Street Park. She's ready to talk to you.

"Thank you," I whispered out loud, thanking Aaron and the universe and whatever other forces had helped to convince Eve to let me explain. I knew my friend and I knew how she could withdraw when she felt hurt. Her being willing to hear me out was a really good sign.

On my way, I texted back before hurrying out the door.

Although I would have loved to jog over and get there as quickly as possible, it really wouldn't be feasible with my sore knee, especially since the sidewalks were still covered in snow and the very last thing I needed would be to slip and fall again. It therefore took me about five minutes to reach the downtown park and as I reached the main thoroughfare of the town, the sight stopped me short for a moment. It couldn't look more picture-perfect with the Bavarian-style buildings gleaming in the bright sunshine, Christmas decorations as far as the eye could see, and the snow-capped mountains in the distance. In the park ahead of me stood a huge Christmas tree, decorated with balls and lights that danced and twinkled in the sun.

This Christmas atmosphere had been the whole reason we came here, and that morning was the first time I saw it, halfway through our trip. If I needed one more indication of just how self-centred I'd been, I'd just been handed it.

Aaron and Eve sat next to each other on a bench in the park, their backs to me, and from this angle, they made a good-looking couple. Aaron had made an effort and Eve looked as naturally stunning as always. For just a moment, it felt impossible that he'd chosen me over her, but when Aaron glanced over his shoulder and saw me, his eyes lighting up and softening at the same time, all my doubts vanished. He really did see me as the prize.

Now, I just had to hope I hadn't made too much of a mess of things with Eve to be able to make things right.

"Here, Noelle, take my seat." Aaron got up so I could sit on the bench next to Eve. "I'm going to go do a bit of shopping for my family. Text me when you're ready, okay?"

I couldn't be more grateful to him for facilitating this conversation. "I will, thank you."

He gave me a quick kiss on the cheek before whispering, "Good luck," in my ear and leaving us in private. Eve still hadn't looked at me, but I sat down next to her and gave her a tentative smile anyway.

"The tree is really pretty," I started, hoping to break the ice as I gestured to the large tree ahead of us. When Eve didn't reply, I gave that up quickly and got to the point instead. "I'm sorry, Eve. I'm sorry about everything I did and I'm sorry that you found out the way you did. I wanted to tell you this morning but you were already upset and I didn't want to make things worse."

"I *was* already upset," she agreed, her voice flat as she looked down at the ground. "Which I told you about because you're my best friend. We tell each other everything. Or I thought we did."

Her words made me wince but I couldn't refute a single one. She had every reason to expect that from me and I'd let her down.

"I don't even know what I'm upset about now," she added, turning to face me at last, and the hurt and disappointment I could see in her eyes nearly took my breath away. "I don't know because I still don't know exactly what you did. I only know that you lied to me and tried to manipulate me and Corey, but I don't even know why. Just because you liked him? Seriously, Noelle? After all the times we said we'd never let a guy come between us?"

My eyes closed in shame at the reminder. We'd sworn on several different occasions that we were not going to be the girls who fought over a guy or let a relationship change who we were. I'd broken that promise, among others.

"Let me start at the beginning," I offered. "The full truth, I promise."

Her pursed lips told me how much my promise meant to her right now, but she waved her hand for me to go ahead anyway.

"Corey is *the* guy," I began, finally letting her in on the secret I'd been concealing for years. "The one I've had a crush on forever. It's always been him."

Eve's dark eyes widened in surprise as she put together all the things I'd ever mentioned about him. I could see the emotions play out across her face as she processed it: the confusion, the understanding, and the dismay. "I had no idea. If you'd told me, I never would have..."

"I know." I cut her off because she didn't owe me any apology. I knew she would never have slept with him if she'd known. I had always known it. "It devastated me when you hooked up with him, but I kept it from you because I didn't want you to feel bad. You hadn't done it on purpose."

"That's why you were so grumpy before we left," she guessed.

I nodded, but I would use an even stronger word. "I was jealous. You said you weren't serious about him, but the idea of you two together still hurt. I've wanted to be you so many times, but never more than when you went to go sit with him on the plane."

"Noelle." Even though she should still be furious with me, and I knew those feelings were still there, concern clouded her face too.

I shook my head, trying to get it all out as truthfully as I could without being distracted. "I was annoyed about having to sit with Aaron, and when we had a few drinks, the reason for my grumpiness slipped out. That's when he told me that he liked you too, and that Corey wasn't any more serious about the relationship than you were. He suggested we play reverse matchmaker and it seemed pretty harmless. I thought if things happened between me and Corey or you and Aaron and you and Corey decided to split up, you'd never have to know how upset I'd been."

"You should have just told me." It sounded so simple when she said it like that, and things would have played out completely differently if I had.

"I know. But I convinced myself Aaron's scheme wouldn't be that big a deal and that you and Aaron might actually hit it off too. We weren't going to do anything crazy. We told you both about how the other person had said they weren't serious about it, and then Aaron rigged the game of Seven Minutes in Heaven, but nothing happened."

Realizing I had left something out, I quickly amended my statement.

"Well, one thing happened. When Aaron kissed me during Spin the Bottle, I liked it way more than I expected to. It surprised me, but I knew he still wanted you, so I didn't do anything about it. Then, the next morning, he wanted me to pretend to hurt my ankle so that Corey would help me, except I actually fell and hurt my knee instead."

"And Corey did help you," Eve remembered. "And I spent the whole time with Aaron."

I nodded again, wincing at the accusation in her words. "That's right, but something weird happened. When you guys got back to the house and Aaron offered to stay with me, he kissed me again and I liked it even more. The whole thing confused me, and then we made the gingerbread house and Corey did the spin with the arrow to choose our shower partners."

Eve's brow furrowed as she thought back. "But he got me in that game. Did something go wrong?"

"No, that game wasn't fixed." She looked confused and I had no real explanation either. "Aaron and I showered together and, like I already told you, I really enjoyed it. I started to have real feelings for him, but I thought he still liked you."

Eve's eyebrows raised but she said nothing, waiting for me to go on.

"Then yesterday, we had the second game of Seven Minutes... or Twenty Minutes in this case... and Corey actually went in and rigged it so that I would end up with him. I think he thought it might make you jealous."

"Corey was in on this too?" Her nostrils flared as even more manipulation came to light.

"He didn't know what Aaron and I were doing, but he fixed that particular game. He would have slept with me then, but when we were alone, I realized that I didn't want that anymore. I'd built him up in my head to be someone he'd never been, and I actually wanted Aaron instead. Except that he was alone with you, and when you came back to the kitchen, I thought you'd slept together and it devastated me all over again."

Eve huffed in disbelief. "Could you have made this any more complicated?"

I gave her a rueful smile in return. "I know. Trust me, I've kicked myself so many times. But last night, he told me nothing happened between you and that he wants to be with me. I'm so excited about it, Eve, but I couldn't be fully happy because of everything that led up to it. That's why I wanted to tell you everything and that's why Aaron told Corey too. So, that's it. That's the whole story. I know I should have just been honest with you from the start and I'm really sorry."

Now that I'd blurted it all out, I pressed my lips tightly together, waiting for whatever she wanted to say to me. She would be well within her rights to shout at me and tell me off and I tried to brace myself for whatever might come out of her mouth.

She didn't yell, though. She looked away from me, looking out over the pretty Christmas scene in front of us in silence as the seconds ticked by, until I began to wonder if this would be her punishment. Would she simply refuse to ever speak to me again?

"Do you know why I was so excited about this trip?" she eventually asked, so quietly that I needed to lean forward to hear her.

Not sure what she was getting at, I shook my head. "Why?"

"I wanted a break from all the drama and pressure at home. I wanted to feel in control again, even if only for these ten days. I wanted to come here and make gingerbread and sing carols with my best friend, the one person I thought I could count on to respect my right to make my own decisions about my life. And instead, this whole time, I've just been a pawn in a game I didn't even know we were playing."

Although I wanted to deny it, I couldn't. Her words were entirely true. I could only apologize again. "I'm sorry, Eve. I never meant to make any decisions for you, but I know I went too far. I screwed up and I'm so sorry."

I couldn't tell if that helped or not. She sighed, still not looking at me. "What is it about me that makes everyone think they know what's best for me?"

I knew she wasn't just talking about me now, but what I'd done certainly hadn't helped matters any. "Well, in your dad's case, he thinks he's doing what you want. In my case, I only thought about myself. Sometimes, you're so perfect to me that I forget you don't have it all figured out. I forget that you can get hurt like the rest of us."

Eve rolled her eyes. "You know I'm not perfect. I'm no different than you, Noelle. I wish you would accept that."

"I know," I surprised us both by saying. "That's my issue and I'm working on it. Talking with Aaron has helped, I think, but I'll keep trying."

At the mention of Aaron, Eve turned to face me again. "So, you guys are together for real now?"

I nodded, the thought of him making me want to smile even though I tried not to look too pleased when she still had every reason to be upset with me. "I've never felt this way about anyone. He's amazing. I just didn't see it before."

"I have noticed you looking happier these last few days. More confident, too. Is that because of him?"

I nodded more energetically this time. "He makes me feel confident. He made it a condition of us getting together that I can't put myself down anymore."

Eve's laugh took me by surprise. "Well, I can get behind that condition. And I like him too. Or I did, until I found out about all of this."

"I want you to like him," I confided. "I want you guys to get along because I think he could be the one, and we always said how we had to approve the guys we ended up with."

Bringing that up was a risk, since it harkened back to how we'd promised to never let a guy come between us either. Eve took a deep breath instead, looking back out over the town.

"I can't pretend I'm thrilled about any of what you did, Noelle, but we promised we'd never let a guy come between us, and I meant that promise. Do you promise to stay out of my love life from now on?"

"I swear," I promised eagerly. "You can date whoever you want or sleep with whoever you want or marry whoever you want. Even if it's Corey."

That made her smile. "I'm definitely not marrying Corey. That guy's got enough issues of his own without adding me to the mix."

"Don't we all?" I smiled back at her hopefully, and she laughed.

"Alright, Noelle. I'm sure I'll have more questions later on, but I'm willing to move on if we can just enjoy the rest of this trip without any more secrets or drama. Can we do that, please?"

I threw my arms around her in relief. "I would love that."

When she hugged me back, things felt right with the world again. Tears sprang to my eyes and when we pulled apart, she dabbed at her eyes too.

"Well, now that we're downtown, let's go do some shopping," she suggested. "And then you can introduce me to this boyfriend of yours properly."

Boyfriend. I loved the sound of that, and I loved the idea of the three of us spending the day together even more. "You're the best, Eve."

"I know." She gave me a smirk that looked so much like her dad, it scared me. "Come on, Noelle. Let's have some Christmas fun."

Chapter Fifteen

REAL LIFE

~Aaron~

I would never voluntarily choose shopping for Christmas presents as a way to pass the time, but with nothing else to do while I waited for Noelle and Eve to finish talking, I ducked into a couple of stores to look at things for my parents and siblings. Nothing jumped out at me for them, but I did notice some engravable pendants in the jewellery section in one of the stores and, on impulse, I bought something for Noelle. Though this relationship had only just begun, I had a feeling she would be the kind of person who never missed a birthday or any other occasion, and with Christmas only a week away, I wanted to be prepared.

I'd just finished getting it boxed up when my phone buzzed with a message from Noelle telling me that she and Eve had finished talking and were going to do some browsing of their own now. She said they'd like my company if I could handle shopping with the two of them.

More shopping didn't particularly appeal to me, but the chance to spend time with Noelle did, and it genuinely pleased me that it sounded like they'd settled things between them.

I met them back by the Christmas tree in the park where Noelle formally introduced us, to my amusement. "We've decided we're going to start over. Aaron, this is Eve Stamer. She's smart and funny and my best friend since the day we were born. Eve, this is Aaron Speelman. He's smart, sexy, and the runner-up for student body president."

Seriously? She wanted to go there? She and Eve giggled as I raised my eyebrows, wondering where this sassy Noelle had been hiding. Fuck, I loved to see her looking sure of herself.

"It's nice to meet you, Eve." I played along by sticking out my hand, which Eve shook firmly. "I used to have a crush on a girl who looked just like you."

"She sounds pretty awesome," Eve teased. "Although possibly out of your league."

"Maybe just in the wrong division," I amended. "When I started looking in the right place, I found exactly what I wanted."

Noelle beamed as I put my arm around her and the three of us headed back to the stores. Watching the two of them together as they analyzed every potential purchase could have tested my patience, but I'd rarely seen Noelle so happy and comfortable. Eve and I teamed up a couple of times to tease Noelle and make her blush, and it all felt easy and natural and right.

Four hours later, with a break for lunch along the way, we returned to the house, to my relief. I was exhausted.

"Let's play a game," Noelle suggested. "Not a dirty one this time, just a regular game. I think I saw Candyland in the hall closet."

Eve eagerly agreed, and after a few rounds of Candyland, the cheating getting more and more outrageous each time, more of the group drifted back and we all had dinner together. If anyone thought it strange that Noelle and I were glued to each other, they kept quiet about it. Maybe it felt as natural to them as it did to us.

"I need to spend the night with you," I whispered in Noelle's ear as dinner finished. "I've been thinking about it all day. Every time you blush that beautiful pink colour, it reminds me of how you look when you come."

Right on cue, her cheeks flushed as her eyes darted around the room. "What about Corey?"

I had a plan for that. James and Sabrina seemed to be joined at the hip after the previous night, the same as Noelle and I were, so after a quick word to the people they'd been rooming with, everyone agreed that Eve would open her room to Sabrina's roommate. James could stay with Sabrina and Corey could take James' spot. A little bit of musical beds, as it were, but as long as Noelle ended up back with me, I would have rearranged the whole damn house if I had to.

She went up to her room to pack up her things, and I had her in my arms as soon as she joined me downstairs. "Fuck, it's been too long since I kissed you."

The suitcase fell to the floor, forgotten, as I pinned her up against the back of the door. Her eagerness matched my own as she pulled off my glasses and tossed them to the side.

"Those are actually kind of expensive," I teased her, pulling her shirt up over her head. "You might want to be more careful."

"And your insurance doesn't cover breakage during sex?" she retorted, grinning as I laughed. She pulled my shirt off too, not messing around any more than I was.

"If anyone could convince them to, I'm sure it would be you." Her pants came off next, and her panties too. No point in wasting time.

"I don't know. I think you're pretty persuasive when you want to be." She tugged at my belt, and when she finally got my pants down, I exhaled in relief. It had been getting awfully tight in there.

"It shouldn't turn me on when you argue with me, but it fucking does anyway." My hands went beneath her thighs, lifting her up as her legs wrapped around my waist, her back supported on the door.

"The talking turns me on too," she admitted, biting her lip as my dick pressed against her wet entrance. "Especially the stuff you say."

"I can tell." With a smirk, I pressed into her, firm and hard, as her grip on me tightened. "Fuck, look at how good you look, Noelle. Look how well you take me."

Following my instructions, she looked down to where our bodies were joined together. I pulled out slowly, letting her both feel and watch as my dick disappeared inside her again.

"Do you see that? Do you feel it? How you were made for me?"

Her bright blue eyes met mine, but rather than looking startled by what I'd said, I could only see happiness.

"Or maybe you were made for me," she replied with all the confidence I'd been dreaming of hearing from her, and I grinned one more time in pure satisfaction.

"That's my good girl."

My mouth covered hers as I increased my pace, thrusting into her harder and faster, the door rattling behind us. Her cries of pleasure were muffled by my kiss but if anyone stood outside the room, they wouldn't have any doubt what was happening inside.

I truly couldn't care less. This woman belonged to me now and I wanted everyone to know it.

"God, Aaron, I'm so close," she whimpered. My hands were busy just holding her up so they couldn't help get her over the finish line, but I had a pretty good idea what would.

"You're going to come for me now, Noelle," I encouraged her. "You'll make me so fucking proud when you come all over my dick. You look so beautiful when you come."

Her body contracted in pleasure as her orgasm hit and I stopped moving, enjoying the sensation of her vibrations all around me.

"Fuck, that's so perfect."

Still buried inside her, I carried her over to the bed and laid her down. Her knee still looked a bit sore so I let her lay back, praising her as I resumed my thrusting, touching and teasing her until she came again, and when she whispered a sweet 'thank you' at the end of her second orgasm, I couldn't hold back either. My whole body flooded with the pleasure of giving her pleasure as I came deep inside her, and when I was fully spent, I lay down next to her and pulled her into my arms.

"Is it really going to be that good every time?" she wondered after a couple of minutes' silence while we caught our breath.

"No," I told her, smiling tenderly at the look of disappointment that crossed her face. I couldn't resist teasing her, but I explained myself a second later. "It's going to get better, Noelle. The more we know about each other, the better it will be. And we've still got five more days here before we have to go back to the real world. I intend to be an expert in every inch of you by then."

"Not if I learn your body first."

I groaned in mock disapproval. "Are you ever going to let me win?"

"I thought you did." She smiled up at me almost tentatively. "I thought I was the prize."

"You bet you fucking are."

We were not going to be getting much sleep that night.

~Noelle~

The rest of our time in Leavenworth flew by in what felt like a matter of seconds. We did all the other Christmas things Eve had wanted to do, including going out to see the Christmas lights at night, going to a carol festival at the local school, and visiting the Nutcracker Museum. The last one made Aaron wince repeatedly, to Eve's delight.

"You know this has nothing to do with your testicles, right?" she teased him.

"Are you kidding? You literally stick a nut in this guy's crotch and crack it open, and the two of you think it's hilarious. How am I not supposed to take that as a threat?"

Eve and Aaron got along even better than I could have hoped, once the awkwardness over our scheming had passed. After a few days, Eve even joked about it. While we were talking about our favourite Christmas movies, she teased us about her plans to write a play based on this trip for the college's drama program, a Noel Coward-style farce called The Poinsettia Plot.

Aaron shook his head. "Love the idea, but hate the name. It should be called The Gingerbread Gamble."

"Why?" Eve and I both asked curiously at the same time.

"Because out of all the games we played, that one wasn't fixed. We let fate play its hand, and that piece of gingerbread paid off better than I ever could have imagined."

My heart melted as he leaned over and kissed me, and Eve snorted at us both. "You really are a perfect match: you're just as sappy as each other."

I couldn't argue with that.

We spent some more time with Corey too, and now that he had no further interest in sleeping with either me or Eve, we all had fun together. He made a few off-hand comments about being concerned about his future after college, and I found myself making him an offer: "Why don't you come have dinner with my parents when we get back? My dad is a huge hockey fan and he's got some connections. He might be able to put you in touch with some people to help you figure out what's available."

Corey looked genuinely touched. "Thanks, Noelle. I'd really like that."

"Wait, you're inviting him over to meet your parents and not me?" Aaron sounded distinctly unimpressed.

"You can come too," I quickly added, which didn't make him any happier.

"So, I'm just an afterthought?"

I raised my eyebrows at him in challenge. "Who's being insecure now? I actually wanted to invite you to join us for my birthday on Christmas Eve, but if you're going to be all weird about it, I might change my mind."

That took him by surprise. "Really?"

"Yes, really." I'd been thinking about it for a few days now. "I mean, if you need to be with your family on Christmas, I understand, but it would be great if you could come for Christmas Eve. Eve's family will all be there too, we usually try and spend the day together even if we have Christmas apart."

He made up his mind remarkably fast. "I don't have any set plans for Christmas. My parents each have other, younger kids they'll spend the day with. If I tell them I'm spending it with someone special, they'll be happy for me."

"Then it's settled," Eve declared. "You get to experience a real Hanmer/Stamer Christmas. You better be prepared for a grilling from Noelle's dad."

Aaron's eyes widened in alarm behind his glasses, making me laugh. "He's a sweetheart," I assured him. "Honestly, after my sister's fiancée, as long as you're not involved in human trafficking, he'll think you're perfect."

"So, I should hide the trafficking ring?" Aaron asked innocently, and my own eyes widened until I realized he was teasing me, of course. Eve and Corey laughed at my gullibility, making me blush, but Aaron leaned over to whisper in my ear. "Don't ever change, Noelle. Everything about you is perfect."

He honestly made me feel that way.

The nights were perfect too. He'd promised me they would just keep getting better, and so far, he hadn't let me down. His words lit a fire in my body and his actions fanned the flames until desire and pleasure consumed me, over and over again. At first, it seemed as though he held all the power, but it quickly became apparent that he drew his own pleasure from my pleasure. If I wasn't engaged and enjoying myself, he wouldn't have had fun either. He never came first, always making sure I'd been satisfied before he focused on himself.

I couldn't believe this perfect man had been hiding in plain sight for so long, and as the cars came to pick us up and take us back to the airport, I took one last look around the house, committing it all to memory. I would always be grateful for this trip and what I'd learned about Aaron and about myself while we were there.

We landed back in New York on December 22nd. I'd already spoken to my parents about having Corey and Aaron over for dinner and they suggested we do it the day we arrived. My dad would drive Corey and Aaron back to campus afterwards.

Eve had been invited too, but she told me she wanted to go home and talk to her dad before all the Christmas celebrations started. I wished her luck and gave her a tight hug before we parted ways. "You're Eve Stamer. You can do anything, and you've got this."

"Thanks." I'd rarely seen her looking so nervous as she did then, even as she tried to put on a brave face. "I'll call you later, and I'll see you on the 24th."

She got in the car her dad had sent for her, while Corey, Aaron and I took a taxi to the Upper West Side street where I'd grown up.

"This is really nice." Aaron sounded slightly awed when we got out of the cab and he looked up at the house strung with Christmas lights, by far the most decorated house on the whole block. The Christmas tree took up the entire front window with all the ornaments Olivia and I had made over the years taking pride of place where anyone passing by could see them.

"It is," I agreed. I loved my house and the way my parents had made it their own. My mom had designed the whole interior when they moved in, and redesigned it a few times over the years. Almost every object had a story, and the house held some incredible memories. "Come on, I can't wait for them to meet you."

We hadn't even made it to the steps before the front door opened and my mom appeared, pulling me into a warm hug as I jogged up to greet her. "I'm so glad you're home!"

"Me too, Mom."

As we hugged, she peered over my shoulder before whispering one more thing into my ear before pulling away. "He's cute! Well done, Noelle."

"Don't do anything weird!" I begged, to no avail. She marched straight down the stairs to give out another hug.

"It's so good to meet you, Aaron. We're excited to have you with us for Christmas."

That didn't sound too bad. In fact, it would have been perfectly fine if the guy she hugged had actually *been* Aaron. Unfortunately, she chose the wrong one.

"Mom?" I winced as she pulled back. "That's our friend, Corey. Aaron's over there."

Corey gave her a charming smile as she looked back and forth between the two of them, while Aaron's smile looked a little more forced. "It's nice to meet you, Mrs Hanmer."

"You too, sweetie." Unflustered as ever, my mom hugged Aaron instead. "Sorry, Noelle never gave me a description."

My cheeks flamed in mortification as we all went inside and my dad came out to greet our guests too. At least he correctly guessed immediately who was who. He took the two of them into the living room, already chatting about hockey, while I cornered my mom. "I told you Corey's a hockey player! His height should have given him away."

She just shrugged. "I don't know anything about hockey and you never said what either of them looks like. It was an honest mistake, but don't worry. Aaron took it well, and he's cute too!"

Luckily, dinner went smoother and my dad ended up being just as helpful to Corey as I'd predicted. By the time dinner ended, they'd made plans for my dad to introduce him to the sports therapists that the New York Rangers used, and he'd invited Corey to join him for a friendly game between employees of Stamer Hotels and one of their biggest rival hotel chains.

Aaron hardly got a word in edgewise.

At one point, my mom asked if he played hockey too, trying to draw him into the conversation, but Aaron shook his head. "My eyesight makes it impossible." No one could say much to that so the conversation moved on.

After dinner, my dad took Corey to his home office to show him some memorabilia. Aaron offered to help my mom tidy up but she sent us both away. "Go and show Aaron the view from upstairs," she suggested, giving me a wink as if we would have our hands all over each other as soon as we were alone.

Another time, she might have been right, but as we climbed up to the top floor of the house, Aaron seemed unusually subdued, and I was pretty sure I knew why.

"I'm really sorry about all of this," I blurted out as soon as we'd gone into my room and closed the door behind us. "My mom meant nothing bad by confusing the two of you, and my dad's just a really big hockey fan, I'm sure he didn't mean to be rude..."

"I get it, Noelle." He gave me a resigned shrug. "You're not the only one who gets overlooked for their best friend at times. I'm used to it. After all, you did the same thing."

That reminder made me wince. "Well, I know better now and my parents will too. Just give them a bit of time."

"It's fine." Although he said that, the words lacked their usual confidence. "It doesn't matter to me what they think. I'd like them to like me, sure, but it's not the end of the world if they don't. I'm not going to change who I am to impress anyone, and as long as you want me, that's all I need. Now, is there really a view up here, or did your mom just give us an excuse for a quickie?"

I rolled my eyes at the question. "There's a view. Come here."

Pulling him over to the window, we looked out together over the city street. The skyscrapers of Midtown were visible just above the rooftop of the building across the street, their lights twinkling against the night sky. For a minute or two, we sat there looking out in silence, both of us lost in thought.

"You must have felt like anything was possible looking out at that," Aaron suggested quietly. "You've always had the world at your feet, Noelle."

I hadn't always felt that way, but he made me feel it. Now, maybe I could return the favour.

"Come on, we're going back downstairs." Without waiting for him to agree, I ran back down the stairs and into my dad's office, interrupting their conversation with Aaron right behind me. "Corey, my mom has asked you and Aaron to help with the dishes."

Aaron's brow furrowed, knowing she'd asked no such thing, but Corey immediately agreed and he and Aaron headed back to the kitchen together as I closed the office door behind them.

"Why have you been ignoring Aaron all night?" I crossed my arms at my dad and his eyebrows raised in surprise.

"What do you mean?"

"I mean how you spent the whole meal talking to Corey and barely said two words to my boyfriend. What's up with that?"

"Where is this coming from?" he asked, and my lips pursed even tighter.

"I just told you, the way you shut Aaron out..."

"I mean, where did this attitude come from?" he interrupted me. "You sound just like your mom."

He clearly meant that as a compliment from the way his eyes softened at the mention of her, but I had no plans of letting him off the hook yet.

"Aaron's trying to get me to stand up for myself more, and so I'm standing up for him too."

"Is that so?" His smile only confused me. Why did he find my anger amusing? "I'm sorry, Noelle. I wanted to help your friend, Corey, and I thought I could get to know Aaron better when he comes back for Christmas, but if you want me to talk to him, I'll talk to him. Go and get him and tell him to come see me."

Well, I didn't mean it like that. I simply wanted him to show more interest. "You don't have to sit down and talk to him right now. I just meant..."

Again, he cut in before I could finish. "Actually, I think I do. Ask him to come here, please, Noelle. It won't take too long."

As I headed to the kitchen to find Aaron, I had a feeling my good intentions might have just backfired.

~**Aaron**~

Our evening really hadn't gone to plan. I'd never been concerned about impressing a girl's parents before, but Noelle wasn't just any girl. We might have only been together for a week but I could see a future for us more clearly than I ever had with anyone else before. From the things we'd talked about, I knew her family meant a lot to her, and I really wanted to make a good impression.

Noelle's mom mistaking Corey for me didn't get things off to a great start, but once the awkwardness of the moment had passed, I decided to take it as a compliment. Corey was a good-looking guy, I knew that as well as anyone, so if her mom mistook Corey for me, it probably meant that Noelle had praised my looks too. While not the ideal start to the night, I could get over it.

Her dad focusing entirely on Corey all through dinner was a little harder to take. As I told Noelle, I'd had to deal with people comparing me to Corey, and finding me lacking in the comparison, ever since we became friends. Normally, I wouldn't let it get to me because I didn't care about those people's opinions, but coming from Noelle's dad, it hit differently. While I really wanted to find some common ground with him, Corey did it without trying. All in all, I couldn't help being left with the distinct impression that they would have been happier if Noelle brought Corey home instead.

Now, Noelle had raced down the stairs like a woman on a mission and sent me and Corey off to the kitchen with her mom. I had no idea what had gotten into her, and when she appeared a couple of minutes later, her face paler than before, I had even less clue.

She pulled me aside to whisper in my ear. "My dad wants to talk to you in his office."

"Am I in trouble?" I asked, only partly joking.

"Of course not." She smiled, but the worry in her eyes belied her words. "He just wants to have a quick chat before he drives you and Corey home."

That didn't make things much clearer, but I could hardly refuse. Following Noelle's directions, I found the open door to the room where her dad waited for me.

"You wanted to see me, Mr Hanmer?" A good-looking man with a bit of a hockey player's build himself, he was still in very good shape for his age. I had no idea what he thought about me and meeting a girl's father could be tricky. Moms were easier, in my experience. They wanted their daughter to be happy and if you were polite and friendly, that usually sufficed. Dads, on the other hand, knew exactly what kind of pigs other men could be, and they wanted to be sure you weren't disrespecting their little girl, even when she wanted you to.

Disrespect had never been my thing, though. I just had to prove that to him.

"Come in and sit down, Aaron." He gestured to the chair on the other side of his desk while he sat behind it. The setup made it feel a bit like a job interview, which I supposed it could be considered in some ways, and as soon as my butt hit the chair, he dove in. "So, Noelle just came in and told me off for being rude to you tonight."

Well, that made things more awkward, but I did my best to smooth it over. "I didn't think you were rude, sir. She asked you to help Corey and you were doing that."

Mr Hanmer nodded. "That's what I told her too, but the truth is, there's more to it than that."

His words sounded rather ominous. "What do you mean?"

He leaned back in his chair and pointed to a photo on the wall to our left. One of several hanging on the walls, the photo showed two couples in formal evening wear outside an elegant building, and I squinted at it to get a better look.

One couple was obviously Noelle's parents: a younger version of the man in front of me and a woman who could easily be Noelle's older sister. The other couple featured a tall, dark-haired man and a woman with hair the exact same shade of red as Eve's.

"That's Cole Stamer and his wife, Gemma," Mr Hanmer explained. "Cole and I have been best friends for around 35 years, so I've always been able to sympathize with Noelle about the unique challenges that come with having a Stamer for a best friend. Without trying, they have a way of stealing the spotlight. Eve's a wonderful girl and I'm so glad she and Noelle are friends, but I know that Noelle's confidence has suffered because of it. No matter how much we try to tell her she's her own amazing person, it's hard for her not to measure herself on Eve's scale."

It sounded like he had a pretty good handle on the situation, so I simply nodded to show I understood.

"Girls would use me to try to get to Cole," he continued. "I know what that's like and I've always been aware it could happen to Noelle. So, when she told us she wanted to bring you over for dinner and that you'd known each other for a while, I asked if you were friends with Eve too. She told me that you actually liked Eve first."

Damn it, Noelle. No wonder her dad had been ignoring me all night. If he honestly thought I simply wanted to use her, he'd actually been very restrained.

"You can guess why that concerned me," he added, and I nodded again. "Some of the guys she's dated in the past, even when they weren't interested in being with Eve themselves, still compared Noelle to Eve. It knocked her confidence even more. I hadn't planned on telling you any of this, but after Noelle came in here and stood up for you, I felt I owed you an explanation."

My mind flashed back to when we were setting the rules for our relationship and how she asked me not to make comparisons between her and other girls. The thought of anyone talking to her that way made my blood boil, but for right now, I needed to convince her father now that I would never do anything like that. I would have to lay my feelings out as clearly as possible.

"Mr Hanmer, I can see how it looks, and yes, it's absolutely true: I was interested in Eve. I went on this trip hoping that something might happen between us, but while we were there, something else happened, something amazing. I realized that when Noelle and I weren't competing with each other over grades or elections, we actually complemented each other very well. I also realized that Eve, while she's wonderful, is not the right woman for me. We don't click in the same way Noelle and I do. So, if you're worried that I'm still harbouring any unrequited feelings for Eve, I can assure you I'm not. And as for comparing Noelle and Eve, I would never to do it intentionally, and if anything ever slipped out subconsciously, it would only be complimentary to Noelle."

He listened to every word I said carefully, and when I'd finished, the corners of his mouth began to turn upward. "Thank you for being upfront with me. As I said, I had no plans to mention any of this to you, but when Noelle came in here, she said something that convinced me I should. She said that you were helping her to stand up for herself more."

She told her parents everything, apparently. Since it was true, I confirmed that too. "Yes, sir. She's incredible and I want her to know it. She might not be Eve Stamer, but that's absolutely fine, because Eve Stamer is no Noelle Hanmer."

His smile grew bigger. "I'm really glad to hear you say that. I happen to agree."

That seemed to go over well, so I kept going. "Besides that, the reasons I liked Eve had nothing to do with her money or her family. I know that's easy to say, but it's true. I liked her because she's smart and ambitious and funny and beautiful. This trip helped me see that Noelle is all of those things too, in a slightly different way. At college, I only knew her as a serious, studious girl, who sometimes tried a little too hard, while Eve always seemed effortless. But when I got to know Noelle better, I realized that when she's not trying to impress anyone, she's actually really impressive. All I want now is to help her see it too."

I could have sworn for a second that his eyes got watery, but when he blinked, the illusion had gone, and he leaned back again, changing the subject. "So, tell me more about you, Aaron. Where's your family from?"

We talked for a while longer about my family and my classes and my career plans. It still felt a bit like a job interview, but not in a bad way. After all, Noelle had already given me the job and she could make her own decisions. Getting her dad's approval would be icing on the cake: nice to have, but not necessary.

Eventually, Noelle knocked at the door and tentatively stuck her head in the room. "Is everything okay in here? It's getting late."

Her dad glanced down at his watch and swore in surprise. "Sorry, Aaron. I should get you and Corey home."

After a quick goodbye to Noelle and her mom, Corey and I got in the car with Mr Hanmer. Noelle's dad invited me to sit in the front with him, and the three of us chatted easily on the way back to campus. When we got to the dorm, he got out and shook Corey's hand, promising to be in touch with him soon about the things they'd talked about. When he got to me, he gave me a friendly, approving nod. "We'll see you on the 24th, Aaron. I'm looking forward to it."

"So am I." Now, even more than ever.

Chapter Sixteen

PERFECT

~**Noelle**~

Christmas Eve had always been my favourite day of the year. The 24th of December marked the start of my new year more than the 31st did: my birthday, shared with Eve, followed by Christmas meant two days of celebration and family and love. I always spent part of the day with Eve, and Aaron would be coming to meet the rest of my family, meaning my sister, Olivia, and her fiancé, Noah Stamer, along with Noah and Eve's parents, Gemma and Cole.

Birthday celebrations that year were at our house, and Aaron would be staying the night to spend Christmas with us. On the 26th, he planned to take me to meet his parents too. His actions made it clear he took this relationship as seriously as I did, even if we hadn't used the L-word quite yet.

As I made my way downstairs to await everyone's arrival, I overheard my parents talking in their own room, and the sound of Aaron's name caught my attention, bringing me to a halt.

"Which room is Aaron staying in?" my dad asked. "I can leave some extra razors and things in the bathroom."

My mom laughed warmly. "Jackson, he's staying in Noelle's room."

"Oh." It sounded as if the thought had never occurred to him. "But they only got together like a week ago."

"And they're already spending Christmas together," my mom pointed out. "Besides, how long did it take you to fall in love?"

I could hear some good-natured grumbling followed by more laughter, and I quickly continued down the stairs before I interrupted anything. Olivia and Noah were already in the kitchen when I got downstairs, taking me by surprise. I hadn't realized they'd arrived.

"Happy birthday, Noelle!" Olivia gave me a warm hug. "You look fantastic! Did you do something new to your hair?"

"It looks great," Noah agreed, hugging me once Olivia let me go. "Happy birthday."

"Thank you. It's not really anything new, I just didn't straighten it like I usually do."

"Well, it really suits you," Olivia told me before giving me a wink. "Or maybe it's just the way you're beaming. I hear we're meeting a new guy tonight."

"Did you hear that from Mom or Dad?"

"Both," she confirmed with a laugh. "Mom says he might be 'the one'. Is that true?"

"I don't want to jinx it, Liv," I groaned. "Can we not label anything yet?"

Olivia shot Noah a knowing look. "I know what that means. They haven't had the talk yet."

"I'd say it has to be pretty serious if you're exposing him to my family too," Noah teased. "Dinner with the Stamers isn't for the faint-hearted."

The doorbell rang, saving me from this conversation. "I'll get it."

My stomach fluttered as I headed to the door, hoping it might be the subject of conversation himself arriving, but when I opened the door, Eve stood there instead, a gift bag in her hand and a forced smile on her face. "Happy birthday, Noelle!"

"Happy birthday to you!" I pulled her inside and gave her a hug. "What's wrong?"

She winced, glancing around to make sure we couldn't be overheard. "I haven't had a chance to talk to my dad yet."

"Eve!" She told me she had changed her mind about me being there and would do it on her own, but when I texted her to ask how it went, she simply said she'd tell me about it when we saw each other. Now, I knew why.

She shrugged unhappily. "Every time I try to bring it up, he gets so excited and goes off on another tangent about how great it's going to be for all of us to be working together. I think I do need you there after all. He's not here yet, is he?"

"Not yet. Liv and Noah are here though."

We made our way to the kitchen where my sister peppered Eve with questions about Aaron, and soon, Eve's parents arrived. Gemma also told me how good I looked, which left me wondering just how bad I'd looked before, but Eve said it simply came down to me looking happy.

Finally, the doorbell rang again, and this time, Aaron stood on the front steps, and the sight of him had my heart racing. He had obviously made an effort with his appearance, his hair styled and a fashionable scarf around his neck. Affection and desire and excitement all ran through me at the same time as he smiled, looking as happy to see me as I felt seeing him. "Happy birthday, Noelle."

He pulled me into a kiss right there on the step where anyone could see, leaving me breathless.

"You look incredible," he murmured into my ear as he pulled back. "I don't know how I'm going to get through the whole evening without touching you."

"You look pretty great yourself. Is this a new coat? And did you get your hair cut?"

"Everything is new," he admitted. "Corey took me out yesterday to get ready. He said I could use the help."

The idea that he had put so much time into making a good impression on me and my family melted my heart. "He did a great job, but you're the one pulling it off."

His warm smile filled me with happiness. "I know it's important to you to fit in. I'll try a little harder and you can try a little less, and we should balance out just right."

That applied to our whole relationship in a way, and as I brought him into the kitchen to say hello to everyone, I had never felt quite so balanced and sure of myself before.

We all sat down with a drink before dinner and, according to tradition, Eve and I exchanged gifts first. We always gave each other a gag gift followed by a real one. Eve laughed when she opened the gingerbread house earrings I got her. "You think I won't wear these, but I will. I love them!"

To prove her point, she pulled out her pretty ruby earrings and replaced them with the cheap plastic gingerbread ones instead. Somehow, she made them look good.

When I opened her gift to me, I groaned while Aaron stifled a laugh beside me. She'd bought me a reusable ice pack. "Since you keep hurting your knee," she teased.

"What's wrong with your knee?" my dad asked in concern, which only made Eve laugh.

"Never mind, Uncle Jackson. It's an inside joke."

Eve and I had a million of those, so nobody questioned it any further. After opening our real gifts, we all sat down to an amazing dinner, and before long, my dad held up his glass to make a toast.

"It's hard to believe these beautiful young women in front of me are the same little babies we met on that Christmas Eve twenty-two years ago. We're so proud of the women you've become and we can't wait to see what amazing things you're going to do. Happy birthday, Noelle. Happy birthday, Eve."

Everyone raised their glasses and Aaron smiled at me as we both took a drink, making me feel that he wanted to be included in whatever that future might bring.

This time, my family included Aaron in the conversation from the start, and Eve's dad took a particular interest in asking him about his plans for work after we graduated. "Stamer Hotels is always looking for smart, ambitious young people to come and grow with us. If you're interested in having a talk about what kind of opportunities are available, just let me know."

Aaron had his mouth open to thank him, but Eve interjected before he got a chance. "Not everyone wants to work for you, Dad."

It could have been a joke, but her tone made it pretty clear she didn't mean it that way, and Cole looked over at her with a touch of confusion. "I'm only suggesting we have a chat."

"You might think that's all it is, but sometimes, you put pressure on people without even knowing you're doing it."

Everyone else at the table, besides me and Aaron, exchanged rather bewildered glances, but I kept my eyes on Eve, waiting to see if she needed help. She probably hadn't intended to get into this now, in front of everyone, but after what she'd just said, I knew her dad wouldn't just let it go.

"What are you talking about, Eve?"

Her eyes darted to me and I gave her an encouraging nod. She'd come this far, she might as well say it.

Even so, I didn't expect her to just blurt it out like she did: "I don't want to work for Stamer Hotels."

The whole room went unnaturally quiet as everyone waited for Cole's response. He still mostly looked confused.

"But we've talked about this."

"No, Dad. *You've* talked about it. You got me the office and made all the plans, but you never actually asked me if it's what I want to do."

Cole looked to Gemma for assistance, but she could only shrug. Eve hadn't told her any of this either. Still lost, his gaze returned to his daughter. "What else would you do?"

Eve let out an almost desperate laugh. "*Anything* else. There's a whole world out there that has nothing to do with rich people going on vacation."

"That's not what we..." Cole started to argue, but Gemma placed her hand on his and he immediately stopped, taking a breath to calm himself. "Maybe we should talk about this later, Eve."

I saw the panic flash in my friend's eyes, worried that her opportunity might be slipping away, and I had to step in. "Actually, Uncle Cole, Eve's been trying to talk to you about this for a while. She didn't want to disappoint you when you're so excited about it, but she's been feeling this way for a long time."

His dark eyes, so like Eve's, moved over to me. "You two have talked about it?"

He knew that Eve and I shared everything, so I nodded in confirmation. "It's nothing against you or the business. She just wants to help people."

"And please, don't tell me about all the donations Stamer Hotel makes," Eve added. "I know all of that, but I want to do something more hands-on. I want to make a difference."

Cole thought all of that over, his lips tightening as he reevaluated all his own plans, but after a few moments had passed, he nodded. "Okay. I respect that, Eve. How about we make a deal?"

"What kind of deal?" Eve asked warily.

"A temporary one," he suggested. "You sign up for some kind of volunteer program for a year or so, doing whatever you want to do. Your job will wait. At the end of that time, we can see how you feel."

"Really?" A look of cautious optimism began to spread across her face. "Anything I want to do?"

"Anything," Cole promised. "As long as it's safe. I'll do a full check on it before you sign up and whoever you'll be working with."

"Dad," Eve groaned, but her tone had softened. She was clearly on board.

"Those are my terms," he insisted. "What do you think?"

"I think that works." Eve gave him a smile of gratitude for the compromise and everyone relaxed as the conversation moved on. They would obviously still have more to talk about, but as I suspected, her dad would put her happiness above anything else, every time.

Speaking of happiness, when the evening had drawn to an end, the Stamers had all headed home, and we said goodnight to my parents, Aaron and I headed up to my room. It had only been two nights we'd been apart, but my whole body was alight in anticipation, and judging from the look on his face, Aaron felt just the same.

As soon as we had the door closed behind us, he gave me an enticing smile. "Are you ready for your birthday present?"

~Aaron~

Dinner with the Hanmers and the Stamers had been very educational. Eve had told me their families were very close and she hadn't exaggerated. I couldn't help thinking about how if I had ended up with Eve as I hoped, I might have been at that table anyway, just sitting in a different spot, but no part of me wanted that anymore.

And not just because Eve's dad intimidated me a lot more than Noelle's.

I might not have got what I wanted, but I absolutely wanted what I got, and I couldn't be happier with the way things turned out.

Especially now, when Noelle and I were alone in her room. I hadn't lied earlier when I told her that keeping my hands off her all evening would be a struggle. Happy and comfortable with the people who loved her most, she shone brighter than ever, and I never wanted to see that light fade again. I wanted everyone to see it and to give her the admiration and respect she deserved.

But most of all, I wanted to make her light up in private.

"You didn't have to get me anything," Noelle protested once I asked if she wanted her present and I gave her a look of mild disapproval, one that I knew would make her just a tiny bit anxious, just enough that she'd want to please me and earn my approval instead.

"You know that's not what I'm talking about. That's not what I want to give to you right now."

Her cheeks flushed with both desire and that mild discomfort that came from not getting the praise she craved from me. I could read her so well.

"Do you want to try answering again?" I prompted, giving her a chance to earn the affirmation she wanted.

She nodded, those sweet blue eyes looking up at me beseechingly. "Yes, I would like my present, please."

The way she squirmed as she said it let me know just how turned on she was, which only made me hotter in return. Nothing compared to the high I got from getting her off, and my dick throbbed in anticipation of her reaction as the next words came out of my mouth. "Good girl. That's better."

The whimper that came out of her mouth would have had me hard in an instant if I hadn't already been there.

"First, we need to unwrap it." My glasses came off first and, moving behind her, I brushed her hair away from her neck and began to kiss my way down it as I reached around to unbutton her shirt. Her sweet little moans were music to my ears, and I told her so while pressing my erection against her ass. "Fuck, I love the sounds you make. I'd love to record them and play them back like music, but I wouldn't be able to get anything done. You feel how hard you make me?"

She nodded, her breathing growing shallower as I unbuttoned her pants, slipping my hand inside to stroke against the fabric of her panties. I expected to find them damp and she didn't disappoint me. Her hips rocked against my hand, looking for more pressure, but I had other plans first. Once I had her totally naked, I ran my hand gently over her knee. The bruise had mostly faded by now but I asked her how it felt anyway.

"Are you going to be okay to put some weight on this? I'd love to get you on your hands and knees."

We hadn't been able to do that yet because of her injury, and Noelle's eyes sparked with excitement at the thought. "Yes, it's okay."

"Tell me if it's not. I don't want you in any pain."

She promised she would and I praised her again for her compliance. Each time I complimented her, her body reacted as if I'd touched her, making me wonder if I'd be able to make her come on praise alone someday. I would love to try, and I had a feeling she would too.

For that night, though, I had more immediate pleasure in mind.

Noelle climbed onto her bed on all fours as I asked her to, perfectly on display for me, and once I had my clothes off too, I took my time exploring her body. My hands ran over every inch of her as I told her exactly what I loved about it and why it turned me on. Fuck, I'd missed her so much in just two nights. We were going to have to figure out a plan for when we got back to campus because there was no way I could handle her sleeping apart from me.

"I love the curve of your hips," I told her, my hands tracing those curves. "I can't look at them without wanting my hands on them. Your tits are so gorgeous, just the perfect size." I took them in my hands now to prove my point. "Just right to hold onto while I'm fucking you from behind."

She whimpered again, her legs spreading wider instinctively in anticipation, and my survey of her body ended in that spot as I took a moment to appreciate her pink pussy, telling her exactly how sexy I found it. "I've been dreaming about this sweet pussy, Noelle. Dreaming about the way it looks and tastes and the way it feels on my fingers, my tongue and especially my dick. Have you been thinking about it too?"

"Oh, God, yes," she groaned, tilting her hips upwards to try to entice me to make good on that fantasy right now.

I still had to explain my plan first though. "So, for your birthday, I'm going to give you three orgasms: one with my tongue, one with my fingers, and one while I'm buried inside you. You're going to be my good girl and take what I give you. Will you do that for me?"

"Yes, please." She had nearly begun trembling in anticipation. "Please, give it to me."

"With pleasure." Spreading her lips with my fingers, I dove right in.

I hadn't been kidding; I really had dreamt about this. The night before, I'd dreamt I had my face buried in her pussy and woke up stiff as a board and unsatisfied. Now, I had the real thing, and I licked her with all the enthusiasm of a starving man, interspersing my actions with reminders of how well she was doing.

"Fuck, Noelle, you taste incredible. I'm going to get addicted. I love the way your clit feels on my tongue."

Each compliment brought her closer until she couldn't take any more. She came sighing my name, sending a wave of satisfaction and arousal through me, making my already hard dick even harder.

"That's one, but I know you've got more for me tonight. My fingers are going to fuck the next one out of you. Open up for me."

She moaned again as my fingers filled her pussy, stroking her gently at first until her need began to rise again and then picking up the pace to bring her to the edge. When I felt her getting close, I added my other hand to focus on her clit as her hips bucked against me.

"I love the way you respond to me, Noelle. I love the way your body wants me, and right now, it wants to come again. Give it what it wants. Give me what I need."

With that encouragement, she couldn't refuse, and her pussy clenched around my fingers as she moaned out her ecstasy once again.

"Such a fucking good girl. Look at me." Her head turned so she could see me and I held up my hand to her, my fingers glistening with her pleasure, and I slowly licked each one clean as she watched me through hooded eyes. "You're delicious. Now, you're going to give me one more. I know you can."

My dick was almost agonizingly hard by now, and as I ran the head of it through her trail of wetness, coating it with her release, we both moaned in perfect harmony, each of us equally anticipating the final stage of her present.

I groaned even louder as I finally slid my dick into her warm, wet pussy. "Fuck, you feel perfect. You were made for me, for this dick. This pussy is mine now, Noelle. I'm claiming it on behalf of my dick."

She laughed breathlessly. "Yes, Aaron, yes. It's all yours. Use it just like you want to."

Fuck, she turned me on. "I'm so glad we agree." With a forceful thrust, I bottomed out, both of us moaning together. My hands on her waist, I pumped into her hard and fast, her previous orgasms making her slick and ready. "I wish you could see how amazing you look right now. The way your pussy looks as my dick disappears into it. You take me so well. You're taking all of me and you're doing so well."

It took a while to get the third one, but I didn't mind. I was having far too good a time, and when it came, her last orgasm ended up being the longest and hardest one of all, leaving me with no choice but to come too as I watched her and felt her coming around me. Her pleasure filled me to the brim.

We both collapsed onto the bed afterwards, her wrapped up in my arms. My heart pounded not only from the exertion of what we'd just done but in anticipation of what I had to say next. Our relationship might still be young, but I knew how I felt and I wanted to make it clear. No more games: we'd made that promise to each other and I intended to keep it.

"I love fucking you. I love spending time with you and debating with you and I love how you make me feel. I love *you*, Noelle, and I'm so glad I got a chance to figure that out."

That startled look in her blue eyes when she raised her head had my dick twitching again even though she'd just drained it. "Really?"

Just what every guy wanted to hear. I shook my head at her in mock disapproval. "Yes, really. Is that all you have to say?"

Her cheeks flushed with that adorable embarrassment. "No, of course not. I love you too, Aaron."

Thank God. Relief and happiness flooded through me even before she went on.

"I love the way you make me feel too, and I love how sexy and smart you are. I love everything about you. I'm so glad we took this chance."

It really did come down to chance sometimes. It came down to taking a leap. A risk. Sometimes, it didn't work out, like with Corey and Eve, but sometimes, that gamble paid off better than anyone could have ever imagined.

I kissed her hard and deep to seal our mutual declaration before pulling back. "Here. I did get you a present you can show other people too."

Sitting up quickly, I grabbed the small box from the pocket of my pants on the floor. She took it from me with that startled look I loved so much, and when she opened it up, her eyes lit up.

"Aaron, I love it!"

The silver pendant I'd bought in Leavenworth had a pretty outline of one of the town's Bavarian-style buildings with a mountain behind it.

"Turn it over," I told her, my excitement almost matching hers as I waited for her reaction.

On the back, I'd had our names engraved with a heart connecting them and underneath, the words 'first Christmas'.

"First?" Noelle looked up at me in happiness and hope, her blue eyes shining.

"The first of many, I hope," I told her truthfully. "I won the prize, Noelle, and I don't have any plans to give it back."

~~THE END~~

IF YOU
ENJOYED THIS...

Eve's story, *Stocking Standoff*, will be released in the spring of 2023! It's available to preorder from Amazon now.

Alternatively, if you'd like to follow along as it's being written, you can join me on Patreon where I share the first drafts of my latest books in daily updates. *Stocking Standoff* will begin on Patreon on December 1, 2022, and you'll find other unpublished works there too.

Visit www.patreon.com/melodytyden to learn more!

MORE FROM THE AUTHOR

Contemporary Romance – New Adult/Clean

It Figures duet
It Figures
Figuring It Out

Historical Romance – 18+

Lady in Waiting Series
Lady in Waiting
King in Training
Princess in Hiding

Paranormal Romance – 18+

Cold Lake Pack Series
The Curse and the Prophecy
The Spell and the Legacy
The Dream and the Destiny

Mismatched Mates Series
Mismatched Mates
Misguided Motives
Mistaken Meanings

Serena's Story
The Alpha's Second Chance
The Returned Mate
The Vampire's Consort

Sacrifice Series
Blood Donor
Life Giver

Paranormal Romance – New Adult/Clean

The Alpha's Prey

KEEP IN TOUCH

My Patreon account has daily updates from my works-in-progress, bonus chapters and more – join me there to comment and read along as my next books are being written: www.patreon.com/melodytyden

You can find and follow me on Facebook at: facebook.com/melodytyden

Join the Facebook group Melody's Romance Corner for fun games, interaction with the author and exclusive news and excerpts.

You can also sign up to my newsletter at www.melodytyden.com for all the latest news.

Made in the USA
Middletown, DE
01 December 2022

16523337R00149